Praise for Nicole H...

The Mc...
'Engaging and heart-w...
for a chilly night...

Lawson's Bend
'Nicole Hurley-Moore has once again proved to me that she
is a trusted figure in the world of Australian rural fiction.
Lawson's Bend delivers on all fronts, providing readers
with the ideal mix of small town intricacies, mystery and
a hearty romance.'—Mrs B's Book Reviews

White Gum Creek
'The perfect summer read.' —Noveltea Corner

Country Roads
'A heartwarming tale of taking chances, facing your
fears and opening yourself up to new experiences.'
—Beauty and Lace

Hartley's Grange
'. . . lives are put back together, lessons are learned, and old
friends resurface in a timeless story of life, love and living.
A wonderful read for a lazy Sunday afternoon which will
leave you with a total dose of that "feelgood" feeling!'
—Blue Wolf Reviews

McKellan's Run
'So very readable—you won't be able to put it down.'
—*Newcastle Herald*

Nicole Hurley-Moore grew up in Melbourne and has travelled extensively, whilst living through the romance of books. Her first passion in life has always been her family, but since doing her Honours in Medieval Literature she has devoted much of her time to writing historical romance. Nicole is a full-time writer who lives in the Central Highlands of Victoria with her family in the peaceful surrounds of a semi-rural town. She is the author of the immensely popular novels *McKellan's Run*, *Hartley's Grange*, *Country Roads*, *White Gum Creek*, *Lawson's Bend*, *The McCalister Legacy* and *Summer at Kangaroo Ridge*.

The McCalister Legacy

Nicole HURLEY-MOORE

ALLEN&UNWIN
SYDNEY•MELBOURNE•AUCKLAND•LONDON

This edition published in 2022
First published in 2020

Allen & Unwin
83 Alexander Street
Crows Nest NSW 2065
Australia
Phone: (61 2) 8425 0100
Email: info@allenandunwin.com
Web: www.allenandunwin.com

 A catalogue record for this
book is available from the
National Library of Australia

ISBN 978 1 76106 555 2

Set in Sabon by Midland Typesetters, Australia
Printed in Australia by McPherson's Printing Group

10 9 8 7 6 5 4 3 2 1

For Ciandra, Conor and Alannah.

*And for Chris because I couldn't have
finished the book without him.*

Chapter One

Stone Gully Farm, 2007

Berenice McCalister waved as her best friend, Jodie, got into her mum's car.

'Bye Berry, it was a great party,' Jodie called out. 'See you on Monday.'

'See you later,' Berry called back before spinning around to her mum, her ponytail whipping behind her. 'Can't I stay at Jodie's place too? Why does Jess get to go?' Just as Jodie and Berry were best friends, so were their little sisters. And tonight Jessica was having a sleepover at the Fords' place.

Her mum shook her head as she pushed a strand of Berry's dark hair back behind her ear. 'No, not this time, sweetheart. I promised your sister that she could have a sleepover with Katie.'

'Yes, but it's *my* birthday,' Berry argued.

'And you've had a big party with all your friends. There've been games and cake and presents. You should be exhausted!'

'Yes, but . . .'

'Let your sister have this, okay? And I promise I'll talk to Jodie's mum next week and we'll arrange a sleepover for you—deal?'

Berry would have given anything to spend the night at Jodie's, but she looked at her mother and reluctantly nodded. 'Deal.'

'Thank you for understanding. I can't believe you're such a big girl now—ten years old. Seriously, I don't know where the time has gone,' her mum said as she bent down and pulled Berry into a tight hug. 'Besides, I need you to help me with your brother. What will Tommy do if both his sisters are gone?'

'I suppose . . .' Berry said. She was disappointed but her mum was right, she'd had a great day and Berry did like playing with her baby brother—as long as he wasn't crying or had a potty-training accident.

Berry leaned against her mother's side and waved at Jessica as the Fords' car drove down the drive.

'Come on, let's see what your dad and grandad are up to,' her mum said as she stood up and held out her hand. Berry took it and together they walked back inside the old farmhouse. 'And maybe you can have another slice of cake?'

'Yes, please,' Berry said as she licked her lips. Her birthday cake had been just perfect: vanilla layers with cream and strawberries on top, lightly covered with icing sugar and pink pearlised dust; pale pink and gold paper encircling the sides of the cake, finished off with a large pink satin ribbon. When her grandma had asked what sort of cake she wanted, Berry had said a grown-up one and not something with a princess on it. And Grandma had delivered—not only was it the loveliest cake Berry had ever seen, it was also the most delicious.

The McCalisters had lived at Stone Gully Farm for generations. Over the decades the family had tried to diversify and hedge their bets by not just running sheep but also planting crops and a small apple orchard, and now Berry's dad was venturing into olives. It wasn't as prosperous as some of the big sheep runs in the area, but Stone Gully had always provided a living for the family. Some years were leaner than others, but it was a living nonetheless. This year hadn't been especially rewarding, but Berry had still got her birthday party and some presents, including a beautiful new bike from her grandparents.

***

Later that evening just before sunset, Berry was out in the back yard riding her new bike. It was a shiny ruby red, with reflectors on the pedals, a light and a straw basket decorated with red daisies sitting at the front. It was the prettiest thing ever, except for the necklace from Mum and Dad, a tiny gold heart outlined in rubies. It was hanging around her neck and it made her feel very grown up.

The late February air was still warm but the light would fade soon as the sun dropped behind the hill in the distance. She had been allowed to stay up later than usual because it was her birthday. It was a Saturday and she'd worked on her father until he'd laughed and agreed. That tactic usually didn't work out so well, but it had tonight.

Berry rode another circuit around the clothesline, all the while wishing she could take off down the track behind the back of the house. It was a great track, it went through Stone Gully and into the bush, and if you followed it right to the end it would lead you to the outskirts of town. She'd only ridden the whole thing once with her father. It had taken almost an hour but it had been worth it. She was good at bike riding and had been doing it ever since Dad had taken the training wheels off when she was six.

Her grandmother opened the back door and stood out on the verandah, wiping her hands on her apron. It made Berry smile; no one else she knew wore an apron like that, but Grandma had a selection of brightly coloured cotton ones that were firmly tied around her waist in a giddy, colourful rotation. Some were check, others striped, but tonight she was wearing her favourite, which was covered in blue and purple flowers with dark purple binding all around the edges. The only time Grandma was ever seen not wearing an apron was when she went into town.

'Hey Berry Cherry, five more minutes, okay?' her grandmother called as she smoothed out her blonde hair. It was the same colour as Mum's but with silvery streaks near her temples. Sometimes Berry wished she had that blonde hair instead of dark brown. Her mum said that she and her brother and sister had the same hair as Dad. Most of the time Berry didn't care but when the sun turned her mum's hair golden she couldn't help wishing that it could have been different.

'Yes, Grandma,' she said as she continued her circuit. 'Thanks again for the bike, I love it,' she called over her shoulder.

'And I love you. I'll come and get you in few more minutes,' her grandma said before disappearing back through the door.

Berry rode and rode, and began to hum. Around and around she went, and the light began to fade. Just as she was on her final lap, she thought she caught the sound of an angry voice so she slowed down. Stopping the bike, she tilted her head and listened in surprise. She had never heard voices raised in anger in her home before, and for a moment she thought that maybe she'd imagined it, as everything appeared now to be quiet, except for the last mournful warble of a nearby magpie. But just as she was about to start peddling again, the noise erupted from inside the farmhouse. It sounded like an argument, and although she couldn't make out the words, she thought she recognised her father's deep voice.

Berry jumped as the back door flew open and her mother ran towards her holding little Tom in her arms. Suddenly Berry felt afraid; she didn't understand what was happening but she knew something was terribly wrong. There was an expression in her mum's eyes that Berry had never seen before—fear.

'Get back on your bike, sweetheart,' her mother said quickly as she placed little Tom in the basket between the handlebars. 'That's it, good girl.'

Berry did what she said and her mother started pushing the bike and running alongside it. She was steering them to the old back gate that opened up to the rest of the farm.

'Mum, what's the matter?'

'Everything's going to be all right, darling. I need you to ride into town, as fast as you can. Get to the Fords' place and tell Jodie's mum to ring the police. Can you do that for me, Berry?'

She was about to answer when suddenly from somewhere in the house came a loud bang, like Grandad's old ute backfiring.

Berry looked over her shoulder and saw her grandmother appear at the back door. Her face was pale and there was a panicked look in her grey eyes. 'Oh God, Cath,' she called out. 'He's coming! Hurry!'

Another bang went off as Mum opened the gate and pushed Berry's bike through. 'Whatever happens, sweetheart, just keep riding. Don't stop until you get to Jodie's.'

Berry looked at her mother and saw that there were tears beginning to fall down her cheeks.

'Mum, where's Dad? I'm scared.'

'You'll be fine,' she said as she squeezed her hand. 'You're my big, brave girl and I love you. Promise me that you'll keep riding as fast as you can and don't look back.'

Berry nodded because she couldn't manage to croak out an answer. She swallowed hard as her eyes began to well.

'Look after your brother and sister. They'll need you.'

'I promise, Mum.'

Her mother gave her a final smile but her eyes were bright with tears. Tom was sitting silently, his face white with fear as he picked up on his mother's emotion. 'I love you all more than anything. Now go, as quick as you can!' she said before giving Berry's bike a final push down the track.

She did what her mother said and didn't look back until she reached the bend in the track. Berry glanced towards the house and saw her mother running in the opposite direction—through the back paddocks towards the dam. The thin saplings that lined the track obscured her view as she rode, but she thought she saw a figure chasing after her mother. She wasn't sure, though, and she had to keep looking ahead to avoid the potholes in the dusty road and make sure Tom was safe in the basket. Her heart beat fast as she tried again and again to catch a glimpse of her mum through the trees. She'd never been so scared; she wanted to turn the bike around and go back but she'd promised to go to the Fords no matter what. A lump was forming in her throat and another in the pit of her stomach as the little red bike flew down the track. Berry pedalled as fast as she could and prayed that Tommy wouldn't start to fuss—but he didn't, not even once, as if he sensed that something was very, very wrong. Ahead by an ancient ghost gum the path veered away from Stone Gully, and as she reached it, another loud bang echoed over the darkening landscape. Berry didn't know what the sound meant but it made her cry harder. Despite the tears blurring her eyes, she did what Mum had asked and kept going all the way into town.

Chapter Two

Berry McCalister pulled off the dirt road and brought her car to a stop. She took a deep breath but it didn't calm her nerves at all. She reached over and grabbed her denim jacket from the passenger's seat before reluctantly getting out of the car.

Berry shrugged on her jacket and pulled it around her. It was the middle of autumn, and even though the sun kept peeping out from a blanket of grey clouds, the wind had a chill to it, making Berry regret not bringing a scarf. She walked around her small red hatchback and leaned against the bonnet. Perhaps it was to give her support or the sense that she was still close enough to jump back into the car and drive off. Berry quashed down the feeling. She was here and it was time to confront the past.

She raised her head. A few metres in front of her was a shabby-looking wooden fence. Most of the once-white paint had faded away. Berry frowned as her phone rang in her pocket. Glancing down at the screen, she saw her sister's name flash up.

'Hey Jess.'

'Hey. Are you there yet? Are you okay?'

Berry smiled. 'I've just pulled up and, yes, I'm fine.'

'All right, good,' Jess said before pausing for a moment. 'You don't have to do this, you know.'

'Yes, I do,' Berry said quickly. 'If we decide to sell, one of us has to see what needs to be done. You've got uni and Tom's in school—so that just leaves me. I'm sure there'll be a hundred things to do to the place; no one's been in it for years.'

That wasn't exactly true. Mr Ford had always kept an eye on the place. He had a spare key and always let Uncle Dave know if there was a problem.

'I know. I just don't know why you didn't wait? I would have come with you and so would've Tommy.'

'I don't know what I'll find.' She paused. 'And I suppose I don't want either of you walking into a wreck.'

'We're not kids anymore, Berry.'

'I know that, I just don't want your memories of the place to be shattered. Just let me see what it's like and what needs doing. Once it's fixed up a bit, then you can come.'

Jess sighed on the other end of the phone, and a flicker of a frown passed over Berry's face. 'What's the matter?'

'I'm still not sure about selling it. I know, I know—we've talked about this again and again, but to be honest, it just doesn't feel right. I mean, it's our home.'

'Jess, our home is wherever the three of us are, as well as Uncle Dave and Nanny and Pop. A house doesn't define who we are and what we mean to each other,' Berry said.

'Yeah, I know. But still . . .'

'I'm not saying that we have to sell the farm—I'm just exploring all our options. Once I get the house tidied up, then you and Tommy can come up and we'll take it from there. I mean, are our lives in Harlington or in Melbourne? Do you want to move back, and if we did, what would we do? These are some of the questions the three of us have to think about. Okay?'

'Yeah, I know you're right. I guess I'm just being a little sentimental about a house I barely remember,' Jess replied.

'There's nothing wrong with that.'

'I suppose it's the last tangible link we have with Mum, and Granny and Pa . . . and even Dad,' Jess said.

Berry heard the pause in her sister's voice. Mentioning their father was always problematic. It was hard to reconcile the image of the broad-shouldered, shaggy-haired, laughing man who had thrown and caught Berry high in the air as a child, with the monster who had destroyed half of her family. 'I understand, I feel it too.'

Jess's voice brightened as she changed the subject. 'So, where are you going to stay?'

'At the house. I brought a sleeping bag and other stuff—it'll be all right.'

'Berry, I don't think that's a great idea,' Jess said quickly, all lightness gone. 'I mean, you haven't been inside yet, it could be trashed.'

'Well, if that's the case—I drove past a B&B, and the pub has rooms.'

'Harlington has a B&B? I didn't think the place was a tourist hotspot,' Jess said with an incredulous lilt to her voice.

'I guess you were wrong.'

'So it seems. Anyway, let me know how you get on,' Jess said. 'Call me, even if it's in the middle of the night.'

'Thank you, but stop worrying. I'll be fine,' Berry said with a laugh.

'All right—but you have to admit that I do it so well. I'll talk to you later. Bye sis,' Jess said.

'Love you. I'll ring you later,' Berry said before she hung up and tucked the phone into her jeans. She glanced at the fence and the drive that led to the old farmhouse, and for an instant she was transported back to her tenth birthday. She could see the children running in the front yard and the colourful bunting her father had hung about, and could hear the sound of her mother's voice. Berry squeezed her eyes shut. She wouldn't let the memories in—she needed to be strong.

***

Nathan Tarant drove his white ute down Lyrebird Road, along the shortcut from his place to town—that is, if you could call Harlington a town. It boasted only a servo, a tiny general store, a community hall and a small pool that sat adjacent to a public park, which wasn't much bigger. Oh, and there was the pub—The Queen's Arms, which was affectionately known as The Queenie. Everyone who lived in or around Harlington drove further afield for pretty much everything, from groceries to school and anything in between. Violet Falls was about thirteen kilometres away and Bendigo was a twenty-minute drive in the opposite direction. But today he was just going to pick up some bread and milk from the general store.

Nate had spent all his twenty-four years at his family's horse stud farm, Tarantale Downs. The Tarant family had been a fixture in Harlington since sometime back in the 1850s when an ancestor had the vision to see that the soft rolling hills could run something other than sheep. It had started small but with each generation grew in both size and reputation. Now, Tarantale Downs was one of the most respected horse studs not just in the area, but statewide.

The dirt road was still wet in places from last night's downpour. The rain had produced ruts where the rivulets of water cut their path, and the side of the road was now soft, a bog waiting to happen. As Nate drove, the ute seemed to hit every ditch and pothole on the way, splashing muddy water all over it. Nate frowned and wondered why the hell he'd bothered to wash it last week.

In the distance he noticed a red car parked outside the old McCalister place. That was odd—no one ever came out here; too many dark memories, and some of the kids around here would say too many ghosts. A town never really got over something like that—most of a family being taken out in such a violent way. At least the kids had managed to survive.

Nate eased his foot off the accelerator as he drew closer. A young woman wearing big sunglasses was leaning against the side of her car. Her almost black hair was pulled back in a ponytail and she was staring ahead at the old house. He stopped the car when his was almost parallel with hers and wound down the window.

'Hi,' he said as he stuck his head out. 'Are you okay? Lost?'

The woman glanced over her shoulder before shaking her head. 'No.'

'All right, I just thought I'd ask. We don't get many people stopping here,' Nate said as he gestured towards the house.

'Why's that?' the woman said as she pushed off the car and walked around the bonnet to face him, pulling off her sunglasses in the process.

'It's a sad place, most people stay away,' he said slowly, distracted by her face. She had high cheekbones, but it was her pale grey eyes that made him pause.

'Well, I'm not most people,' the woman said as she hooked her sunglasses on the neck of her top. 'I'm Berry McCalister.'

Nate was stunned for a moment before shaking himself into action. He pulled on the hand brake and got out of the ute. No one had seen any of the McCalister kids since their uncle had bundled them into his flashy car all those years ago.

'Hi, I'm Nate Tarant—my place is just down the road. So, I guess we're neighbours.' Nate winced at the words as they poured out. God, that was lame. If she was Berry McCalister, then she'd probably know who the Tarants were.

'I guess we are.' Berry gave him a smile. 'Are you going to leave your car there . . . in the middle of the road?'

He smiled. 'It's quiet around here and this road hardly gets used. Besides, if anyone turns up they can drive around it,' he said with a shrug before sticking his hand out to her. 'Listen, I'm not sure what sort of state the house is in. As far as I know, no one's been in it for years but the town does keep an eye on it.'

'I know that Mr Ford does,' she said as she shook his hand.

'Yep, him and several others. They come out here on a regular basis to make sure the house hasn't been disturbed.'

'I didn't know that.'

'We weren't sure if you'd come back, but if you did, the town wanted to make sure that you had a house to come back to.'

'That's very kind. Would you pass on my thanks?' Berry said.

'Of course. So, are you back in Harlington for good?' Nate asked as he relinquished her hand.

'I don't know. I don't think so,' she said. 'It's the first time I've been back since . . . well, we're just wondering what to do with the place.'

'We?'

'My brother and sister—Tom and Jessica,' Berry said. 'Look, I'd better get on with it.'

'Right, well, I'll leave you to it, then. And if you need anything, I'm just down the road,' Nate said with a smile.

* * *

Berry watched as Nate sauntered back to his ute. He gave her a final wave before driving off down the dirt road. A brief smile flitted across her lips as she remembered the tall, gangly teenager she had secretly idolised when she was a kid. Not so gangly now. She turned her attention back to the house, before Nate had made it to the cross-road at the end of the track.

It was funny really, she'd spent last week assuring her family that she was quite capable of checking out Stone Gully Farm by herself and now that she was here . . . well, maybe she wasn't so sure. Berry dragged in another deep breath. Nate was right, it was a sad place, and it was filled with ghosts—but they were her ghosts and she alone had to confront them.

Berry eyed the overgrown path that led to the front door. A feeling of desolation had settled over the farm. Perhaps the weather added to the gloom—it was cold with a strong wind whipping through the bare branches of the trees in the front yard. The sky was grey with a sprinkling of rain. Like tears, Berry thought as she looked across the paddocks to the storm-filled clouds on the horizon.

Annoyed with herself because maybe she wasn't as strong as she thought she was, Berry yanked open the car door and grabbed her backpack. *Oh, this is stupid,*

I'm being stupid, she told herself before she slung the bag over one shoulder and marched towards the house. She pushed open the old wire gate, which creaked and scraped against the broken cement paving. Beyond the row of trees at the fence line, the garden opened up to what used to be a spacious lawn, which she and Jess used to play on. Now it was knee high with weeds and blackberry bushes.

Berry stepped up the one step to the verandah, which ran around two sides of the house. She blocked out the childhood memories that swarmed in her mind and focused on getting the damn key into the lock. After a moment or two jiggling the key, the lock finally clicked and Berry pushed open the door. The musty air hit her face as she stepped over the threshold into a dark corridor. Her hand went instinctively to the light switch and flicked it on—nothing. Berry frowned, she had organised for the electricity to be put back on but obviously there had been a delay.

She grabbed her phone, switched on the flashlight and stepped inside. The open door cast a little light but it didn't reach the end of the hall. But Berry didn't need the light to find her way around, the floor plan of the house was burned into her memory. She turned to her right and opened the door into what used to be the lounge room. It was partially open plan with the dining area and kitchen located through the dated arch at the end of the room. She hesitated for a second as she saw some large white objects across the other side of the room. Holding up her phone, she saw that it was coversheets over pieces of furniture. Annoyed at her own skittishness, she marched over to the windows, drew back the heavy drapes and threw open one of the sash windows. The pale light flooded the large room and the cold breeze blew the staleness from the air.

Berry walked over to the first dust cover and pulled it off, knowing full well what she would find. Beneath it was an old wine-coloured couch with carved wooden armrests and feet. The couch had been in the family for generations, patched and chipped and patched again over the years. Berry squeezed her eyes shut as the memory of her mother sitting on it bubbled up. That was the place her mum would read a bedtime story to her daughters every night. In winter they would cuddle up and listen to fairytales and watch the fire in the grate, and Berry would imagine the characters of the story in the flames.

She walked deeper into the room, pulling off the dust covers in her wake. She needed to turn her back on the couch and all the memories it conjured. The last dust cover revealed an empty crystal cabinet with glass doors, which had belonged to her grandmother. Once again Berry closed her eyes, this time picturing the little treasures that used to be housed there—Granny's favourite pieces, the hand-blown glass horse, her mother's Royal Doulton teapot, and a handful of other knick-knacks. Until this moment, Berry had forgotten all about them . . . but, now, she wondered where the little glass horse was.

Adjacent to the fireplace was a large bookcase, still filled with books, now covered in a thick layer of dust. Berry glanced at the spines as she walked past and headed to the kitchen, where she stopped to look at the pencil marks on the doorframe. She smiled to see her and Jess's growth over the years; lower down was the first line for little Tommy. They were still as fresh as the last time she'd seen them. The room seemed smaller than she remembered, but the familiarity of it wrapped itself around her. Berry opened the blind and then the back door to let the light filter in, and somehow it made the old house a little more welcoming.

She let out a breath as she made herself keep going towards the bedrooms on the other side of the house. Her footsteps echoed on the old wooden floor as she walked through the sunroom and to the bedroom she used to share with her sister.

The door was open and the corner of the curtain had been pushed back, creating a shaft of light that cut through the darkness. Berry went over and pulled back the rest of the faded curtain. As she turned around, she saw that the room was empty—gone were the bunk beds, the dressing table, the posters that had covered the walls. It had always been such a bright and happy place, filled with toys, games and midnight whispers. But not anymore. Now, it felt empty, neglected, sad.

After the tragedy, Berry had been back to the house only once, and that was under the watchful eye of her Uncle Dave. She and Jess had been allowed in this room, but the rest of the house was off limits. He'd given them each a suitcase and an instruction to fill it up with their favourite toys, clothes and books, then left them alone for a while as he went to pack a bag for Tommy.

Jess and Berry had stood in the middle of the room looking at the empty cases. She wanted her mother, she needed to feel her arms around her but that was never going to happen again. Berry glanced at her sister and took comfort in the fact that at least they still had each other and little Tommy. She squeezed her sister's hand for a moment, realising with a sudden sad weight that she now had new responsibilities for her siblings, before urging her to hurry.

'Come on, Jess, don't forget to pack Caramel,' she had said, pointing to a scraggly and well-loved teddy bear that lay threadbare and forlorn on her sister's bed. 'You don't want to leave him behind.'

The first thing Berry had put in her case was the photo from last Christmas of her and Jess with their mum. It was the way she wanted to remember her mother—smiling at the camera and hugging her daughters to her. After that, she grabbed some clothes and her favourite fairytale book. The last two things she stuffed into her bulging bag were two soft toys—Minty Tat Cat and Rabbit. She'd had them ever since she could remember, and even if she was ten and almost grown up, there was no way she was going to leave them behind. Not long after, Uncle Dave had walked in with a sad smile and Tom in his arms, and ushered the girls back out of the house and into his waiting car.

Berry looked around her childhood room as the memory settled in the back of her mind. God, she hadn't thought of that in forever. She turned to the window and looked outside. The rain was getting heavier, dimming what light there was. The room seemed to close in on her a little and again she wondered if she should have put off the trip until Jess and Tom had been able to come. She walked over to the light switch and flicked it—still nothing.

Berry felt . . . she wasn't entirely sure, maybe a little skittish, a little melancholy, a little uneasy. The rain was beginning to drum on the old iron roof; if she had a bit of light and a cheery fire it might have been comforting, but instead she had a silent and chilly house that only served to give the bad memories the power to overwhelm the good.

Berry quickly walked to the back door and locked it. She paused for a second as the silence of the house enveloped her. She was all of a sudden aware of the sound of her breath sucking in and blowing out against the backdrop of the rain. The air was still, as if she were holding her breath, and as the moments passed the more constricted her lungs began to feel as an ever-growing panic began to coil within her. She looked down the darkened hallway and took in a gulp of air, reminding herself there was nothing to be afraid of, but with each passing second the more rattled she became. She turned back to the door and double-checked that it was locked, and as she did, a shiver ran down Berry's spine. She could almost hear her mother faintly calling out her name. She knew that the voice came from memory rather than reality, but as she stood in the silent, shadowed house, both worlds seemed to merge. 'It's just in my head, it's just in my head,' Berry muttered. She turned around and headed to the front door, keeping her eyes straight ahead, not daring to glance over her shoulder.

To hell with this. She was going to stay at the B&B. She would come back when she had sunlight and electricity to frighten away the ghosts.

Chapter Three

Berry pulled up outside a quaint cottage just off what was regarded as the main street in Harlington. A charmingly painted sign next to the wrought-iron gate said *Cumquat Cottage—Guests Welcome*, and a welcome was just what Berry needed after the sad stillness of Stone Gully Farm.

She grabbed her bag and headed towards the front gate. Light spilled out of the cottage windows and Berry caught the scent of smoke in the wet air. A shiver skittled up her back; she would be glad to get into the warmth and, she hoped, in front of an open fire.

Berry walked up to the tiny porch and rang the bell. From within came the sound of a deep bark, and Berry braced herself at the sound of footsteps both human and canine coming towards the door. The door swung open to reveal a trim woman, perhaps in her late thirties, with a ready smile, and a large Irish Wolfhound sitting by her side.

'Well, hello—and welcome to Cumquat Cottage.'

Berry nodded and smiled. 'Hi, I was wondering if you had a vacancy.'

'Sure do—come on in. I'm Andrea, and this is Darby.'

Berry bent down and let Darby smell her hand. His tail thumped against the polished wood floor and she gave him a pat. 'He's gorgeous,' she said as he excitedly licked her hand.

'Yes, he is and he knows it,' she answered with a laugh. 'So, are you just staying the night?'

'Um . . . no, I think I'll be here for a few days. That is, if you're not booked out.'

Andrea shook her blonde bob. 'No, we don't get many visitors this time of year. There's a bit of a spike during school hols but generally it's quiet right through autumn and winter.'

'That's a shame, it's pretty here at this time of year.'

'It is but it's okay because I'm generally run off my feet during spring and summer. Come on through and I'll show you the room, then you can see if it suits,' Andrea said with a smile. 'The room is self-contained with an ensuite. It's attached to the main house but it has its own entrance. There are another couple of rooms, but I think this one is the best.'

Berry followed Andrea and Darby down a hallway to a small extension that had been added off the right side of the house. The room wasn't overly large but it had everything Berry needed for a short stay. There was a double bed, a small desk and a window seat overlooking a tiny courtyard and a cumquat tree.

'The door over there leads through the courtyard and to the front gate,' Andrea said.

'It's lovely. I'll take it.'

'Great, come on back through and we'll fill in the book. And after that, I think you'll need a cup of tea and a sit by the fire in the parlour.'

'That sounds wonderful.'

Back at the desk by the front door, as Berry finished signing in, Andrea pushed a large old-fashioned guest-book in front of her.

'It's not compulsory to write in it, just a bit of fun. When I envisioned the Cumquat, the idea of having a big leather-bound guestbook was always part of it. Maybe I've just watched too many old movies but I get a kick out of it.'

Berry gave her a smile. 'I'll be happy to add my name,' she said as she filled it out.

'Thanks,' Andrea said when Berry slid the book over the desk. As Andrea looked down, she stared at Berry's name, and a frown flickered across her face.

'Is there anything wrong?'

Andrea glanced back at her. 'No . . . sorry. I just made a connection, that's all. Your surname, it's familiar around these parts. But I'm sure you've got nothing to do with the story I was told when I first moved here.'

Berry was quiet for a moment. She should have realised that her family would still be spoken of in town. It was only natural—people wouldn't forget a murder–suicide, especially when it happened in such a small town like Harlington.

'Actually, I daresay I am connected to that story you

heard. I used to live here with my family when I was a kid. Our farm was down on Lyrebird Road—Stone Gully.'

'Oh, I'm so sorry. I should never have mentioned it,' Andrea said quickly as her cheeks infused with colour. 'There I go again, talking without thinking first.'

Berry shook her head. 'It's all right, really. It was a long time ago. I'm actually here to check out the farm. My brother and sister and I need to work out what we should do with the place. I've just come from there, actually; it's the first time I've been back in years. Anyway, I was going to stay at the farm, but the electricity isn't on and it was a bit cold and dark and . . .' Berry finished her sentence with a shrug.

'You went out there by yourself?'

Berry nodded.

'Perhaps you needed to take someone with you—at least the first time?'

'Maybe you're right. I found it harder than I thought.'

'Well, come on then, it's high time you were by the fire. Go and warm up. Darby will keep you company and I'll make a nice pot of tea.'

***

It was almost dark when Berry's phone rang. She was on the window seat, staring out at the rain-drenched courtyard, and had to dig the phone out of her pocket.

'Hey Jess,' she said.

'Hi. I just wanted to make sure that everything was okay. Are you still at the house?'

'No, that didn't pan out. The electricity wasn't on. And there was—well, still is—a storm, so the upshot was that it was pretty dark at the house and I couldn't see anything.'

'Oh, so where are you now?'

'Cumquat Cottage B&B,' Berry said. 'I'm going to stay here for a few days. It's nice and so is the woman who runs it.'

'Does she know who you are?'

'Yeah, seems we're kind of famous. Andrea isn't a local, she only moved here about three years ago but she already knew about what happened at the house.'

'Yes, well, that's not surprising,' Jess said.

'I guess. Anyway, I'm going to head over to the pub and grab something to eat. Hopefully, tomorrow will be more productive.'

'Okay. Have a good night, and give me a call tomorrow.'

'Of course. Night.'

Berry stared out the window for another minute before walking over and pulling out her quilted parka from her backpack. It was a dull olive green with faux fur around the hood. She put on the parka, grabbed her wallet and headed out the door. Despite the rain she felt refreshed as she walked the two blocks to The Queen's Arms. The place was familiar, not because she remembered visiting it but rather as a landmark in the town.

Berry pulled her hood up as she walked towards the pub, the wet footpath shining in the light of one of Harlington's four street lamps. As she looked about, the town was deserted; even the lights of the service station across the road were turned off. There wasn't another soul on the street, and after years of city life and bustle, it felt a bit creepy. She was used to crowds and noise and traffic, but here silence was the norm and it took a bit of getting used to. The only sign of life came from the pub. A handful of cars were parked outside, and as Berry neared, the sounds of voices, laughter and music wafted towards her. The warm glow of the pub's interior lights spilled out and reflected in the puddles that had formed on the roadside. She paused for a moment as she reached the door and took a deep breath. She always radiated a sense of strength and determination, but mainly that was for her family. Ever since the loss of their parents, Berry had taken it upon herself to be strong, not just for Jess and Tom, but also for Uncle Dave. But she had moments when being the rock that everyone could lean on was too much, and her vulnerability came through. But she wouldn't give into it, she couldn't. The one thing the past had taught her was that you needed to be strong to survive and that was what she would continue to be. Taking another deep breath, she centred herself before yanking open the door.

A wave of hot air hit Berry when she walked into the pub. She pushed back her hood and unzipped her jacket. Ahead of her was a small room filled with about a dozen tables and to her left was a large archway that led to the bar. Berry nodded to the four people at the nearest table before heading towards the back of the room. On one side of the old open fire was a table for two. Slinging her jacket over the back of the chair, Berry sat down and studied the limited menu. After a couple of minutes she made her way to the bar and ordered a lemon squash and the obligatory chicken parmigiana with salad.

'Is that it, love?' the elderly man behind the bar said. He had a thatch of white hair, red cheeks and more than a hint of a beer belly.

'Yes, thanks.'

'No worries. Just take a seat, love, and it won't be long,' he answered with a smile.

As Berry turned to go back to her table she heard him shout out behind her, 'One parma and salad!' She wasn't sure who he was shouting it to, as from her vantage point she could only see him and another old guy who was propping up the bar.

Returning to her table, Berry was aware of several sets of eyes looking at her. A middle-aged man in particular from the table further down kept turning around and staring. Berry wasn't sure if she should just ignore it or call him out, but she glanced back just in time to see him stand up and head her way. Berry groaned inwardly. All she wanted to do was eat her meal in peace and then turn in for an early night; the day had been emotionally draining enough without having to make chitchat with the locals.

Berry momentarily toyed with the idea of running off and hiding in the loo but dismissed the thought; she might have been a child the last time she was in this town, but not anymore. So, she watched as the man with salt-and-pepper hair neared, and prepared to deflect his questions. But as he drew closer she was struck by something familiar about him, although as hard as she tried she couldn't place what. He was dressed in a white shirt and jeans and he radiated a middle-aged dad vibe. But the main thing that struck her was that he had a kind face.

He stopped in front of Berry and gave her a small smile. 'Um, sorry to disturb you, but would you be Berry McCalister?'

'Ah yes. I'm sorry, I don't . . .'

The man's smile arced into a grin. 'You know, I was sitting over there and I thought it was you. It's wonderful to see you again,' he said before looking back over his shoulder and calling to his friends. 'I told you, Lynette—it's Berry!'

Berry frowned and felt suddenly like she was the last person to be let in on a joke.

'I'm sorry, I don't remember . . .' Her voice trailed off.

The man turned back and gave her another reassuring smile. 'It's all right, my dear. You don't remember us, do you?' he asked as a woman a similar age joined them. 'It's been a long time and you were only a kid.'

'Um . . .'

'Lynette and Jack Ford,' he explained. 'Jodie's parents.'

As everything fell into place, Berry stood up from the table and gave them a tight hug. These people had protected and comforted her on the worst day of her life.

'I'm so sorry I didn't recognise you,' Berry said.

'That's okay, darling,' Lynette said as she hugged Berry again. 'You were very little last time you saw us. It's so good to see you. Are Jess and little Tommy with you as well?'

'Not yet. They'll be up in a few weeks.'

'But they're fine?'

Berry nodded. 'Oh yes, Jess is at uni and Tom's in high school. They're both doing really well.'

'That's wonderful,' Jack said. 'Come on and join us at our table.'

'Thanks, as long as I'm not intruding.' Berry's wish for a solitary night suddenly seemed less important than reconnecting with this link from her childhood.

'Of course not,' Lynette said. 'Come on, we'd love to have you.'

'Georgie,' Jack called out to the man behind the bar as they walked back to their table. 'Berry is joining our table, so send her dinner there.'

'Righty-oh,' the barman called back.

'Good,' Jack said as he ushered Berry to a spare seat. 'This is Sarah and Bill Higgins. You might remember their son, James. He was in the same grade as you.'

Berry had to think for a second but she made the connection. 'Yes, I remember James from school,' she said. 'It's lovely to meet you.'

The couple smiled, making Berry instantly feel at ease.

'So, how is Jodie?' she asked. 'I feel so bad that we lost contact once I moved away.

'Oh, she's fine. She's up at uni in Bendigo at the moment. She took a while to settle on a path but that's okay, not everyone knows what they want to do after they leave school,' Jack explained.

But before he could expand, Lynette broke in. 'You shouldn't worry about losing contact. Those sort of things happen all the time, especially when someone moves away. Besides, I bet once you and Jodie catch up it will be just like you were never apart.'

'She's still the same?' Berry asked with a smile. 'I seem to remember us always getting into trouble.'

'Well, Jodie would say that was all on you,' Jack said with a laugh.

Berry shook her head. 'Oh, I think she's got that one backwards. She was always the instigator, I just followed along.'

Lynette giggled. 'Well, I guess you'll be able to fight that one out once you meet up.'

'So, what've you been up to and what brings you back to Harlington?' Jack asked.

'I finished uni last year and I took the beginning of the year to try and work out what I want to do. I've been waitressing while I figure it out. Now I'm here to check out Stone Gully Farm. Jess, Tom and I have to figure out what we're going to do with the place,' Berry answered. 'We're not sure if we should keep it, sell it or rent it out. The only thing we all agree on is that it seems a waste to leave the house standing empty.'

'Well, let us know if there's anything we can do to help,' Lynette said.

'Thank you, that's very kind.'

'Nonsense, we're more than happy to help,' Jack said before he tapped his glass with a knife. 'I'd like to make a toast,' he said.

Everyone raised their glasses and waited for Jack to speak.

'Whether or not you choose to stay, I'd just like to say Harlington has missed you. Welcome home, Berry—welcome home.'

Chapter Four

Doherty's Farm, 1906

Edward Doherty was sitting in his mother's garden by the vegetable patch. His mother was busy hanging out the washing not far away. He glanced over his shoulder and saw her pegging out a white sheet, the sunlight almost blinding as it reflected off the material.

The day was hot and the back of his neck was sticky—he'd wanted to go with his brothers to the dam for a swim but their mam was in the middle of being talked out of it. It wasn't fair that his brothers were always off doing that sort of thing. Was it his fault that he was only six and couldn't run as fast as Gabe and Samuel? Sometimes they let him tag along, but more often than not they shooed him away like a pest.

'Aw, Mam, Neddy can't swim yet. We'd have to watch him like a hawk,' Samuel had said. 'Besides, we can only go for a quick dip because I promised Da I'd help him fix the fence in the far paddock.'

Their mother straightened up from the washing trough

33

and placed her damp hands on her hips. 'Maybe you should have thought of that earlier.'

'Please, Mam, can't he stay here? Promise we'll take him next time,' Gabe said with an encouraging smile. 'And Sam's right—Da will be back from town soon and he'll expect us to crack on with the fence.'

'I'll pull up a bucket of water from the well so Neddy can cool off without getting into trouble,' Sam bargained as he gave him a fleeting glance. 'He can water the beans— you'd like to do that wouldn't you, Neddy?'

Sam didn't wait for a reply but rather turned around and gave Gabe a nod. As if on cue, Gabe squatted down in front of Neddy.

'Come on, Neddy, let's go and get the water,' Gabe said, holding out his hand as he stood up.

Neddy waited next to his big brothers as they pulled up the water from the well and filled an old metal tub, before carrying it back and placing it near the veggie patch.

'There you are—now you can water all the beans,' Sam said with an encouraging smile.

Neddy picked up the cracked willow-pattern teacup and dipped it into the tub, the water cold on his fingers. He smiled up at Sam and let out a giggle.

'Now, you water them beans well, 'cause I'll check when we get back,' Gabe said.

Neddy filled the cup and carefully tipped the contents over the plants. He was so intent on what he was doing that for a moment or two he forgot about swimming in the dam. He repeated the task a couple of times, but when he looked up to get some sort of encouragement from his brothers he realised they had disappeared.

With a sigh he put down the cup and looked towards the gate. Outside the fenced cottage garden, the Dohertys' farm consisted of a couple of large paddocks that swept gently downhill towards a large dam. Even in the height of summer the water never dried up.

The cottage was just out of Harlington and sat on a dusty track over a rise of a hill. The family owned a few acres between the small creek and the track. Unlike the majority of families in the area, they weren't farmers. Instead, Neddy's father, James, was a carpenter who occasionally picked up labouring jobs on the side to make ends meet. They still kept a few animals—a handful of chickens, a couple of goats and a cow—but that was for the family's needs rather than any commercial pursuit. They didn't have much, but neither did most of the folk around here.

Grandfather had built the four-room wooden cottage when he'd settled here from Ireland as a young man. Over the years Da had added a laundry with a small copper in the back garden and a sleep-out just outside the back door— that's where Neddy and his brothers slept. There were more impressive houses in Harlington, but none of them were as nice as the little whitewashed cottage on the hill.

Neddy turned his head towards the open door as the sound of little Rosie crying wafted over on the summer breeze. He stood up and started towards the cottage; he was her big brother, after all, and even if his brothers thought him a nuisance he would never act that way with Rosie. She couldn't help it if she cried a lot and was close to bald. A frown flicked across his face. He hoped her hair would grow quickly, then maybe she'd be almost pretty.

Neddy was about to step up onto the slate front step when his mother's voice came from behind.

'You can keep playing, if you like,' she said as she carried the empty laundry basket towards the door. 'Our Rose probably wants feeding anyway. Why don't you keep watering the garden and watch for Da to come home?'

Neddy nodded, but Mam had already disappeared into the cottage to tend to the baby. He went back to the tub of water and for the next few minutes made a half-hearted attempt to water the plants, although there was a possibility that he managed to drop more water on himself than the beans. After a while he realised that Rosie had stopped crying and there was a peaceful lull over the garden except for the occasional song from a bird in the crab-apple tree and the faint rustle of leaves. The sun was warm on Neddy's back and made him a little sleepy—that was until a movement by the gate caught his attention.

Neddy looked cautiously over towards the wooden fence, then edged closer until, through the slats, he could see the long ears and the soft brown fur of a rabbit. He glanced over his shoulder to see if his Mam was there—she wasn't, which was probably just as well, as she was partial to putting rabbits into pies. Neddy would much prefer to play with them. She called them nothing but pests that kept trying to eat her garden, but Neddy thought they looked soft and cute and he had always wanted one for a pet. He took a few steps forwards as quietly as he could. The rabbit didn't move.

Hopeful, Neddy took another step and then one more. The rabbit nibbled on some half-dry grass and ignored him. The summer had been hot and a lot of the grass had dried up and died, except by the fenced cottage garden. Because they had a well, Mam had made sure that most of her vegetables, fruit trees and even her one rose had enough water to flourish.

Encouraged, Neddy crept all the way to the gate. The rabbit, intent on eating, still disregarded him; perhaps he was too small to be considered a threat. He watched the rabbit and smiled, and after a moment's hesitation he slowly opened the gate and slipped through. At the soft creak of the gate's hinges the rabbit took a couple of slow hops towards the dusty track, and Neddy followed.

Chapter Five

The sun was shining when Berry rose early the next morning. Perhaps it was the change in the weather or her chance meeting with the Fords last night; whatever the reason, Berry felt ready to take on Stone Gully.

Yesterday, Berry had expected memories to resurface as soon as she walked in the door of her childhood home, but not that they would almost bowl her over. In the past few years she had told herself that she had come to terms with the death of her parents and her grandparents. It was a terrible, life-shattering event that had changed how she saw the world and her sense of belonging. But it was in the past and Berry now had two options—either deal with it or let the tragedy define her entire life. She chose the former. It was what it was, and no amount of thinking about what had happened to her family would change the outcome.

According to her Uncle Dave, her father had been under financial pressure, something that as a child of ten she wasn't aware of. Apparently, the pressure had been building and there was a chance that the family would lose Stone Gully.

At the time Berry couldn't really comprehend what had happened. In the beginning the truth had been kept from them. They were told that her parents, along with Granny and Pa, had been in a terrible accident and had died. But even at ten, that explanation never rang true for Berry. It wasn't an accident; so many years later she could still see the fear in her mother's eyes as she told Berry to ride to the Fords' in town. *Whatever happens, sweetheart, just keep riding. Don't stop until you get to Jodie's.* Something terrible had happened, and it wasn't until she was eighteen that Uncle Dave finally told her the truth. She had come across a folder containing the funeral notices for her parents, carefully cut out and placed in a plastic sleeve. Except they were not for her parents . . . they all seemed to be about her mother, and her father was never mentioned. She had asked her uncle why this was, and he sat her down and told her the truth.

There never was an accident. Berry's father had snapped and shot his parents as well as his wife, Berry's mum. Finally knowing the truth had turned her world on its head, but within that was the comfort of actually knowing what happened.

Every way she looked at it, she couldn't fathom that her father would ever hurt her mum—he loved her, Berry was sure to this day about that. She remembered how he would bring her mother a bunch of flowers for no particular reason. Sometimes he would shell out money and buy them from the servo, while the rest of the time he would go out of his way to pick some. Most of the time they were just wild flowers he'd found on the way home, but occasionally he'd go on a midnight raid of Mrs Jenkins' prize-winning rose garden. But something had gone terribly wrong, and in a matter of a few brief minutes, her dad had shattered their perfect life.

But the past was dead, a closed chapter that couldn't be rewritten. Berry knew she probably would never know why her father did what he did and that she just had to accept it. He had taken away her mum and for that she wanted to hate him, but try as she might over the years she couldn't. The conflict left her feeling as if her heart were torn in two. There was the deep sense of loss for her family and a realisation that it was a hole she would never be able to fill. But mixed in with that was the guilt that she should hate her father but couldn't. So, Berry did the only thing she could: she buried the events of the past deep inside her, along with the turmoil of emotions that were all wrapped up with it. This was the only way she could function—the only way she could be the Berry that her brother and sister depended upon.

And that's what she intended to channel today: no-nonsense determination. She had a job to do and she would just get on with it. Emotions aside, she needed to assess Stone Gully and whip the place into shape before Jess and Tommy turned up. The sun was out, which was an optimistic start, and the electricity provider had promised her that the power would be on by this morning. She could only hope they would keep their word.

Berry packed her gear, and along with cleaning products and a vacuum cleaner, she included her laptop and external speaker; if she was going to spend the day at Stone Gully she would make sure that she had music to get her through instead of enduring hour after hour of deafening silence.

Berry parked outside the general store, the street as deserted as it was last night except for an elderly man walking his little terrier and a couple of kids playing in the park. Berry headed into the store and was struck by just how small it was—she had always remembered it being bigger.

Nothing seemed to have changed. There was a small counter on the right-hand side as you walked in, a fridge that housed the milk, cheese and pre-packaged meat, and the entire back wall was covered in shelves that held a higgledy-piggledy array of products.

'Morning,' came a disembodied voice from somewhere behind the counter.

For a moment Berry was taken aback as she tried to work out who was speaking.

'Um, good morning,' she replied, craning her neck over the rack of chewing gum and lollies.

An old lady stood up and smiled at her. She was plump with pink cheeks and her white hair pulled up into a bun.

'Oh, Mrs Appleby, I didn't see you there.' As a child she had always thought that Mrs Appleby was ancient, so the fact that she was still there kind of blew Berry away. 'I didn't realise that you still ran the shop.'

'Yes, I've got nothing better to do,' she answered with a wink behind her gold-rimmed glasses. 'Now, if my memory serves me correctly, I'd say you're young Berry McCalister all grown up.'

'That's right. I didn't think that you'd recognise me. I was just a kid when I left.'

'You're the spitting image of your mum—darker hair, of course, but other than that you're just like her.'

'Thanks.' As always, the mention of her mum caused her breath to stop and her heart to flutter with a pang of sadness, but at the same time she felt happy—it was the first time anyone had ever said such a thing. In fact, it was the first time in ages anyone had even mentioned her mother. Uncle Dave never spoke about his sister, and if Berry ever asked him a question about her, she'd get a brief answer with no extra details.

'So, if the gossip is correct, you're back to sell the farm?' Mrs Appleby asked.

'Possibly. I haven't decided.'

'Well, it will be good to see the lights on again. I understand why but I always think it's sad to see a place abandoned.'

'I guess so.' Berry didn't really know what else to say. 'Anyway I'd better get moving. The house won't fix itself.'

'Well, that's the truth,' Mrs Appleby said.

Berry grabbed a couple of snacks and a bottle of flavoured milk and headed back to the counter where she handed over the money.

'It's good to see you again, dear. And I hope everything goes well for you, whatever you decide.'

'Thanks, Mrs Appleby,' Berry said with a smile before picking up her items and turning towards the door.

* * *

Nate crested the hill, riding his bay stallion, Ronin. He paused for a moment as he took in the sight of Tarantale Downs. He would never get sick of this view, it was in his blood but also in his heart. Before him the soft undulating ground swept down to the old house and extensive paddocks, stables and large training arena.

The stud had the reputation for breeding champions, which meant its services were always sought after, making Tarantale a lucrative family business. The Tarants had been on this bit of land for more than a century, and as far as Nate was concerned they weren't going anywhere.

Nate stroked Ronin's neck before urging him forwards and galloping down the dirt track towards the house. Ever since the family settled here, Tarantale Downs had been in a constant flux of improvements. Once one building project or renovation was finished the next generation would want to shore up the business and expand it further. When Alexander Tarant arrived in the late 1850s with his wife Alice and their son Henry, he pitched a tent on his hundred acres, quickly replacing it with a tiny wooden cottage, the remains of which were now nowhere to be found; the only evidence that the cottage ever existed was a small watercolour painted by Alice.

At the beginning Tarantale Downs was a livery stable, but Alexander had an eye for horse flesh, and as the years went by he began to trade horses as well as breed them. Family lore had it that he even supplied horses to Cobb & Co.

By the time Henry took control of Tarantale Downs, it had become an established horse stud and a blossoming success. Henry, who had developed more than a hint of respectability, decided that the family needed a grander home than the little cottage, so as well as building a new stable on the edge of the north paddock he set about having the homestead built; it was large and impressive with bull-nosed verandahs skimming three sides. And just to make his new wife, Emily, happy he spared no expense and included wrought-iron lacework, elegant steps leading up to the verandah and a dozen rose bushes, all to make Tarantale Downs the envy of Harlington.

As Nate rode down the drive, the homestead loomed ahead. From the front the house looked like it had in Henry's day, but as you got closer you started to see the extension out the back along with a conservatory. Of course, inside it had been updated over the generations and it now had all the mod cons, and thanks to Nate's dad, a state-of-the-art kitchen.

Ronin's hooves clattered on the road as he trotted around the house towards the stables. The stables had been built only a few years ago, and just like Tarantales' kitchen, they were state-of-the-art. Beyond the stables were fenced-off pastures and a training arena.

Nate pulled back on Ronin's reins and slowed him down.

'Hey Nate, you want me to stable Ronin?'

Nate looked up and saw one of the stable hands, Justin, sauntering across the yard. Justin was just seventeen and working here as a last-ditch effort to keep him out of trouble. He'd fallen in with the wrong crowd and Nate had taken him under his wing six months ago in the hope that working at Tarantale might help turn his life around. Nate had treated him like a younger brother. He made a point of keeping Justin busy, too busy to spend time with his old friends. He was a good kid, or at least Nate thought so—besides that, he was great with the horses and didn't mind doing the less fun jobs like mucking out stalls and stacking hay. There were only two things that worried Nate: that the kid might slip back into his old ways, and that he might be too handsome for his own good. Nate had overheard his fourteen-year-old sisters whispering about 'hot Justin' with his shaggy dark hair that made him look somewhere between a gypsy, a pirate and the lead singer of the boy band that Lia and Em worshipped. Nate had thought the twins were only besotted with horses but he'd recently started to rethink that notion.

Nate swung off Ronin's back and gave Justin a grin. 'Thanks, mate, appreciate it.'

'No worries.' Justin reached for the reins.

'Is the family still in?' Nate asked as he gestured to the house, before turning back to Ronin and giving him a pat.

'As far as I know,' Justin said before he started to lead Ronin towards the stable. 'I saw one of the girls about ten minutes ago. Catch you later.'

'Yeah,' Nate said, biting back a question about which sister Justin had just seen. 'See you later.'

Nate didn't live at the old house. A couple of years ago he realised for his own sake, and if he was going to maintain a relationship with his dad, he needed to move out. He loved his dad but the man had the need to micromanage nearly every aspect at Tarantale. Nate had converted the original stables into a home, meaning he was still on his beloved Tarantale Downs and close to his family, but not living on top of them. The place was a bit of a bachelor pad—furnishings a little on the sparse side—but it was his own domain, one that his dad couldn't impinge upon.

Nate entered the back door of the homestead and found his family in the kitchen. His mother and Em were bustling about cooking pancakes and making school lunches. Lia was finishing up a bowl of cereal and his father, Sam, was engrossed in the local paper, oblivious to everything. It was a familiar picture, one that Nate had witnessed most of his life. His father was always present but in some way or another he was always removed, never fully engaged with what was happening around him.

'Hello, darling,' Nate's mum, Jackie, said as she looked up from the stove and gave him a smile. 'Have you eaten?'

'I had some cereal earlier, but those pancakes look great,' he said as he scruffed Em's hair on the way past.

'Hey, get off—I just did that,' Em said before giving him a grin and a half-hearted shove.

'Well, sit down and I'll make you a couple,' Jackie said.

'No, it's all right.' Nate eyed the half-full mixing bowl. 'You sit down and I'll make them.'

Jackie hesitated for a moment but Nate kissed her on the cheek and gestured to the table. 'Go on, sit. I'm more than capable of flipping a couple of pancakes.'

Sam Tarant glanced up as his wife pulled out a chair and sat down. It was only then that he appeared to notice Nate.

'Nate, take a seat—one of the girls can do that.'

Em and Lia looked at each other and rolled their eyes before going back to what they were doing.

Nate shook his head. 'She's right, Dad. They'll only take a minute.'

'Well, hurry up, I've got something to discuss with you,' Sam said gruffly before turning back to the paper.

Silence fell over the kitchen. His mum and the girls sat quietly, the only cheery sound that of the kettle boiling and the hiss from the pan as Nate poured in some pancake mixture. It was moments like this that reminded him why he'd moved out in the first place.

'I hear that one of the McCalister girls is back,' Sam broke the silence as Nate sat at the table with his pancakes. 'The whole town's buzzing with the news. They say it's the eldest one, Berenice.'

'Well, small towns are like that,' Nate replied as he sprinkled brown sugar and lemon on his pancakes before digging in. 'Always talking about something or someone.'

'I guess I should go and say hello, welcome her back and all of that,' Sam said.

'I suppose, though you might want to give her a couple of days. Yesterday was the first time she'd been back to the farm, and I imagine that she'd have a lot to sort through.'

'You mean with the contents?'

Nate gave Sam an incredulous look. 'No, Dad, I mean it must be tough facing the house where most of your family was murdered. The bad memories would outweigh any of the good ones, wouldn't they?'

Sam put down the paper and looked at him with an intense and uncompromising expression, which always felt a bit unnerving, but eventually he nodded. 'You're probably right. I'll give her a few days to settle in. I doubt I'd even recognise her. She was just a kid when they left town.'

'You can't miss her,' Nate said as he glanced up from the pancake. 'Long dark ponytail, pretty, not scared to speak her mind.'

His father stared back at him. 'Since when did you meet her?'

'Yesterday, when I drove to the shop. Berry had just arrived, so I stopped and talked to her,' Nate said with a shrug as he felt his sisters' eyes burning into him.

'So, do you know why she's here?' Sam asked.

'Well, it's their house,' Nate said, ignoring the twins.

'You think she might want to sell it, after all this time?'

'I don't know. Maybe. I guess she'll have to talk that out with her brother and sister. She said it wasn't just her decision.'

'Hmm, I guess not.'

'I was always surprised that they kept the place,' Jackie said before taking a sip of orange juice.

'I thought it was odd as well,' agreed Sam. 'I mean, why would you want to live in such a place? All those terrible memories.'

'Maybe they decided to let the McCalister kids decide,' Lia added as she polished off the last of her cereal. 'I think I'd want to make that decision rather than have someone else do it. Guess her family decided to wait until they grew up so they could say what they wanted.'

Jackie nodded. 'You're probably right, sweetheart. It would make sense if the family could afford to keep the property, that is. I always thought they were struggling at the time of the . . . well, you know.'

'They were,' Sam said. 'That's what everyone believes pushed Jordy McCalister over the edge—the financial strain. But apparently the other side of the family was loaded.'

'So, why didn't he ask for help?'

'Too proud, I guess. Anyway, I was told at the time that the kids' uncle paid off the mortgage so they could keep it. Always thought it was a waste, that good land sitting idle for all these years.'

'Well, it looks like things are about to change,' Nate said. 'Guess we'll just have to wait and see what happens. Were you friends with him, Dad?'

Sam took a moment and stared across the table. 'Yeah, I was. It was a terrible business. Jordy McCalister was always a bit of a dreamer. I never could believe that he'd do something like that. I know that depression and financial strain can eat at a man, but I never thought he'd snap like that. He worshipped his wife, I can't see how he could have hurt her.'

Nate studied his dad for a second. 'Are you saying you don't believe he killed his family before taking himself out?'

Sam shrugged. 'They say he did but I've never been able to believe it.'

'Do you know something? I mean, if you have doubts you should have told the police.'

'I don't have any evidence, it's just a gut feeling that the guy I knew would never have done what they said. I talked to the police at the time but they said it was a cut-and-dried case. Jordy had snapped and killed his parents and his wife. Thank God the kids got away, though that must be an awful burden to live with, especially the eldest, because she would remember more.'

Nate nodded. 'I reckon so.'

'It's a tragedy, all right. And one that should have been buried by now. Whether Jordy did it or not, it's in the past. The family should have got rid of the place back then rather than letting it fester.'

Chapter Six

The first thing Berry did when she arrived at Stone Gully was to open every window and door to let the breeze and sunlight cleanse the house. The next thing was to set up her portable speaker so she could pump music through the place. Once this was done, Berry stood back and marvelled at how some sunshine and music could change the atmosphere.

The farmhouse had taken on a different feel today. There was still an undercurrent of melancholy but not the sense of foreboding doom that surrounded her yesterday. It was just a house that needed to be cleaned and put in order. She ferried in the vacuum cleaner and other cleaning products she'd brought up from Melbourne and set to work, tackling the kitchen first.

Halfway through the morning, just as Berry wiped down the final bench, there was a loud knock at the door. Berry frowned as she wiped her hands on a tea towel before heading to the front door. Standing on the verandah was a middle-aged man in a smart grey suit and aviator sunglasses. His dark hair was slicked back and he exuded an air of self-importance.

'Hello, can I help you?' Berry said.

The man shoved his sunglasses up until they were sitting on his head.

'Oh, hello. Miss McCalister?'

Berry nodded. 'That's right.'

'It's lovely to meet you,' the man said as he extended his hand. 'I'm Laurie Worth.'

Berry took his moist hand and then wished she hadn't as he pumped hers up and down a couple of times before releasing it. It took all of Berry's willpower not to then rub her palm on the leg of her jeans. 'Okay. So, how can I help you?'

'I'm a local businessman. I have interests in several of the towns around this area but my home is in Harlington. The town's buzzing with the news that you've come back, so I thought I'd stop by and welcome you.'

'Thanks,' Berry said with a small, wary smile.

'No problem at all,' he said, leaning against the doorway. 'So, are you planning to move back permanently? Or maybe sell the old place?'

'I haven't made a decision on that yet,' Berry said, now on her guard.

'Right ... right,' he said and Berry wasn't sure if he was addressing her or himself. 'Well, if there's anything you need, please don't hesitate to call,' he continued as he whipped out a business card and handed it to her.

Berry took the card without looking at it. 'Thanks.'

'Right then,' Laurie said after a few moments of silence. 'Well, I'd best press on as I'm sure you've got a busy day ahead. Once again, welcome back to Harlington.' He finished with a smile.

Berry nodded and then took a step back. 'Bye.'

He paused for a moment as if he were going to say something and then seemed to change his mind. 'Yes, see you later,' he said as he turned to go.

Berry watched him walk down the drive to where his shiny black car was waiting. She didn't know much about cars, but she would bet her dinner that Laurie Worth's car was expensive. She glanced down at the business card in her hand: *Laurie Worth—Worthy Development*.

Berry shut the front door, screwed up the business card and carried on with her cleaning.

She broke for lunch—which consisted of the raspberry muffin and chocolate milk she'd bought at the store that morning—sometime after one o'clock. She had grabbed a handful of tea bags from the B&B but quickly realised when she got to Stone Gully that she didn't have anything to make it with.

Taking what was left of the milk, she wandered outside into the back yard for the first time since coming back. Ahead of her was the old Hills hoist. For a moment she closed her eyes and blocked out the memory of riding her new bike around it.

Steadying herself, she walked on. Further down the overgrown garden was a large metal shed, where some of the contents of the house were boxed up. The door was padlocked. There were more structures to her right, though they didn't seem to be in the best shape. The roof had collapsed on one, and the door of the old chicken coop was hanging off two of its three hinges.

Past the sheds Berry could go either into the back paddock or follow a path to the small orchard down by the dam. She followed the skinny track, almost over-grown with weeds and dandelions, as the land dipped down towards the huge dam that reminded her more of a lake. A jetty overhung the water's edge and looked out to a large island in the middle. The winter rains had filled it up and Berry stopped for a moment to listen to the silence of the place. Not far away was the orchard, which mainly comprised almost an acre of Red Delicious apple trees, though at this end her mother had included several other fruiting trees—pears, peaches, plums—which had always been used for the family rather than sales. They were all overgrown and in desperate need of pruning, and the ground beneath was littered with broken branches, twigs and the detritus of years of unharvested fruit.

Stone Gully Farm had once been four times bigger than its present fifty acres, but over the years and genera-tions, slices of it had been sold off to keep the creditors at bay—which is why in her father's day, the sheep-running aspect had been scaled back to almost nothing and he had pursued other avenues. He'd planted half an acre of olive trees next to the apple orchard. Added to that, there had been a small flock of sheep, chickens and even a few grape vines. Stone Gully Farm was a hodge-podge of different ideas, none of which had truly paid off. Her father had tried so hard to run the place but ultimately had failed. If it wasn't for Uncle Dave and her maternal grandparents the farm would have been lost not long after her parents had died. He was a barrister and worked long hours but never complained when the children came to live with him—in fact, he had insisted on it. Uncle Dave was a bachelor, and Berry often wondered if he would have settled down and married if he hadn't devoted his life to his nieces and nephew. He had given them a sense of family, stability and belonging. And for that Berry would be eternally grateful.

Berry wandered through the apple orchard, running her hand across the trunks as she passed each one. The trees were gnarled and in need of pruning but they were still here, they had endured—just like her. There was something comforting in that.

***

'How did it go today?' Andrea asked as she and Berry sat in front of Cumquat Cottage's open fire.

Berry sipped her Earl Grey tea and sank back into Andrea's comfortable couch. 'Okay. I managed to clean a couple of rooms and air out the place. There's still a lot to do, and regardless of what we end up doing with it, it still needs a new kitchen, bathroom and several coats of paint.'

'A lot of work ahead.'

'That's the way it's shaping up.'

'And pretty pricey, I'd say.'

Berry let out a sigh. 'Yeah, I guess it will be. Uncle Dave will be funding the improvements but I'm determined to pay him back.'

'So, what do you do—I mean work wise?' Andrea asked.

Berry sighed. 'I haven't decided. I worked as a waitress and a barista while I went to uni, but now that's finished I have to start looking for something more permanent.'

'What did you do at university?'

'I started out in Teaching but I quickly discovered that it wasn't for me, so I switched to a BA, focusing on literature and history. Which means that now I'm a really well-educated waitress,' Berry added with a grin.

Andrea reached for her cup and took a sip before asking, 'What about your dreams or passions? I only ask because I suppressed my dreams until only a few years ago. I always wanted to move out of the city and have a quaint B&B but my head wouldn't allow it. So, for years I stayed in a job that I didn't love. I was a good accountant and the last firm I worked for were great, but my heart wasn't in it.'

'Well, I think that's the problem—I don't really have a goal to aim for. Not like my sister Jess, all she wants to be is a writer and I think that's what she'll do. I'll support her any way I can so she achieves what she wants.' Berry couldn't admit it aloud, but she had never allowed herself to have personal dreams and goals because she needed to look after Jess and Tom, and their welfare and happiness were the only things that mattered to her.

'Do you always take care of your brother and sister?'

Berry nodded. 'Yes, I made a promise.'

Andrea gave her a small smile. 'Well, just remember that you need to look after yourself as well.'

'You know, sometimes I feel like I'm treading water, like I'm waiting for something to begin but I don't know what.'

Andrea reached over and squeezed her hand. 'It'll come. All I'm saying is, when you decide what you want to do, don't wait until it's too late to go for it.'

'Wise advice,' Berry said.

'Well, I'm a very wise woman,' Andrea said with a wink. 'Now, I don't know about you but I'm starving. Why don't we pop over to the pub for dinner?'

Berry put down her cup. 'Sounds like a plan.'

Saturday night at The Queen's Arms was a lot like a Friday night—a few souls in the bar and a handful of people enjoying a meal.

'Does it get busier than this?' Berry asked as they settled at a table near the fireplace.

'Yes, but this is off season. There's just enough local traffic to keep the doors open. Once we hit spring, things begin to liven up.'

'Same as the B&B?'

Andrea nodded. 'Yes, but I do get a few bookings. You know, couples wanting to explore the orchards and wineries around this area. And there's nothing nicer than sitting in front of an open fire, sipping hot chocolate when it's cold outside.'

'Wait, what's this about hot chocolate and why am I only finding out about it now?'

Andrea laughed. 'Best in town . . . um, maybe in the entire area.'

'You've been holding out on me,' Berry said with a grin.

She was about to ask Andrea about what she would recommend on the menu when a commotion broke out in the bar.

'Are you calling me a liar?' a gruff voice sailed through the air.

'Now, Ned, I didn't say that. You just took it the wrong way,' came a placating tone.

Berry looked over at the bar and tried to pinpoint where the fuss was coming from.

'You know the story and it's as true as we're standing here. My grandfather saw it when he was a nipper. Everybody knows it.'

Berry glanced at Andrea, who in turn rolled her eyes and leaned closer over the table.

'That's Young Ned. Let's just say he's one of Harlington's characters.'

Berry looked back to the bar and saw the profile of an old man with white hair that hit his shoulders.

'Young Ned? The guy has got to be in his seventies,' Berry said as she glanced back to Andrea in surprise.

'That's because his dad goes by "Old Ned"—he is ninety-three years old and still spritely,' Andrea explained.

The conversation continued in the bar with whoever had offended the old man now trying to settle him down. 'Now, now, Ned, I didn't mean it. Come on and I'll shout you another beer.'

Berry heard a bit of mumbling before Young Ned turned back to the bar. 'Bloody young whippersnapper, you're talking through your hat. You got no respect for town history.'

'Come on, Ned, I didn't mean to upset you. Here, the pint's on me.'

As peace appeared to settle over the bar, Berry made her way over to order dinner and a round of drinks. As she paid for the food she made the mistake of looking over at the other side of the bar, catching Young Ned's eye. He put down the beer he was drinking, got off his bar stool and made a beeline for her. Berry hightailed it back to Andrea but Young Ned almost beat her back. For an old guy he could move fast.

'Evening ladies,' he said with a nod of his head.

'Hello Ned,' Andrea said with a smile. 'This is Berry McCalister. She's staying with me at the B&B for a few days.'

'McCalister, I know that name,' he said as he studied Berry. 'I seem to remember that there was a bit of bad business years back.'

Before the conversation could take a turn down a road that Berry didn't want to go, Andrea jumped in. 'So, what was all that about in the bar?' she asked.

Young Ned screwed up his nose. 'That young Tarant kid just asking dumb questions. Asked why my grandad didn't go after the vein,' he harrumphed.

Berry looked at Ned and then to Andrea, without a clue of what he was on about.

'Sorry, Berry,' Andrea said. 'Ned's talking about the gold his grandad discovered when he was a boy.'

Ned looked at Berry. 'Oh, doesn't the young lady know about the Harlington Vein?' he asked expectantly.

Berry smiled and shook her head. 'No, I'm afraid not.'

Without another word Ned grabbed the nearest chair and sat at the table. 'Well, it all started when my grandad was a little nipper. I'm not sure when exactly, back around 1906 give or take a few years. He was only little—five or six, maybe—and one day he wandered off from home and got lost in the bush. The town was in an uproar and searched for him day and night. When he turned up two days later he said he'd seen a big golden vein running through rock. Some people thought he was making it up but others believed him. Problem was that he couldn't remember where he'd seen it, he was so little, you know. Over the next few years the townsfolk went out to try to find it but no one ever did. But he saw it, he said he did and I believed him. It's out there, just waiting to be found, I can feel it in my bones.'

'So, there was gold in the area?'

Andrea nodded. 'Oh yes, all through here was dug up during the gold rush.'

'Well, I hope one day you do find it,' Berry said.

Ned nodded sagely. 'It's not about what's it worth— it's proving to everyone that my grandad was right. You understand that, don't you, missy?'

'Yes, I get it,' Berry answered. 'I really do.'

'Oh come on, mate, you left your beer on the bar. I wondered what happened to you,' Nate Tarant said as he appeared behind Ned's chair and placed his hands on his shoulders. 'Hi Andrea. Berry, it's good to see you again.'

'Hello Nate,' Berry said as she glanced up at him. She felt an extra beat of her heart that caught her by surprise. Their eyes locked for a moment before she looked away.

'I didn't realise that you knew each other,' Andrea said.

'We crossed paths yesterday,' Nate explained before looking back down at the old man. 'Anyway, come on, Ned, let's go and finish that beer.'

Ned stood up and gave a nod. 'Ladies,' he said before he let Nate lead him away.

'Bye,' Berry and Andrea said in unison but it was Berry who caught the glance that Nate sent as he looked back over his shoulder.

'Well, thank goodness for Nate,' Andrea said with a smile. 'If he hadn't distracted Ned, he would have sat here for the next two hours telling us about gold fossicking. Don't get me wrong, I like him, just in contained doses.'

'So, do you believe in the gold story?'

Andrea shrugged. 'I don't know, maybe, but sometimes family legends aren't always founded in truth.'

'I guess,' Berry agreed as the waitress walked up with a smile and bearing two loaded plates.

Andrea looked over towards Nate and gave a small nod. 'He's such a nice lad, so different from his father.'

'Is he?' Berry picked up her cutlery and looked at Andrea, expectantly.

'Well, one doesn't like to gossip . . .'

'But go on anyway,' Berry said with a grin.

Andrea laughed. 'It's just that I've never warmed to him. Which of course means absolutely nothing—if we all liked and agreed with everyone it would be a bland sort of world. He tends to be the standoffish type. You know what I mean—a bit cold.'

'I don't know him or the family now, but I'm pretty sure that Nate's father was a friend of my dad's.'

'That's interesting, he always seems such a loner. I guess I could be wrong. The rest of the family are lovely. You didn't hang out with his family at all?'

Berry shook her head. 'No, from what I can remember Nate's sisters are about the same age as my brother Tom. Nate was a few years older than me. So, let's face it, there wasn't much incentive to hanging out with a scabby-kneed kid when you'd just turned into a cool teenager.'

'So, was there a big age difference between you?'

Berry looked over at Andrea and smiled. 'It seemed so at the time. I think the year we left he'd just started at the high school in Castlemaine. I used to see him every now and again, you know, across the paddocks, but he always seemed so much more grown up. He was never interested in talking to little old me.'

Chapter Seven

Later that night, Berry was distracting herself with a book when her phone rang. She smiled as she picked it up.

'Hey Uncle Dave, how are you going?'

'Good. I just thought I'd check and see how you were faring up there.'

'I'm okay,' she said a little too brightly.

'That doesn't sound very convincing. What's up, Berry?'

She sighed. 'It's nothing, really. It's just, well, coming back is a little harder than I thought it would be.'

She heard him sigh. 'I wish you'd waited a couple of weeks. I would have taken the time off and headed up there with you. I should have known better than to let you go by yourself.'

'You didn't *let* me do anything,' Berry said with a laugh. 'My mind was made up.'

'Hmm, yes, and we all know how . . . determined you can be,' Dave chuckled. 'So, how are you doing, really? Are you okay?'

'Yes. The first time going to the house was a bit rocky but it's all right now. It's going to be hard for a while for all of us—we've all lost so much here, including you. But I think that with time and work, we can move on, and fixing the house is just the start.'

'And how's that going?'

'I've been cleaning it up and making a list of things that have to be done. It's going to need a damn good renovation.'

'What are you thinking?'

'Hmm, new kitchen and bathroom, and a total paint job inside and out for starters. Some of the outbuildings look as if they need repair, and one of the water tanks needs replacing,' Berry said.

'What about the floors?'

'I haven't looked under the carpet yet but I was thinking about pulling it up and polishing the wooden boards.'

'That's a good idea,' Uncle Dave said. 'Well, draw up a list and we'll get things started. Maybe you can inquire about finding some local tradesmen who can take on the job.'

'I'll start looking into it in the morning. Oh, and Uncle Dave—thanks for everything.'

There was a slight pause on the line. 'You don't have to do that. We're family. The three of you have been with me so long I think of you as mine anyway, you know that.'

'I know and I can't think what we would have done without you. You didn't have to take us in but you did.'

'Don't be silly, there was never any question. Cath was my big sister; there's no way I wouldn't have stepped up.'

'Yeah, but you had your own life. You didn't have to be saddled with us,' Berry said softly.

Again there was a pause on the other end of the phone and Berry thought she heard his voice crack a little as he replied.

'I wasn't saddled with you. I took you guys in because I needed to. I did it for Cath and I did it because I love you all, but most of all I did it for myself. By looking after all of you, I got to keep a little bit of Cath with me. And that means everything,' he said before trying to lighten the tone a little. 'Besides, if I hadn't, Cath would have found a way to whip my butt even from the afterlife.'

Berry smiled. Uncle Dave was never very demonstrative. She had never doubted that he loved her and her siblings, but when he said something like he just did, Berry wanted to hold onto it.

'Love you.'

The line was silent for a moment. 'I love you too, Berry.' The words lingered for a second or two before he cleared his voice and carried on. 'Now, I expect you to keep in touch and tell me how everything is going.'

'I promise.'

'Good. Now I'd better go, and you probably need an early night.'

'Yeah, you're right. Night, Uncle Dave, I'll call you soon.'

'Night, Berry. Take care.'

Chapter Eight

Harlington, 2007

Lynette Ford had just served the kids dinner when a frantic banging on the front door startled her.

'Stay here,' she said to her children. 'I'll be back in a tick.'

With a frown she headed towards the ongoing noise. It didn't seem right, and alarm bells were ringing even before she'd yanked the door open halfway.

'Berry what are you doing here?'

The child was pale, tracks of tears had washed a clean path down her grubby cheeks. She stood on the doorstep looking small and frail and clutching her squirming baby brother. Lynette glanced towards the road half-expecting to see Cath McCalister, but the only thing on her lawn was a bright red bicycle lying on its side.

'Good God, Berry, did you ride all the way here?' she asked as she bent down and took the struggling Tom from his sister's arms. Once he was settled on her hip, she placed a comforting hand on Berry's back. 'It's all right, sweetheart. Everything is going to be all right. Come on inside, Berry,' she soothed as she applied a little pressure in an attempt to guide the child into the house.

Berry stared straight ahead, her eyes open and wide, and Lynette was sure whatever the child was seeing was a memory replaying in her head. She gathered Berry towards her with her free arm and felt her tremble.

'You're safe, Berry, I promise.'

There was a small commotion near the kitchen door, along with some fairly ill-disguised whispers. Lynette glanced in the direction and saw her girls, Jodie and Katie, along with little Jessica McCalister staring back at her.

'Jodie, I think Dad's in the garden—will you please tell him that he needs to come in, I have to speak to him.'

Jodie didn't have to be asked twice, she sprinted down the small hall and out the back door.

'Now, Katie, I need you and Jess to go back and finish your dinner,' she said. She was surprised that her voice sounded so calm and level, the opposite of how she felt.

The two girls looked at each other before Katie took a step forwards. 'But Mummy, Berry's here with the baby. Can't we stay?'

Lynette shook her head. 'No, off you both go before your dinner gets cold. Quick now.'

Reluctantly the two little girls walked slowly back into the kitchen, one by one looking over their shoulders to see what was going on.

Lynette waited until they were out of sight before turning back to Berry.

'Come on, sweetie, come inside and sit down. It looks as if you've ridden a long way—you must be tired.'

Berry didn't speak but this time she allowed Lynette to usher her into the living room. Once she had settled the three of them onto the couch, Lynette tried again.

'Berry, can you tell me what happened? Why did you come all this way on your bike, and bring Tom?'

A heavy silence hung over the room and Lynette was beginning to think that the child wasn't going to answer her. 'Sweetie, can you tell me?'

'Mummy told me to come.'

'Did she?'

Berry nodded.

'You're very brave to ride all that way in the dark, especially with little Tommy.'

'Mummy said I had to be brave.'

The words sent a shiver down Lynette's spine. No parent would send their children into the night by themselves for no good reason.

'Sweetie, can you tell me why she said that and what does she want me to do?'

The child finally turned her head and looked at Lynette. Her eyes were overbright as tears welled and began to trickle down her face.

'Ring the police. Mummy needs you to ring the police.'

Lynette caught a movement out of the corner of her eye. Her husband was standing in the doorway with a shocked expression on his face.

Chapter Nine

Berry looked up from her paint samples to the sound of knocking on the front door. She frowned as she got up from the old couch, and when she opened the front door she was more than surprised to see Nate standing there. He was wearing a red plaid shirt, jeans and work boots. His dark blond hair was swept to one side, and Berry's gaze lingered on the slight stubble of his chin and the light in his eyes.

'Hey,' he said as he gave her a brief smile. 'I didn't disturb you, did I?'

Berry shook her head. 'No, not really.' He looked a little uncomfortable as he took a step back. 'Do you want to come in?'

'Um, thanks,' Nate said as he started to walk in.

Berry glanced over her shoulder as she headed towards the kitchen. 'Coffee?'

'Oh, thanks—sure, but only if you're having one. I don't want to put you out.'

'You're not,' she replied as she started to fill up the kettle. 'So, what can I do for you?'

'You said the other day that you might renovate this place, and I was thinking you might need some suggestions about contractors seeing as you haven't been in Harlington for a while?'

'Well, I'm certainly open to suggestions,' Berry said with a smile. 'I've researched a list but I'm not sure if they're any good.'

Nate leaned against the kitchen bench. 'Do you want to tell me who's on your list? Maybe I can point you in the right direction.'

'Sounds good. I'll just go and grab it.'

Nate waited until Berry returned holding onto a notepad. 'From what I can gather, there aren't any contractors in Harlington, is that right?'

Nate nodded his head. 'Yeah, you'll have to go to Lawson's Bend or maybe Bendigo. Harlington's pretty small, so the main thing that's going on here is farming. Some of the residents live here because they're still hanging onto the family land but they work further afield.'

'I kind of figured that was the case. Harlington doesn't seem big enough to support all its population.'

'Yeah, it used to be, apparently—you know, back in the day—but now many people use it as a base. Most work in the larger towns and a few people even travel to Melbourne each day.'

'That's a bit of a journey, isn't it?'

'About an hour and a half by train and add another fifteen minutes to drive to Lawson's Bend to get to the station. I've asked a friend of mine why he does it—seems it would be a bit wearing after a while—but he said that he gets the best of both worlds: his dream job and living in a place he loves. He figures if travelling is the price he has to pay then he's happy to do it.'

'I guess even if you live in the city your commute's going to take a while,' Berry said with a shrug. 'I get that some people would choose to commute. At least you'd get to wake up to that each morning,' she gestured to the window.

'Yeah, maybe it's because I've always lived here, but I can't imagine being anywhere else.'

'I like both. It's beautiful here but the city is great too. I love the movement and the bustle and the fact that I can get a great coffee at two in the morning.'

Nate laughed. 'Well, you're not going to get that here unless you make it yourself.'

'I guess I'd better brush up on my barista skills then,' she said with a wink as she handed Nate the notepad. 'Here's the list I've made so far. Are any of these contractors any good?'

Nate scanned the list. 'Yeah, I recognise some of them. The Grants from Lawson's Bend are good, same with this guy from Violet Falls.' He said as he pointed to the paper. 'We've contracted work from both of them over the years and they were excellent. The only one I wouldn't recommend is *Big Jake—Wonder Builder.*'

'Bad?'

Nate smirked. 'He does a good job, I won't take that away from him, but unfortunately he's not that reliable. We tend to "wonder" if Jake is actually going to turn up to finish the job.'

Berry smiled. 'Well, maybe we should cross him off the list.'

'Yeah, probably a wise move. So, what are you thinking about doing to the place?'

Berry gave Nate a rundown.

'You're not playing around, then?'

'Not when it comes to renovation,' Berry said with a laugh. 'If I'm going to do it, I might as well do it right. And—' she looked around '—the house . . . no, the whole place needs a facelift to shake the past off.'

Nate glanced up at Berry and for a moment their eyes met. 'Will that work?'

'I don't know,' Berry answered in a soft voice. 'I guess we'll have to wait and see.'

The light-hearted banter seemed to disappear within an instant and Nate wished he hadn't asked the question. It was stupid, the last thing Berry needed was a constant reminder of what happened here. The silence lengthened, as Nate shifted from one foot to the other while he tried to work out what to say next.

Berry seemed to snap out of it first. 'Sorry, here I was going on and I haven't even made you that coffee yet,' she said quickly as she started to grab a couple of mugs from the dresser. 'How do you have it?'

'White with one, thanks.'

'No problem.'

Wracking his brain to find something else to say, Nate came up with the first thing that popped into his head. 'Do you ride horses?' He winced as soon as the words were out of his mouth—of all the lame things to come up with.

Berry glanced over at him with a slight frown on her face.

Yep, this would definitely have to be the lamest thing he'd ever uttered.

'Um, I've never ridden a horse.'

'Oh, I thought that you probably did when you were a kid—I mean, growing up on a farm and all.'

Berry shook her head as she poured the water into the coffee plunger, the scent beginning to waft in Nate's direction. 'Nope, it wasn't that sort of farm. About the only animals we ever had were half a dozen chickens, a few sheep and a cat.'

Damn, he was clutching at straws now. When did talking to a woman get so hard? There was something about Berry that made him more self-conscious than usual, and he was starting to understand that her opinion of him meant more than that of other girls he knew.

'Um, if you want . . . you can come over and I'll teach you. That is, if you've got time.'

'What?'

'I mean, you don't have to. It's just that you're next door to a horse stud, so I thought . . . It doesn't matter . . .'

'Thanks, that would be great,' Berry said before he could finish. 'I'd like that, I've always wanted to learn how to ride.'

Nate looked at her and slowly smiled. 'Good, I'd be happy to teach you. Shall we say, Saturday morning at nine?'

'That sounds good. I'm afraid that you'll have to be patient, I've never really been near a horse, let alone ridden one,' Berry said.

'You'll be right, I've got a sense for these things.' Nate grabbed a pen that was sitting on the kitchen bench and jotted something down on her pad. 'Here's my number, just in case you need to get in touch.'

'Thanks,' Berry said as she swapped the notebook for his coffee. 'I mean it, that's very kind of you to offer to teach me.'

'Not a problem,' Nate said as he watched her turn to grab her coffee, his gaze lingering an instant too long.

***

Soon after Nate left, Berry stepped out for some fresh air to clear her head. As she walked out the back door she took a deep breath. She had no business even thinking about Nate Tarant, but his handsome face lingered in her mind's eye. She was here to do a job and that was all. Yet, she couldn't deny even to herself that there was something about Nate that quickened her heart. And she had agreed to riding lessons! She couldn't even tell herself why. It's not like she had the time to take on a new hobby like horse riding, yet she couldn't bring herself to turn down his offer. In fact, she hadn't even hesitated. The idea excited her—but it was not the thought of riding a horse that quickened her pulse.

Berry headed through the back yard towards the sheds. She remembered them from when she was a kid but had barely taken notice of them. Her dad had kept the tractor in the big shed because it could be locked, as well as things like his chainsaw and any other tools that were a bit pricey. The first shed was a big metal one, which was the size of a couple of rooms, and it appeared to be the newest and the one in the best nick. Its door was shut but the fat padlock was hanging open.

Not too far away were two more smaller sheds that had seen better days. Both were made of wood and one had a little cracked window that she could peer through. Berry pulled out a tissue from her jeans pocket and rubbed the dirt layers from the glass and looked in. It was fairly dark and she couldn't make out much except for an old mower and a couple of boxes.

The last shed had been there for decades. The door stuck a couple of times but Berry eventually managed to push it open, and the sunlight cast a beam into its gloomy depths. There was a jumble of old boxes, ancient suitcases and enough cobwebs to make Miss Havisham proud. She stood in the doorway for a moment as the scent of dust, stale air and the discarded past wafted around her.

She took a tentative step into the shed but the floor-boards creaked. Glancing around, she saw another pile of boxes in the corner, several stacks of newspapers and a couple of worn-out old-fashioned baskets. Everything was covered in a thick layer of dust and there was a stillness within the room that Berry found a little unnerving. She took a step back and regrouped. The only way she was going to get this shed cleaned out was with gloves, a broom, copious amounts of insect spray and very loud music.

Going back to the big shed, Berry fiddled with the padlock until it came clear. Poking her head in, she saw that it was almost empty. The tractor wasn't there, nor at first glance were any of her father's tools. Berry frowned, unsure what was meant to be there. She looked down to the padlock in her hand—had the stuff been sold off or had it been stolen? She would get to the bottom of it but first she'd have a look around. There was a work bench sitting across the far wall and next to it an old metal filing cabinet.

Berry sighed as she pulled out the first drawer; just as she suspected, it was empty except for half a dozen discarded suspension files. The second drawer was hiding a hammer, two paintbrushes of varying sizes and a small empty Vegemite jar half-filled with gold drawing pins— not exactly treasure by any stretch of the imagination.

She pulled open the third drawer and found a couple of manila folders filled with old photocopies and a stack of handwritten notes. Berry took out one of the sheets and recognised her father's bold handwriting. For an instant a memory popped into her head. It was almost as if she were seeing through a faded yellow filter of a long-gone summer. She remembered that he had a habit of writing notes in varying notebooks and scraps of paper. She frowned for a second as she focused on the picture in her mind. She remembered wondering what he was writing about, that day she found him in the kitchen with a pile of old maps, books and, of course, notebooks.

'Dad, whatcha doing?' she had asked as she pulled up a chair and sat by him.

'Homework,' he answered with a slight smile.

'You don't go to school,' Berry said with a scoff. 'You're too old.'

He laughed and ruffled her hair. 'Too old! Geez, Berry Cherry, you certainly know how to hurt a man. Just how ancient do you think I am?'

Berry shrugged. 'I don't know, not as old as Grandpa.'

'Wow,' he muttered under his breath as he brushed his dark hair away from his eyes.

'Anyway, what's all this?' Berry asked as she gestured to the table full of papers.

'As I said, it's homework,' he replied.

'Dad,' Berry said with a whine, 'aren't you going to tell me?'

He looked down at her, shook his head and held one finger up to his mouth. 'Nup, it's a secret.'

As she stood in the shed immersed in her memory, a lump formed in the back of her throat and for an instant her head began to swim. She dropped the page, took a step back and leaned on the workbench until the sensation passed.

'Get a grip,' she muttered. 'It's just a piece of paper. Don't be an idiot.'

It was just a stupid bit of paper, but with it came the mental picture of her father smiling down at her. These were the memories she didn't want—these were the ones that she feared the most because they were the most confronting. How could someone she had loved so much turn out to be the monster who had destroyed everything?

Berry dragged in a breath and straightened up. 'This is ridiculous—just get your act together,' she said in a firm voice.

Turning back to the open drawer, she picked up the manila folders and placed them on the bench to go through later back at Cumquat Cottage. Finally, she turned her attention to the last drawer. Instead of it being empty like she thought, it was full of more papers, an old briefcase and several slim volumes. Berry picked one up and saw that it was a history of Harlington and the surrounding area. Another book was a collection of reminiscences and local legends.

Berry frowned as she found more of her father's handwritten notes and scribbles. Whatever this was, it was obvious that it had been important to him. For a second she almost wanted to shut the drawer and walk away but something stopped her. Instead she scooped the material out of the drawer and stacked them on top of the manila folders.

It didn't matter if it hurt. Berry was going to discover what he had been working on and why. Decision made, she carried the papers into the sunshine and placed them on an old outdoor chair until she could take them home.

She looked back to where the tractor should have been, and pulling out her phone, decided to ring the only person who would know what happened to it.

'Hey, Uncle Dave.'

'Berry? Is something wrong?'

'No, no—I'm okay, I just had a question. I was poking around the old sheds and I remembered the tractor. What happened to it after we left?'

'Ah, it was sold, along with other bits and pieces—tools, and the cars. Jack Ford organised it for me. They held an auction and all the money that was made was put towards your education, and Tom's and Jess's. It seemed like the right thing to do.'

Berry paused for a moment. There was so much about her past that she didn't know, and she felt as if she was intruding on decisions that affected her own life. 'Oh, I see.'

'I thought someone getting use out of the tractor was a better idea than locking it up for years. Was I wrong?'

'No,' Berry said quickly. 'Of course not. I just wondered what had happened.'

'You shouldn't worry about the sheds. I doubt there's much in them. But if you want to empty them, I'll arrange for someone to come and do it,' Uncle Dave said.

'No, it's okay. I can do it.'

'Are you sure? You've got enough on your plate with getting the house fixed.'

'You're right about that. I'll get the house organised before I tackle the sheds, okay?'

Uncle Dave gave a small laugh. 'Okay. Just let me know if you need anything. Promise?'

'Promise.'

'Good, I've got an appointment, so I'll talk to you later.'

'Bye. Love you.'

'Love you too,' Uncle Dave said before the phone went dead.

Berry stared across the paddocks to the distant hills. Her uncle was right, she really did need to get the house squared away before she started tackling outside. Reluctantly she turned towards the house after giving the old shed a final glance. She needed to organise a contractor for the renovations and get this project moving. If she didn't stop procrastinating, she would still be here next winter. In a way it didn't really matter as she had no pressing business in Melbourne, but she didn't want to burden her uncle's finances too long. If there was a considerable hold-up she'd have to look for a part-time job somewhere up here.

With a little more determination in her step, Berry walked back to the house. Even though she'd only been back in Harlington for a short time, she knew deep down that she was dragging her feet on starting the reno. This was partly because she didn't want to make a mistake and hire the wrong contractor, but mainly because even though she hated to admit it, seeing the house as it was brought back all her childhood memories. The more she was at the house, the more memories came back—flashes of her mum and grandparents . . . and even her dad. As she allowed herself to remember her childhood, Berry came to the realisation that in most ways it had been idyllic. There was never a lot of money to go around and sometimes they all had to make do with what they had, but still there was a comforting glow about the past that she couldn't ignore any longer. The crackling of the open fire, the hot sweet porridge her mother would make each morning in winter, and how her breath would steam in the cold May air as she helped her mother pick apples in their orchard. How could Berry have forgotten how it felt to run barefoot across the paddocks when they were carpeted with spring grass, or the joy of taking the dingy with Jess and paddling over the island to play.

Her childhood had been snatched away by that one terrible day, and she had spent the rest of her life doing her damnedest to block everything else out. Berry had thrown herself into her studies and keeping her promise to her mum by looking after Jess and Tom. Perhaps she should have tried to hold on to some of her childhood memories, but instead she'd locked them up because remembering how happy she'd once been was just too painful. As soon as she started to think, the same question would always raise its ugly head: *How could Dad do what he did?* And equally as terrifying, if Jess and Tom had been there, if she had been there . . . would he have killed them too?

Chapter Ten

2007

As Constable Rob Mendez drove down the dirt road towards the McCalisters' place the moon was high in the night sky, illuminating the flat paddocks dotted with clumps of tall gums and the odd shed. The house was not far ahead on the left, but if it hadn't been for the light of the moon, Rob would have missed it.

It took about fifteen minutes to drive to Harlington from the Lawson's Bend police station. This trip, however, was taking a little longer. One, because Stone Gully Farm was on the other side of Harlington and, two, he had his boss in the car.

He glanced over to his companion. 'Do you know what's going on, Sarge?'

'Nope, only that the McCalister kids arrived by themselves at the Fords' place. Young Berry told Mrs Ford that she had to call the police,' Sergeant Adam Harris said as he kept his gaze on the road ahead. 'I guess we'll find out what's going on when we get there.'

They were silent for the next couple of minutes, Rob

scanning the side of the road for any kangaroos that might decide to jump out without warning. Having grown up in inner-city Melbourne, he thought his co-workers were winding him up when they warned him about this when he first moved to Lawson's Bend. That was until driving home one evening, from Bendigo, he had to swerve to miss a kangaroo as it bounded across the road—it had scared the life out of him and he'd been vigilant ever since. Over the past couple of months he had tried to settle into country life, but he reckoned he'd never get used to this.

Rob pulled off the dirt road onto a patch of withered grass outside the McCalister property. A small dark-coloured hatchback and a white ute sat in the driveway, but not a single light shone from the house.

'Come on, let's go,' Sergeant Harris said as he cracked open the door. 'Keep on your toes, we don't know what we'll find.'

Rob nodded before he got out of the car and headed towards the front door with Harris. As it was midsummer and the air was still warm, he could detect a hint of jasmine mixed with the scent of far-off rain—it was clear and sweet and made him draw in a deep breath. He flinched as Harris rapped forcibly on the front door, the sound was sharp and echoed through the darkness.

'Hello, this is the police. Is anyone there?'

They stood by the front door for a moment as the silence enveloped them. Harris shook his head before knocking again.

'Hey, it's Adam Harris. McCalister, are you there?'
He glanced over at Rob before he turned the doorknob
and slowly opened the door. He reached over and ran his
hand up the inside wall until he found the light switch
and flicked it on. The light illuminated a small hallway and
spilled out the front door.

They stood together on the threshold for another
moment. Rob tilted his head and strained his ears in
an attempt to pick up a sound, but there was nothing.
The stillness sent a shiver up his spine. He hadn't been
a policeman for long, but even with his inexperience he
sensed that there was something very wrong.

Harris gave him a nod before taking the lead and
walking into the house, guns drawn. The door on the
right was closed, and Rob knew in his gut that something
awful was waiting behind it. He opened the door and
pushed it open, a shaft of light from the hall falling into
the dim room. Old Mr McCalister was on the floor, a pool
of dark blood had seeped from beneath him and edged its
way towards the doorway.

'Are you all right?'

Rob pulled his eyes away from the sight just in time
to see Harris give him a quick glance. Everything inside
him wanted to scream *No, I'm far from all right*, but he
pushed it down and nodded back. He was determined to
hold it together, no matter what. He was a professional
and had a bloody job to do.

'Yeah, I'm okay.'

'Good, come on, then,' Harris said.

Rob followed the older cop further into the room. It didn't take them long to find Jordy McCalister. He was slumped in an old armchair with a handgun near his feet. His temple was shattered by a bullet hole, and blood dripped down the side of his head. Rob quickly turned away and kept moving in Harris's wake; they went through the kitchen and towards the back door. They paused only for a second while Harris flicked on the light switch and opened the back door. Immediately it flooded the steps that led down to the back yard in a pool of light. That's where they found Jordy McCalister's mother, on the path, face down with a bullet in her back.

Rob wasn't from Forensics but it didn't take a rocket scientist to see that she'd been trying to run away. He reckoned he might never get the image out of his head. They doubled back and checked the remainder of the house, but Cath McCalister wasn't in there.

'Do you think Cath got away?' he asked as they went down the back stairs and into the yard.

Harris shrugged as he grabbed his radio. 'We don't know what's happened here, not for sure, anyway. I'm calling this in.'

* * *

Rob stood in the front yard and watched a steady stream of headlights bump their way down the dirt road outside the McCalister place. A squad car was already parked behind Rob's vehicle, but it took a bit longer for everyone else to arrive from Lawson's Bend and Bendigo.

Within another few minutes the almost silent property was abuzz with action, voices and the bustle of people getting on with trying to work out what exactly had happened. The house was cordoned off, and as the night wore on, the kinetic atmosphere of the place seemed to intensify. Rob kept his vigil by the front gate just in case any curious neighbours showed up. He doubted that would happen now as he glanced at his watch and saw it was approaching four a.m. A cold sensation trickled up his spine and he shivered, closing his eyes for a moment as he tried to get the images of the McCalisters out of his head, but he couldn't seem to shift them. He tried to imagine what Cath went through—knowing something so bad was about to happen she sent her children away, not knowing if they would reach safety. The thought haunted him as he wondered what had happened to her. Rob was tired, maybe that was just from the initial shock, but he reckoned he could do with a hot coffee or perhaps even something stronger.

Headlights travelling from the opposite direction caught his eye. He watched as the vehicle approached; at first he assumed it was a paddy wagon but then he realised it was a large dark blue ute. It pulled over to the other side of the road, and out stepped a tall man wearing jeans and a plaid shirt that by the look of things had been hurriedly buttoned. As the man strode over the dirt road, Rob could see that he was in his early forties.

'Hey, what's going on?' he asked as he started to walk through the gate.

Rob held up his arm. 'I'm sorry, sir, you can't go in there. It's a crime scene and is cordoned off at the moment.'

'Listen, I'm Sam Tarant—I own the horse stud up the road. The McCalisters are friends of mine. Is everything all right?' he said as he tried once again to walk through the gate.

'I'm sorry, sir, but you can't come in,' Rob said with a shake of his head.

'Geez,' Sam Tarant said, his eyes rounding as the realisation began to dawn on him. 'Oh God, are they all right? I was just talking with Jordy this morning. Are Cath and the kids okay? Tell me!'

'I'm sorry, sir, but—'

'Jordy! Cath! Are you okay? Jordy!' Sam cried out with rising panic in his voice as he tried to push his way past Rob.

Adam Harris sprinted over and gave Rob a quick glance. 'Come on, Sam, let's go back to your car,' he said as he placed his arm around the man's shoulders and started to guide him back over the road.

'Adam, what the hell's going on? I've got to get in there.'

Harris shook his head. 'Nah, you don't want to go in there.'

The words made Sam's steps falter and for a moment Harris had to hold him up. 'You mean . . .'

'It's bad, Sam. I can't say much, but Cath's parents have been called and . . . and, well, at least the kids are okay.'

'What?'

'Go home, Sam. There's nothing you can do here,' Harris said as he opened the car door and urged him to get back in.

Sam Tarant slid into the driver's seat with a look of shock on his face as he stared ahead.

'Hey, are you all right to drive?'

'Huh? Yeah, I'm fine.'

'Okay, then. We'll know more tomorrow.'

Sam gave him a nod before starting up the car and heading back home.

Adam Harris paused as he walked back to Rob. 'Listen, you've had a hell of a night—you can take off if you want. Your shift's almost over anyway.'

Rob shook his head. 'Thanks but I think I want to stay for a bit. There're a couple of teams beginning to search the property for Cath McCalister. I thought I'd lend them a hand.'

'Okay, but remember to get some rest. I'll see you tonight,' Harris said and clasped Rob on the shoulder as he moved past him. 'You did good, kid.'

Rob went around the back of the house, walking under the old Hills hoist and out towards the paddock beyond the yard. There was a skinny track that ran behind the old wire fence and Rob turned right to see where it would take him. There were flashes from torch lights further into the paddock. As he looked around he saw several groups of police and emergency services workers walking over the paddock, searching. He knew what they were looking for—Cath McCalister. For a moment he wondered if he should join them, but something made him want to follow the little path, so he did. He flicked on his torch and carried on.

The track rose uphill for a little way before dipping back down towards what he took to be a small orchard. There wasn't anybody else searching near him. He knew it was standard procedure to start near the house and fan out, and that this approach made sense. And, yet, there was something compelling him to keep going.

Time seemed to fly by as he combed every inch of the orchard, to no avail. He leaned against the trunk of a pear tree and took a breath. He was exhausted but there was also a shot of adrenaline that kept firing deep within him and he knew that he had to keep going. The night sky was beginning to lighten with the oncoming dawn. Looking up, he could still make out a scattering of stars.

'Please let us find her,' he whispered. 'Please let her be okay.'

Leaving the orchard, Rob continued down the track, a clear and sweet breeze buffeting him along. With each step the sky brightened and he could easily make out the lake-like dam that appeared before him. It was expansive, with poplar trees skimming along the far side, and a large overgrown island in the middle of the rippling water. As he walked closer he noted a concentration of reeds by the water's edge that didn't thin for several hundred metres, and a little further up the bank was a long jetty that jutted out over the water. As the first hint of the rosy dawn began to break over the far-off hills, he paused for a moment and took in the scene. It was so perfect it could have been on a postcard. How could there be so much death in such a peaceful and beautiful place?

Rob took a last moment of silence in the cool summer air and then moved on. He had a job to do and he wasn't going to go home until Cath McCalister was found.

He scoured his way through the thick reeds, looking for any sign that she had come this way. The birds began to sing as the first faint rays of the sun crept into the sky. Being from the city, he couldn't make out most of the birds except for a magpie that warbled nearby, and the only reason he knew about the magpie was because he'd heard all the horror stories from his co-workers about being swooped.

A movement caught his eye and he looked out across the water to the island. Several herons were stirring from their sleep—he stood transfixed for a moment and watched as they unfurled their wings.

Rob forced himself to keep walking; he followed the curve of the bank and fought his way through the tall reeds as he headed towards the jetty. He imagined Cath taking the same route in panic and desperation. How terrified she must have been. He paused every few minutes to scan the area but everything appeared as it should. He pressed on until he reached the jetty. His footsteps echoed on the rough wood as he walked out to the end of it and stared out across the water in the hope of finding something . . . anything.

From his vantage point he could see that a group of searchers were beginning to fan out on the other side of the dam. Rob turned around and looked back at the bank, and for a second he thought he caught a glint of light. He hurried back down the jetty and then made a path through the reeds to the water's edge.

It took him a moment to register what he was seeing. A stone dropped in his stomach as he edged closer, his breath came short and sharp. Hot tears threatened and he squeezed his eyes shut to stop them from falling. He had wanted so much to find her alive. Rob liked to think of himself as a hardened professional, but the truth was that today was his first experience seeing dead bodies like this. Cath McCalister was lying on her side as the water lapped against her—staring unseeing towards the island.

Chapter Eleven

Berry kept telling herself that she should fix up her old room at the house and move in, but she enjoyed being able to escape back to the B&B after another day of solitude, joining Andrea for a chat over a hot chocolate. But she also knew that there was more to it. As the night drew in, the atmosphere of the house began to change. Berry realised that she was being fanciful, but she couldn't seem to shake the mood. It was fine during the day as she kept busy with music pumping through the entire place, but at night . . . well, that was different. Winding down meant you had more time to think, and even worse, remember.

The renovation was scheduled to begin the next Monday, so Berry decided it was time she took stock of the land that comprised Stone Gully Farm. Up until now, she hadn't gone much further than the old orchard and the dam. The farm consisted of several other large paddocks, a winter creek and, of course, the large quartz reef that cut across a corner of the property. As a kid she used to follow the creek that wound around the base of the reef. It was unfortunate, at least that's what her grandfather used to say, that the reef was there because it made that bit of land almost useless. But he'd then follow it up by saying you had to work with what you had and that was that. Berry had always liked collecting bits of pretty quartz, so she would just nod to her grandad and say nothing.

Berry spent much of her day walking along the boundary fences and checking the state they were in. For the most part she was surprised that the majority of the fenceline was okay. There were some sections that needed work, but on the whole it was better than she expected—until she came to the fence that they shared with her closest neighbours, Tarantale Downs. A large gum had crashed down on a section of the fence and had managed to flatten the whole thing. It looked like it had only happened fairly recently. Berry stood for a moment and then another as she tried to work out how the hell she was going to fix it. The tree was huge and she had no idea of where to begin.

The fence being down wasn't really a problem for her but she realised that it could be for Nate and his horses. She pulled out her phone and scrolled through until she found his number. He answered after two rings.

'Hello?'

'Hi Nate, it's Berry McCalister. I'm sorry if I've interrupted you.'

'No, no it's fine,' Nate said quickly. 'What can I do for you?'

Berry had barely finished telling him about the fence before he offered to come to meet her.

* * *

It was only about ten minutes before Berry saw Nate's ute bumping its way down the paddock towards her. Nate gave her a wave through the windscreen as he pulled up by the fence.

'Hey,' he said as he got out of the car and motioned towards the fallen tree. 'I can see we've got our work cut out for us.'

'Yeah, it's huge, isn't it?' Berry said as she glanced back to the gum before turning back to the newcomer who had stepped out of the ute after Nate. 'Hi, I'm Berry.'

'Oh, sorry—this is Justin. I dragged him along to give us a hand.'

Justin gave her a smile and a nod. He was younger than Nate but almost as handsome. Berry frowned at her own thought. She had no business toying with the idea of handsomeness, especially when it came to Nate. She was smart enough to know how vulnerable she was.

'So, do you go to school around here?'

'No, I wasn't very good at it,' Justin said with a shrug.

'More to the point he didn't put enough effort into it,' Nate said.

'Hey, are you my dad or something?'

'Lord no, it would be a twenty-four–seven job keeping you out of trouble,' Nate laughed as he nudged

Justin's shoulder with his own. 'Justin is one of our stable hands at Tarantale.'

'Oh, I see,' Berry said, and then after pausing for a moment, continued. 'So, any ideas on how to get rid of the tree and fix the fence?'

'We'll repair it, you don't have to worry about this,' Nate said with a smile. 'I'll grab a couple more guys and we'll take care of it.'

'Thanks, but don't you want me to help or at least pay for some of the fence?' Berry asked with a frown. 'I mean, it's only fair that I contribute to getting this sorted.'

'Have you ever used a chainsaw?'

Berry bristled a little. 'No, but that doesn't mean I can't give it a go.'

'Sorry, I didn't mean that to sound like how it came out,' he said and Berry caught Justin rolling his eyes behind Nate's back.

Berry stared at him for a moment to gauge if he was actually telling her the truth. She raised a questioning eyebrow and waited for the next words out of his mouth.

He took a step closer and looked her in the eyes. 'Look, I'll take care of it but if you want to come down and help, you're more than welcome. I'll teach you how to use a chainsaw and mend a fence, okay? I didn't mean to make it sound like you weren't capable.'

For a second he stared at her with puppy eyes and she had to admit it was hard to maintain her annoyance when someone that damn handsome was gazing down at her.

'Okay, we'll do that,' she said grudgingly, slightly irritated at herself for being manipulated by a handsome face.

Nate grinned, and Berry wondered if he was aware of what he was doing.

'Good, we'll go back and grab some help and tools and be back in an hour or so,' he said as he held out his hand waiting for her to shake it.

'Fine,' Berry said as she took his hand. She tried to ignore the warmth of his skin and the tiny buzz of electricity as they touched. 'I'll see you then.'

***

Back at the house, Berry was about to dive into a sandwich when there was a knock at the door.

'Hello,' the middle-aged man said with a brief smile that didn't quite reach his eyes. He seemed familiar but she wasn't sure why. He was tall with a lean face and his dark blond hair was silvered around his temples. 'I'm one of your neighbours—Sam Tarant.'

'Oh hi, I'm Berry. I know your son.'

'Yes, he said he'd met you when you first arrived.'

'That's right, but I actually just left him.'

Sam Tarant's eyes widened a little in surprise. 'What, just now?'

Berry explained before she gave an embarrassed smile and took a step back. 'Sorry, I don't know where my head's at. Please come in, can I make you a cup of tea?'

'Thanks, that sounds good,' Sam said as he started to follow her back towards the kitchen.

Berry noticed that he paused, took a deep breath and blew it out.

'Are you okay?' she said as she glanced over her shoulder.

He nodded. 'Yeah, sorry. It's just that I haven't been in here for a long time.'

Berry indicated a stool by the kitchen bench. 'Please, take a seat,' she said before putting the kettle on. 'Did you know my parents, Mr Tarant?'

He nodded again. 'I was friends with your dad. You don't remember?'

Berry shook her head. 'I'm sorry, things from back then are all pretty hazy.'

'Well, it was a long time ago and you were only a little kid.'

'Coffee or tea?'

'Coffee, thanks—just white and no sugar,' he said. 'So, I was a little surprised when I found out that you'd returned. Harlington is a sad place for your family, it must have been difficult to come back, especially by yourself.'

Berry smiled. 'I'm fine. Really.'

'Still, I suspect it was a bit daunting when you first arrived.'

'Yes, I suppose it was. Although I'd have to thank your son for stopping by when he did. It really helped.'

'So, do you mind if I ask what you are going to do with the place? I mean, I figured that you and your brother and sister must have lives in Melbourne.'

'I guess we do. I've finished my Arts degree and I'm taking a break to work out what I want to do. That's why I decided to come here and check out the house. One way or the other we have to come to a decision on what we're going to do with it.'

'I suppose that's a hard decision,' Sam said as he took a sip of his coffee.

'It is. On one hand I feel that we should fix it up and sell it, but on the other . . . it was our home,' Berry said as she pulled out the other stool and sat down next to him.

'You'd have a lot of memories invested here.'

Berry sighed and gave him a smile. 'I was quite young at the time. I do have memories of my parents and grand-parents, but as I said before they're a bit hazy. I remember feelings and snippets, like planting trees in the orchard with my mum or paddling over to the island with Jess. Although we only did that a couple of times because if Mum had found out she would have hit the roof.'

Sam Tarant chuckled. 'I would have felt the same way if any of my kids had done something that dangerous. At least until I knew that you both could swim.'

'Probably not as well as we thought,' Berry admitted. She paused for a moment, gathering herself to ask the question foremost in her mind. 'Did you know Dad well?'

'Yes, I did. We'd hang out quite often. He was a dreamer, you know. Always looking at ways he could improve Stone Gully. Some of his ideas were solid while others . . . well, they were a bit out there.'

'Mr Tarant, did you talk to him before . . . the incident?'

He was silent for a moment. 'It was a long time ago, but I think I saw him a couple of days before. He was worried. I'm not exactly sure what about because he didn't tell me. I can only guess that it had something to do with money.'

'Why do you think that?'

'Look, I don't know what went on in his head. If you had told me that he'd snap like that and hurt your mum, I would never have believed it. They were devoted to each other and because of that I jumped up and down at the time that the police had got it wrong. I believed an outsider must have killed your family because the Jordy I knew would never have raised a finger to anyone, not his own parents and especially not your mum.'

'And yet that was the verdict.'

'Yes, that's true. I guess you never really know someone. Your dad was under financial pressure. Oh, he never told me the details. I guess it must have just been too much for him and he snapped. At least that's what I tell myself—he couldn't have been in his right mind. I don't know if that helps but—'

Berry broke in before he could finish his sentence. 'Actually, I think it does.' He wasn't telling her anything that she didn't already know, yet somehow it seemed comforting to have someone else say it.

Sam looked at her. 'I can't imagine what you've been through. And your brother and sister. It was a terrible tragedy, but you have to remember sometimes things like this just happen—people reach breaking point. Back in our day no one ever talked about mental health, especially in rural areas; you just had to get on with it. There's a lot of pressure on families to make ends meet, not being the son of a bitch to lose the family land, enduring drought, fire and everything else that gets thrown at you. Basically, from an early age you're told to man up. At least I know I was and I bet your dad was the same. There's more support available now but still there are people who don't ask for help and think that problems and mental-health issues are seen as a weakness.'

'You think my father was like that?'

'I can't say for sure but it would explain what happened. Because Jordy would never had done what he did if he'd been in his right mind. I think there must have been a culmination of things that just piled onto him until he broke.'

Berry stared at her coffee. She'd spent years trying to forget her tenth birthday, trying to reconcile the father she'd loved with the man who had destroyed nearly everything.

'I'm sorry, I've just met you again and I take you back down into the dark past that you're probably trying to forget.'

'No. Thank you. I think you've made me understand what happened better. My uncle didn't tell me the truth until a few years ago. Up until that point my brother, sister and I all knew that our parents had died, but not the circumstances.'

'That must have been difficult.'

'Understatement. For the second time my world was turned upside down,' Berry said with a shake of her head.

Sam Tarant took another sip of his drink. 'Listen, I know that you don't know what you're going to do with the place. I'm not pushing you one way or the other, but if you and Jess and Tom decide not to keep it, I'm more than willing to buy it for a decent price.'

Berry sat back, startled. 'Why would you want it?'

'Because you kids have been through enough. And, if I'm being honest, I could use the land. I guess, above all . . . because your dad was my friend.'

Berry nodded. 'We haven't come to a decision, but thanks. I promise I'll keep it in mind.'

'Good. And listen, if you need anything, don't hesitate to get in touch with me or Nate.'

'Thank you, I really appreciate that. I was a bit worried about coming to Harlington but everyone I've met so far has been very welcoming.'

'It's a small town and generally people stick together. It's been like that for generations.'

'There's something nice about that.'

'Oh, one other thing,' Sam said.

Berry glanced up and gave him a questioning look.

'I'll take care of the fence, you don't have to put anything into it. Keep your money to fix up this place.'

'That's very kind of you, but I wouldn't feel right about not helping to pay for the damage. I mean, the tree was actually on my side of the fence,' Berry explained.

'Think of it as a welcome home present,' Sam Tarant said quickly.

'Oh no, I couldn't.'

'If you feel that strongly about it, why not supply the guys with some refreshments. That'll be enough and I figure they would appreciate the thought.'

'Um . . . okay, I guess, but that still doesn't seem fair.'

'That's all I'm willing to accept,' Sam said before he drained the last mouthful of his coffee and stood up. 'Thanks for the cuppa and let me know if you need anything.'

'I will. Thanks again, Mr Tarant.'

'Well, I hope we'll run into each other soon.'

'There's a possibility,' Berry admitted as she stood up and pushed the stool back against the kitchen bench.

'Oh?'

'Actually, Nate's suggested he could teach me to ride. I'm keen to learn, so if it's not too much trouble I think I'll take him up on his offer.'

Sam Tarant gave her a smile. 'It's no trouble at all. I'm sure Nate will be looking forward to it. Right, I'd better be off—there's no rest for the wicked,' he said as he headed towards the front door.

Chapter Twelve

True to his word, Nate turned up at their shared fence line an hour and a half later. He arrived with a couple of utes, several chainsaws and a handful of men of ages ranging from Justin's late teens to about fifty. They got to work straightaway, cutting up the fallen tree and clearing it away from the fence.

Nate grabbed one of the chainsaws from the back of his ute and frowned. He glanced towards Berry's house and wondered when she would turn up, before putting on his protective goggles and starting up the chainsaw. He wasn't sure why he'd felt a burst of excitement when he'd answered her phone call earlier, but he had. It was beginning to become apparent that the more he saw Berry McCalister the more he wanted it to keep happening. She had crossed his mind more than once and he found himself thinking of excuses that would take him to see her.

He started cutting one of the branches of the fallen tree. The scent of petrol mixed with the eucalypts and wood filled the air along with the sawdust as he cut deep into the bough. The noise from multiple chainsaws began to swell and Nate hoped that Berry could hear it at her house, so she would come back.

After about twenty minutes she arrived. He pulled off his goggles and shook his head in the vain attempt to shake off the sawdust.

'Hey,' he said as he put down the chainsaw and walked over to meet her a little way from the others. 'I wondered when you were going to turn up.'

She gave him a bright smile as she leaned against a ghost gum. 'Yeah, sorry about that. I can see you started without me.'

'Everything okay?'

'Yes, actually I just met your dad. That's why I'm a bit late.'

'My dad?'

'Uh-huh, he turned up at my place just as I was having lunch. He seems really nice.'

'Wait, are you sure you're talking about my dad—Sam Tarant?' Nate asked with a confused look.

'Yes, your dad. Oh no—have I walked into the middle of a family feud or something?' Berry said with a laugh. 'Okay, let me rephrase that—he was really nice *to me*.'

'And he just rolled up to your place?'

Berry nodded. 'About half an hour ago. He came to introduce himself and tell me that he and my father were friends—did you know that?'

'Sort of. He doesn't generally talk about what happened.'

'I guess most people would want to forget.'

Nate looked at her for a moment. 'It doesn't sound like you do.'

Berry shrugged. 'It's different, I suppose. Part of me wants to erase the whole thing from my mind. The enormity of what took place makes it hard to get my head around it. But there's another part of me that wants to know what happened and, more importantly, why. I feel torn, which is stupid, really, because whatever I do, it won't help. Nothing will bring my parents and grandparents back.'

Nate was silent for a moment as he tried to think of something to say. He was never good at that sort of thing, but somehow it didn't seem to matter. Where the silence could have been awkward, they shared the moment, and it felt natural. 'I can't imagine what it must have been like for you,' he finally said.

'Well, it is what it is,' Berry said quickly with a slight smile as she stepped away from the tree. 'So, are you going to show me how to use one of those things or what?' She pointed to the chainsaw.

He smiled. 'I guess I am.'

***

It had taken more than a few days but the tree was now a stack of firewood weathering for next winter and the fence was fixed. The whole process had taken a little longer than Nate had expected as he and the guys had to squeeze the task between their normal work that kept Tarantale Downs going. Because of the irregular nature of

105

trying to fit in the job he had seen little of Berry. Damn near every time he turned up he'd just missed her. The whole thing annoyed him more than it should have. It wasn't as if there was anything between the two of them but, still, he was disappointed in not being able to see her. At least now that the bloody tree had been dealt with and the fence was done, he could go over to her place and tell her.

It wasn't much, but it made him feel better.

He was tossing up whether he should visit Stone Gully that afternoon when he got a call from his mum asking if he could pick up the twins from school. She'd been held up in Bendigo and it was too late to get in touch with them.

With a sigh Nate put his plans on hold and went into the main house to pick up the keys to the family car. As he walked into the kitchen he was surprised to see his dad sitting at the table.

'Hey, I didn't realise you were here,' Nate said.

Sam glanced up. 'Yeah, I just stopped in for a minute to pick up some paperwork. I'll be heading back out as soon as I finish this,' he said as he lifted up his coffee mug.

Nate walked over to the line of key hooks that were near the door. 'Mum rang, apparently she's been held up and wants me to pick up the girls.'

'Oh, right. Listen, I'd do it but I've got a meeting,' his father answered.

'It's okay, I don't mind,' Nate said as he grabbed the keys to the SUV.

'Have you got a minute?'

Nate glanced at the wall clock. 'Sure, I'll have to leave in about fifteen.'

'Won't take long.'

Nate pulled out a chair, sat down and waited for his dad to start.

'I was just wondering what you think about Berry McCalister?'

Nate sat back in his chair and frowned. 'Where did that come from? What exactly do you mean?'

His father shrugged. 'It's just a question.'

'Kind of a weird one.'

'I just thought that since you'd been spending a bit of time with her, you must like her,' Sam said as he took a mouthful of his drink.

'I hadn't even thought about it,' Nate lied. There was no way in hell he was going to have this sort of conversation with his dad of all people. And why the sudden interest in his love life?

'She's pretty.'

Nate frowned. 'Yes, I guess she is but that doesn't mean . . . listen, I don't even know if she's going to stay here.'

'That's true, but what if she does? Maybe she'd stick around if she had something to stay for. Or someone.'

Nate gave him a look that encapsulated *God, this is uncomfortable* and *What the hell are you talking about?* Unfortunately, it seemed lost on his father. He stood up and took a step away from the table. 'Well, I'd better take off and pick up the twins.'

'No need to get twitchy. I was just curious, that's all. I thought there could have been something between you. Maybe I was wrong.'

'Yeah, maybe,' Nate said as he began to walk away. 'I'll see you later, Dad.'

Sam Tarant nodded but said nothing.

Slightly rattled without really knowing why, Nate jumped in the car and headed off towards Castlemaine to pick up his sisters from school.

***

Sometimes being in the presence of his sisters was akin to what he imagined it would be like to stand in the middle of a typhoon—deafening and terrifying at the same time. This was one of those times.

The girls were waiting for him outside the high school with their friend, Beth. The girls waved and clambered into the car as it stopped.

'Hey Nate, do you mind giving Beth a lift home?' Lia asked.

'And can we please stop at the newsagent and the supermarket? I need to buy some more binder paper and felt tips,' Em asked. 'And can I please borrow the money off you because I spent all that I had at lunchtime?'

'Sure,' Nate said as he forced himself not to roll his eyes. He leaned past Lia and said, 'Come on, Beth, I'll take you home first and then we'll go shopping.'

***

Nate sat in the car outside the supermarket and checked his watch for the fifth time. How in the hell could it take thirty-five minutes to buy paper, snacks and pens? Finally, he saw the girls walking over to the car.

'Sorry, Nate,' Em said as she slid in. 'We met Casey and Heather,' she explained.

'Didn't you just see them at school?' he asked.

'Yeah, what's your point? Oh, and here's your change. And I got you this,' she continued as she gave him a handful of coins and a bottle of iced coffee.

'Thanks,' he mumbled. He never quite worked out how his sisters could be both annoying and thoughtful at the same time. 'Okay, let's go.'

'I'm glad we're going home,' Lia said as they made their way out of the car park. 'I'm so tired.'

'Me too, but I have to finish off that assignment for History and the report for English,' Em grumbled.

'Oh, I finished the English report. I handed it in today,' Lia said.

Em screwed up her face and gave her sister a look.

'Well, actually, I just need to swing by Berry McCalister's place on the way home,' Nate said.

'Really?' the girls said in unison.

'Yeah, really,' Nate replied with a smile.

Chapter Thirteen

To avoid a lot of the noise, not to mention dust from the kitchen being ripped out, Berry decided to revisit the sheds. She started out mid morning with high hopes about what she would find, but after three or so hours that state of starry-eyed anticipation was beginning to wane.

She didn't think there would be anything of value, because as far as she knew the McCalisters as a whole had always been pretty poor, but she was hoping for something personal to her family, perhaps even something that had belonged to her mum. But so far all she'd found was a stack of old newspapers, a couple of car tyres and a rusty old hand mower that looked a hundred years old.

The second shed was as disappointing as the first. So far it had given up:

Seven dried-up paint cans
A plethora of cardboard boxes and old rust-pitted tins
A Golden Fleece Service Station wall calendar from 1962
More stacks of newspapers

Assorted old tools, including eight different chisels
Five glass marbles
One dainty cup and saucer, surprisingly unchipped
Two jars of half-rusted nails
A half-filled bottle of turpentine
Three candles
A box of matches
A ball of string
An old brown leather briefcase
And, finally, several copies of the *Australasian Post* from
   the 1960s.

Berry carried the items out of the shed and dumped them in a box outside. She was just about to bin it all, but hesitated as she held the old cup in her hands. It was shallow with a pale blue band wreathed in flowers and a fine gilt line running around the rim. In the sunlight, Berry could see that the cup had an almost translucent quality and it was obvious that it was very old. Berry smiled; maybe she'd found a little family treasure after all.

She grabbed a smaller box and placed the cup and saucer in it, along with the marbles with their colourful swirls frozen within the glass. The brightly coloured covers of the old magazines caught her attention. Celebrities of the day were pictured along with beautiful bikini-clad models posing on the beach by a brilliant blue sea. Berry picked up the top copy, from August 1964; the cover was graced by a stunning model with long dark hair, and a list of articles that made Berry's eyebrows involuntarily shoot up.

In particular, the one that said in large bold type, *What's Wrong With Women? Why women have more power and freedom than ever before, but they're not happy about it.*

'Well, I guess I've found my reading matter for tonight,' she laughed, putting the magazine into the box with the teacup.

Glancing at her watch, she saw that it was nearly four p.m., so she picked up the box of treasures she was keeping, as well as the old briefcase jammed full of papers and a couple of maps, and walked back to the house. As for the rest of the junk she had hauled out of the shed, Berry would deal with that tomorrow.

Just as she was opening the boot of her car, the sound of a vehicle crunching up to the house made her look up. She frowned at the SUV that had just come to a stop. She didn't know the car and she couldn't see through the tinted windows to work out who was behind the wheel. Putting the box in the boot, she turned and waited for the occupants to get out of the car.

She smiled when she saw Nate slide out of the driver's seat, but she quelled it before he was close enough to notice. Damn, that was the last sort of reaction she wanted. It wouldn't take much for her to become entangled with Nate—Berry would have been a fool if she failed to recognise the chemistry between them—but the last thing she needed was an interlude, romantic or otherwise. She needed a clear head and she sensed that Nate had the ability to mess her up, if she let him.

'Hey,' he said as he sauntered over towards her.

'Hey,' she responded trying hard not to notice just how good he looked in jeans. 'I didn't know you were stopping by today.'

'I just had to pick my sisters up from school, and as I was driving by, I thought—'

Nate didn't get to finish his sentence as the doors of the SUV banged open and two identical blonde girls in school uniforms got out and hurried over.

'Hi! You must be Berry,' one said. 'I'm Amelia and this is Emily, or you can call us Lia and Em, everyone does.'

'Were you scared when you came back? I mean, I walk past here all the time and it's creepy. Do you think it's creepy—with what happened and all?' the other girl babbled.

The girls talked over each other and Berry felt like she'd been hit with a blast of teenage exuberance. It took her a moment to gather her wits, and when she glanced at Nate he simply rolled his eyes.

'Sorry, these are my sisters ... my baby sisters,' he explained.

'Geez, Nate, we're not babies,' Em said. 'You should stop saying that.'

'Well, you're not exactly rational adults either. Don't be so nosey and watch your tongue, Em,' he said.

Berry smiled at the girls and Nate. 'It's okay. And yes, Em, when I first arrived I thought it was a bit creepy. But maybe the cold rainy day had something to do with that. It feels very different now.'

Amelia looked over at the house. 'Why's that?'

'Because it's being renovated, and that can change the whole feel of a place.'

'Can we look inside?'

'Em!' Nate said as he sent her a look.

Em ignored him and grinned at Berry. 'Please, can you show us around? I've always wondered what it was like inside.'

'All right,' Berry said. 'But it's just a house and I doubt it's anywhere near as grand as Tarantale Downs.'

'You know, Nate was right,' Em said as she fell into step next to Berry. 'You *are* really pretty.'

Berry bit back a smile not because of the compliment but the half-strangled, 'Geez, Em,' that Nate muttered under his breath. She took a quick peek in his direction and saw that his cheeks were flushed.

'So, are you going to live here?' Lia asked.

Berry opened the front door. 'I'm not sure what's happening yet. It's something that I have to talk over with my brother and sister.'

'How come they're not here?' Em asked as she stepped past Berry. 'Shouldn't they be helping you fix up the place?'

'It's not that easy. Jess is at uni and Tom's still in school,' Berry replied as she looked at Em. 'I think he's probably about your age.'

'Really,' Lia said. 'Are they going to come up?'

Berry nodded. 'Yes, but I'm not sure when exactly.'

'So, who's looking after Tom if you're here?'

Berry smiled as she ushered them into the lounge room. 'We all live with our uncle and have done ever since we

114

moved to Melbourne. My mum's brother. Our grand-parents are down there as well, so to be honest I'm not sure if we'll keep Stone Gully Farm.'

'It's been in your family for a while now, isn't that right?' Nate asked.

'Yes.'

'Seems a shame to get rid of it,' he continued. 'I mean, any one of you might change your mind later down the track. Once it's sold, that's it.'

Lia nodded before flicking her long blonde hair over her shoulder. 'You could rent it out—that way it would pay for itself and you still get to hold onto it. If your brother is the same age as me, what he wants now might be different to when he's, like, Nate's age.'

'Hey, you make it sound like we're stupid kids who don't know what they want,' Em said quickly.

'I'm not saying that. It's just, I don't even know what I want to do when I finish school. How would I know if I wanted to keep a house or not?'

Nate gave Berry a shrug. 'Hate to say it but she may have a point.'

Berry was quiet for a minute. 'I hadn't thought about it that way. You might be right, Lia. Tom may regret selling this place. It's certainly something I'll have to discuss with him. And Jess.'

'When are they going to visit?' Lia asked.

'Soon, I suppose. The truth is I didn't want them here in the first place. I didn't want to trigger any bad memories.'

'Won't just coming here do that?' Nate asked gently.

Berry shrugged. 'Maybe . . . I don't know. Jess is a couple of years younger than me, so her memories are a bit blurry, and Tom was just a baby. Perhaps it wouldn't have turned out so badly after all.'

Em gave her a smile. 'You were just trying to protect them.'

Berry smiled. 'I probably was. But, now, the house is the same but it's also going to be so different. It's getting a facelift and a brand new feel—so maybe that's scared away the darkness.'

Berry gave them a quick tour of the house and introduced them to some of the workmen, before they wandered down the steps into the back yard.

'I really like your place,' Lia said with a smile. 'I can't wait to see it all finished. I mean . . . that is, if you invite us back.'

'Of course you're invited back. You can drop in anytime you see my car parked out the front.'

'Thanks, Berry!'

'What's down here?' Em asked as she pointed to the old sheds. 'Anything interesting?'

'Only if you like dust and cobwebs,' Berry replied. 'I've been going through the sheds but so far all I've found are some really old magazines, a handful of glass marbles and a very pretty teacup. Unfortunately, not one bit of hidden treasure, which was more than a little disappointing.' She led them downhill towards the sheds.

'Yeah, well, people generally don't put anything very valuable in sheds. That is, other than cars or tractors,'

Nate said as he pushed himself off the railing and followed her.

'So, there wasn't anything pretty?' Lia asked.

'No, except for the teacup and the marbles.'

'That's a shame, it would have been really cool if you'd found something old and important.'

'Yeah, I guess it would have been.'

They continued past the sheds and made their way towards the orchard. The girls walked slightly ahead and Berry was conscious of Nate striding along beside her. It was becoming disconcerting to say the least.

'So, you haven't said what brought you over today.'

Nate glanced at her. 'Um, I just wanted to let you know that the fence is fixed. You don't have to worry about any stray animals wandering in.'

'Thanks, I appreciate it.' Berry looked away. Why did half her conversations with Nate end up feeling weird? *Thanks, I appreciate it.* She directed an internal eye roll at herself.

'Oh, there was one other thing. We've cut up the tree and stacked it on your side of the fence. I figured you'd still have at least one open fire. It has to dry out, so you probably can't use it until next winter but it's there anyway.'

'You didn't have to do that. But thanks.'

'If you want . . . when I've got a spare minute, I can bring it up to the house. We could stack it over there near the sheds. At least that way it's closer than halfway down the back paddock.'

'I wouldn't want you to go to any more trouble,' Berry said quickly.

Nate shrugged. 'No problem at all. I'll get it sorted.'

Em stopped ahead and turned back to Berry and her brother. 'Berry, what sort of orchard is this? The trees look different.'

'You've got a good eye. It's made up of all sorts of different fruit trees,' Berry said as she pointed past Em. 'Apples over there, and over in that direction are pears, plums and a few nut trees.'

'Quite a mixed bag of varieties,' Nate said.

'Well, thinking back I suppose it was more like a hobby farm. Not like the majority of sheep runs in the area. My grandparents ran it as a proper farm, but Dad just didn't seem to have the knack when it came to sheep.'

'Oh, I see . . . sorry, I shouldn't have said anything,' Nate said.

Berry gave him a friendly nudge with her shoulder and then immediately regretted the close proximity. 'Don't be silly, it's okay. Dad always wanted to try new things, most of which never quite panned out like he'd hoped. I remember Mum used to use the fruit from here to make jams and chutneys and sauces that she'd sell to local shops and cafes around the area. Also, there used to be big raised beds of strawberries closer to the house, and blackberries too.'

Lia stopped walking and turned back around. 'Is that where you got your name from?'

Berry smiled. 'Partly. Berenice was my great-grand-mother's name, but my dad called me Berry because he said that I was sweet. I guess it stuck, because no one calls me Berenice anymore. Well, except for my uncle if I've managed to really annoy him,' she said with a laugh.

'And does that happen often?' Nate asked with a raised eyebrow.

'No, not at all. Well, maybe once in a blue moon,' Berry said. 'My uncle can come across as a little formidable, and he's not particularly demonstrative. I guess that makes him well suited to being a lawyer! But once you get past the hard exterior he's kind and squishy inside, especially when it comes to me and my siblings. He didn't have to take us in after our parents died, but he did and I think that says a lot about him.'

Nate nodded. 'I reckon you're right. So, you're close?'

'Yep.' She paused, then added thoughtfully, 'I guess that happens when a family goes through a tragedy.'

Nate watched her. 'I suppose you can appreciate what you have, and who you have, and draw strength from each other.'

'Yeah,' Berry said. 'Something like that. Is your family close?'

'Yes, I get along pretty well with these two nut jobs,' Nate said with a grin as he gestured to his sisters. 'And my mum. Dad, on the other hand, can be . . . difficult.'

'Yeah, well, every family I know fights and argues and thinks that they're the only dysfunctional one around, but I reckon no one does it perfectly.'

'Mmm, I suppose I should be thankful, but Dad and I tend to rub each other up the wrong way. He believes he's right about everything all the time and insists on treating me like I'm a sixteen-year-old idiot.'

Berry winced. 'Ouch, really?'

'He's always saying that I'm the future of Tarantale Downs and yet he won't give me a voice in how the place should be run. Look, he's my father and the business belongs to him, I get that, but you'd think he'd start giving me a little bit of responsibility. Sometimes I don't feel much more than a glorified stable hand, the only difference is my pay packet might be a bit heavier than Justin's.'

'I'm assuming that you've tried talking to him?'

Nate gave her a look.

'Sorry, I guess you've already done that,' she said with a sheepish grin.

'Yeah, I've tried. More than once. I always get the same answer—*You're not ready yet*. I get frustrated because half the time he's telling me to man up and take responsibility for my actions all the while he's saying that I'm not ready to handle any aspect of the management of Tarantale.'

'That must be hard.'

Nate shrugged. 'It can be. As I said, we tend to butt heads a lot—it's one of the reasons I moved out of the main house.'

'Oh, where do you live? Still on the property?'

'Yep. I had the old stables renovated. I'm still at Tarantale but far enough removed so I can have a little breathing room.'

'Sounds like it was a good move,' Berry said with a smile.

'Berry, what's down here?' Lia called out as she reached the edge of the orchard.

'If we keep going we'll hit the dam.'

'Oh, okay,' Lia said as she turned back to continue walking down the path.

Nate glanced at Berry. 'Listen, we just sort of showed up—are we keeping you from something?'

'Nah, I've spent most of the day by myself in the sheds. It's nice to have some company.'

'Well, if you're sure. Shall we keep going to the dam?'

'Good idea. I've been walking down here a lot. I don't really know why, maybe because it's just peaceful,' she said as the dam came into view.

'Oh, look, Nate—it has an island in the middle,' Em said with a grin. 'It's so lovely!'

'Have you been over there?' Lia asked.

Berry shook her head. 'No, not yet. As far as I know, that's where the herons nest. I wasn't sure if I'd disturb them, plus I don't have a boat. It's on my list of things to do, I just haven't got there yet.'

'Maybe we can all go together?' Lia suggested.

'Lia, will you stop inviting yourself,' Nate said half under his breath.

'That's all right,' Berry said. 'It sounds like a great idea . . . if we can find a boat.'

Nate said, 'Leave it to me. Maybe we could aim for next weekend or the one after that?'

Berry nodded. 'Sounds good.'

Berry meant what she said. Everything about this place needed to be cleansed, and the dam was no exception. In her mind, the dam held a handful of golden memories of her mucking about on the water with Jess—a time that was precious to her, but also painful in the way it brought back all the things that had gone.

Chapter Fourteen

As Berry drove up to Cumquat Cottage after an early-morning shop for supplies, she noticed Andrea and an elderly man on the porch. Assuming he was another guest, Berry parked and grabbed her small grocery bag from the passenger seat and walked up towards the front door. She smiled to the gentleman as she passed.

'Oh, Berry, this is Harvey Wainwright. Apparently he's been waiting for you,' Andrea said as she turned her back on him, faced Berry and rolled her eyes.

Berry bit back a smile before saying, 'Oh, I'm sorry but I don't believe we've met.'

'You haven't but he insisted on waiting even though I said that I had no idea when you'd be back,' Andrea said quickly, before adding an exasperated sigh. 'Come find me in the kitchen when you're done, Berry.'

'All right.' Berry turned to Mr Wainwright, trying not to notice his incredibly bushy eyebrows. He was a thin man with a shot of windswept white hair and eyebrows reminiscent of a seagull's wings about to take off in flight. 'Now, why did you want to see me?'

He stood and looked intently at her. 'Well, to make you an offer, girly—and a damn good one at that,' he said bluntly.

A frown flitted across Berry's face as she braced herself for another one of *these* conversations.

'Oh, I assume you're talking about Stone Gully.'

'Well, of course. I've been thinking about the property and you'll be happy to know that I'm willing to take it off your hands,' he blustered. 'I know for a fact that it's in a shabby state and the land hasn't been worked on in years.'

Berry took a steadying breath. 'Thank you, Mr Wainwright, but the decision isn't entirely up to me. I must discuss it with my brother and sister, and until we decide whether or not we're going to sell Stone Gully, I can't give you an answer.'

Mr Wainwright's eyes opened a little wider. 'Are you saying that you're going to keep the place?'

'I'm saying we haven't decided yet.'

'Gah, you don't need to be mouldering out there. Get your pretty face back to the city where it belongs. You've got a life ahead of you; you don't want to bury yourself in a backwater like Harlington.'

'That may be, Mr Wainwright, but whether or not I belong here is not for you to say,' Berry said firmly as she took a step towards the door, hoping that he'd get the point—he didn't.

124

'But I'm willing to offer a fair price. I've done the research and I think you'll be surprised,' he said as he pushed a folded piece of paper into her hand.

Berry didn't bother looking at it. 'I'll put it with the other offers.'

'So, you've got other offers, girly?' he said quickly.

'Yes, quite a few,' Berry said as she made it to the door.

'You're not playing hardball with me are you, in the hope of upping the price?' Mr Wainwright said with a frown that made his eyebrows meet in the middle to form the perfect seagull.

'Not in the least. Now if you'll excuse me I have a lot to do around my *shabby* place. Goodbye Mr Wainwright,' she said as she stepped through the door and shut it behind her.

Berry made her way down to Andrea who was just pouring two cups of tea. She pushed one towards Berry.

'You look like you need this.'

Berry accepted it gladly. 'Thanks, I think that's an understatement. Can you believe that was the third offer for Stone Gully in the past week?'

'How many all up?'

'Seven, and I have to admit this one was the least palatable,' Berry said as she took a sip of tea.

'Not a good price?'

'Awful delivery,' Berry said with a wink.

Andrea laughed as she opened the biscuit barrel and offered it to Berry. 'Here, you'd better take a couple of these too. I can't tell you much about Harvey Wainwright other than he's a grouchy old man who makes it his business to rub people up the wrong way.'

'Well, I guess he succeeded again. And grouchy old man isn't exactly how I'd describe him,' Berry said with a smile, 'but I'm much too polite to say what I really feel.'

'Okay, I get it,' Andrea said. 'So, did he offer you a decent price at least?'

Berry unfolded the piece of paper and stared at it in disbelief for a moment before handing it to Andrea.

'A decent price? This is a joke!'

'Well, apparently he did the research and Stone Gully Farm is in a shabby state,' Berry said as she took the paper from Andrea, screwed it up and dropped it in the rubbish bin. 'I understand that there's an interest in the place because I've come back, but what I don't get is that so many people think I'm just here to sell it.'

'I suppose they believe you've got a life in Melbourne, but you're right, they're assuming a lot.'

'At this rate I feel like keeping the farm just to spite them all,' Berry said.

'Have you had any real offers?'

'Maybe two. Sam Tarant told me he'd buy it for market value if we chose to sell.'

'Really?' Andrea sounded surprised.

Berry glanced up at Andrea. 'I know you don't like him but he seemed sincere. And unlike everyone else, he wasn't pushing. He said if we decided to sell it would make sense for him to buy it because Stone Gully borders his place. And the other reason was that he was friends with my father and he'd feel that on some level he was helping out.'

'He always seems so . . . oh, I don't know, unapproach-able. Then again, maybe he's just like that with me. But at least he's given you an option, whether or not you take him up on it,' she said with a smile. 'Are you going out to your place today?'

'Later. First I thought I might drop by the Fords' place.'

'Ah, yes, you were friends with their daughter, Jodie?'

'Yeah, we went to school together. We tried to keep in touch after I moved to Melbourne, but it all ended up being too hard. It wasn't my fault and it certainly wasn't Jodie's, it just happened.'

'Do you think you'll reconnect now?'

Berry nodded. 'Uh-huh, she's coming back next week from uni. I'm a little apprehensive but at the same time I'm really excited. Anyway, while I'm here I thought I'd talk to her mum about my parents. They were friends, I remember. And they were the ones Mum sent me to when . . . well, they looked after us until the police came.'

Andrea took a sip of tea.

'You don't think it's a good idea?' Berry asked with a frown settling on her forehead.

'I don't know,' Andrea answered. 'I guess because you were so young you'd like to get an impression of your parents, but do you really want to open up the past? I mean, you sound like you want to move on, so is dragging up things that happened a long time ago really in your best interest?'

Berry considered this for a moment. 'I understand what you're saying. The truth is that I'm a little torn—part of me wants to know what my parents were like and the other part wants to slam the door on the past and try to forget. I've been thinking about it a lot since I came back, and I figure that if I don't find out what I can now, maybe I'll regret it in the long run.'

'I get it. I'm just worried that you might end up finding out something you wish you hadn't.'

'I suppose that's a risk I have to be prepared to take. If we end up selling Stone Gully and leaving Harlington, then any information I might have been able to learn will be lost.'

'I just don't want you to get hurt,' Andrea said with a smile.

Berry reached over and took her hand. 'Thanks, Andrea. I promise I'll be careful.'

***

That afternoon Berry found herself sitting around the bench in the Fords' kitchen. The warm familiarity brought back memories of happy childhood days, and in some ways it felt like she had rolled back the years to that innocent, trouble-free time before her world collapsed around her.

'I'm so happy that you took me up on the invitation,' Lynette Ford said with a smile.

'No, thank you, I really appreciate being able to drop by.'

'I talked to Jodie last night. She's so excited about next weekend and seeing you again.'

Berry smiled. 'I'm excited too. I hate the way we lost touch.'

Lynette nodded. 'Well, things like that happen even under the best conditions and intentions. There were a lot of things conspiring against the both of you but at least you can find each other now.'

'We've got so much to catch up on,' Berry said with a grin.

'You do,' Lynette agreed as she pushed the banana cake closer to Berry. 'Have a piece, I made it this morning.'

For a moment Berry almost refused, but the temptation was too great and she snagged a piece and took a bite. 'Oh my God,' she said as she held her hand up to her mouth. 'This is amazing! I'd forgotten how good your cake is. You used to make this for us as kids.'

Lynette laughed. 'Well, thanks—I think that's the best compliment my cake has ever got.'

Berry swallowed. 'No, seriously, it's fantastic. I could eat the whole thing.'

Lynette poured a little more tea in Berry's cup. 'Did you have anything you wanted to ask me?'

Berry was silent for a moment. Lynette had given her an opening and now all she had to do was be brave enough to take it.

'I guess there is, but I'm not exactly sure how I should word it,' Berry said.

Lynette looked at her kindly. 'I usually find that the best way is just to come out with it.'

Berry nodded as she focused on her teacup for a second too long. Finally, she glanced up at Lynette. 'Could you tell me about my parents?'

Lynette paused for a moment as if trying to find the right words, and Berry realised that she was holding her breath.

'I was friends with your mum, as you know,' she began. 'We met because of ... well, you and Jodie actually. Your mum and I just kind of hit it off when you two started kindergarten together. She was a good friend, the type who would do anything for you, whether it was emergency babysitting or a shoulder to cry on. I miss her every day and even now when something goes wrong, in those first few seconds as the shit hits the fan, Cath is the first person I want to turn to—and then I remember I can't.'

A silence hung over them for a breath and then another one. As Berry studied Lynette, she saw that the older woman was holding back her emotions, and obviously trying to stay strong. She gave her a fleeting, awkward smile before wiping her eyes with the back of her hand.

'Sorry, I don't know what came over me. My loss is nothing compared to yours—your whole family's. But all I can say is that I lost my best friend in the most horrible way, and it still hurts.'

Berry forced herself to smile. 'There's nothing to be sorry about. I'm glad you were friends and had each other. Because I was so young, a lot of my memories are kind of fuzzy. I remember my parents and grandparents, of course, but sometimes it's like looking at a faded picture.' Berry sighed and ran her hand over her hair. 'I'm not explaining this very well at all, am I?'

'No, I think I get what you mean.'

'You know, some of my memories merge and I'm not sure when things actually happened. Except for my tenth birthday—I think I can remember pretty much everything until I got here.'

Lynette nodded. 'I couldn't believe what I was seeing— you'd ridden your bike all the way into town with little Tommy. I knew something was terribly wrong but I could never have imagined what actually happened.'

'Lynette, I know this could be a difficult question, but what did you think of my dad? I mean, I know what he did but I've always found it really hard to accept it. When my uncle told me the truth of what happened, I couldn't reconcile the dad I knew with a man who could kill his family.'

Lynette nodded sadly. 'I know. I had to explain to my kids that he had a breakdown and wasn't in his right mind when he killed your mum. Never in a million years would I have thought Jordy would do that—he always doted on all of you,' Lynette said, then gave a small laugh. 'Sometimes I was a little jealous of the way he treated your mum.'

'What do you mean?'

'He just loved her so much. He always remembered their special dates, and not just their anniversary or birthdays, but little things—like when they first met. He'd bring her flowers for no reason, and even though there were times he could drive her crazy, she loved him too.'

Berry closed her eyes as snippets of memories began to resurface. Lynette hadn't been wrong when she said that her dad doted on her mum. She remembered him handing her a bunch of flowers he'd picked. It was almost as if Berry were looking through a hazy lens or staring into an old photo that was fading and tinged yellow with age. No, there had been love in their family, so how could it have gone so wrong?

Berry hesitated for a moment before she went on. 'Did Mum ever say anything to you, I mean about Dad having a temper or that she was worried?'

Lynette shook her head. 'No, not at all. Look, no marriage is perfect and they had their fair share of troubles, but generally any problems centred around money. I know that sometimes cash was a little thin and your mum had to be creative to make ends meet.'

'Did she resent him over that?'

'I don't think so, at least she didn't say anything to me. She'd get exasperated sometimes and even a little annoyed because he was such a dreamer, but never enough to blow things up into a full argument. I know she felt frustrated that he tended to flit from one idea to the next without seeing anything through.'

'I never knew any of this,' Berry said with a sigh. 'I guess Mum didn't want us to know about it. That might explain why we had an orchard full of different varieties of fruit trees. Or occasionally the odd paddock planted with canola or sunflowers.'

'Yeah, and don't forget about the trout in the dam. You could probably still catch one for your dinner,' Lynette said with a grin.

'Oh, I think I do vaguely remember a robust discussion about alpacas,' Berry said as the memory popped out of nowhere.

Lynette laughed. 'Yes, that's right. He was about to launch into raising them and your mum put her foot down.'

'He didn't have the knack when it came to farming, did he?'

'No, he didn't. It was a shame, because the farm had been in the family for generations, and it ended up whittled down to not much.'

'You mean it was bigger?'

'Oh yes, when dad took it on Stone Gully Farm was probably twice the size. When times got hard the family would sell little chunks of it. But it was your grandfather who put an end to that, he told my dad if they kept selling it off there wouldn't be anything left to leave to you or your brother and sister. So, I know he resisted selling any more land even when they could have done with the funds.'

'He wanted to pass it on to us?'

'I guess so,' Lynette said as she reached over and patted Berry's hand. 'But remember it's what *you* want that's important. Don't think you have to stay because of what your grandad wanted. It can sound a little harsh but

133

we can't be swayed by the ghosts of the past. If we live that way, we end up living someone's else's life and not the one we're meant to.'

Berry smiled. 'I think you're right.'

'Oh, I know all about family expectations and the guilt trip that can come with it,' she said with a wink.

'That sounds like a story.'

'And not a pretty one.'

'I'd like to hear it.'

'I'll tell you but maybe another day. It's long and tedious and I think I may need something stronger than tea to get through it,' she answered with a laugh. 'Let's just say, I was expected to marry the boy next door—not because I loved him or we were destined to be together, but so my father could expand and secure the family farm. I felt I was being sold off in a marriage contract from the damn Dark Ages.'

'How did you get out of it?'

'I ran away with Jack and never looked back. Truth is, my father still hasn't forgiven me and it's been almost twenty-five years.'

'It sounds very romantic,' Berry said with a sigh.

'It was,' Lynette said with a wink.

Chapter Fifteen

2007

Jordy McCalister was a bit of a screw-up. He knew it and so did most of the inhabitants of Harlington. Though to be fair, most of them had the decency not to say it to his face. He tried really hard but nine times out of ten things blew up in his face. No matter what he turned his hand to it would never pan out like it was meant to—especially if it had anything to do with farming. God only knows why Cath stayed with him.

He leaned back in his chair, linked his fingers behind his head and stretched. Glancing at his research on the small desk in front of him, he smiled. This time was different, this time everything would work and, just once, Cath would be proud of him and the kids would have the life he dreamed for them.

Jordy sat forwards and shuffled through a stack of paper until he pulled out the old map of Harlington he'd accidentally-on-purpose borrowed from the Historical Society. He ran his finger over the heavy paper and for a moment allowed himself to dream a picture of what his life was going to look like. And he wouldn't fall into the same trap he always did; he wasn't going to get excited, announce his plans and run at full speed. This time he would be clever and not tell anyone anything until it was all in place.

He ran his hand through his dark hair. No, he couldn't even tell Cath, not yet. She'd stood by him for each of his grand ideas and stayed there as they crumbled into dust. The only time she objected was six months ago when she refused to agree to turn Stone Gully into an alpaca farm. Even a saint had her limits.

If he was right, then this could be the making or at least the rebirth of the McCalister family's standing in the community. But more than that, he would finally be able to protect Cath and the kids and give them everything they deserved.

Chapter Sixteen

Berry's stomach fluttered as she arrived at the pub on Friday night to meet Jodie for dinner. It was crazy to be worried, Berry told herself as she walked into the lounge. Jodie had been her best friend when they were kids; there was nothing to be nervous about.

She scanned the room hoping to recognise Jodie from the couple of photos that Lynette had shown her. She needn't have worried. From across the room came a shriek followed by, 'Berry! Berry, over here!'

A slight figure with nut-brown hair was jumping up and down while waving madly, evidently not caring that every eye in the place was focused on her. Berry grinned. Some things never changed.

She hurried over only to be caught in a vice-like hug.

'Look at you! It's *so* good to see you,' Jodie said.

'I've missed you so much,' Berry replied, embracing her old friend.

'Come sit down and tell me *everything*.' Jodie gestured to the nearest chair. 'It's been too long. What are you up to?'

Berry sat down and smiled at her friend. There wasn't any of that dreaded awkwardness she'd been half-expecting. She should have known better—Jodie was just Jodie.

'I'm fixing up the old house,' she said.

Jodie nodded. 'Yeah, Mum told me. Are you going to move back?'

Berry shrugged. 'I'm not sure—probably not.'

Jodie frowned. 'That's not like the Berry I remember. You were always so decisive.'

Berry laughed. 'Oh, I don't think so.'

'Yeah, it was always you leading us into trouble,' Jodie said with a widening grin.

'Hah, yeah—I think you've got that backwards. You'd rush in and I'd stupidly follow.'

Jodie pretended to think for a second before she continued. 'Hmm, how about when we snuck into the Stringy Bark Orchard and stole apples? That was your idea,' Jodie said, and before Berry could deny it, she kept going. 'Oh hang on, how about when old Mrs Taft told us off and in retaliation you hijacked her beloved garden gnomes and put them in the front yard of the school. And then there was the time . . .'

Berry held up her hands in a sign of surrender and laughed. 'Okay, you win. That's enough.'

'Just refreshing your memory,' Jodie said. 'So, how's the renovation going? Is it weird being back in Harlington?'

Berry paused for a moment. 'I guess it is. I told myself that coming back wouldn't worry me. I mean, I was only ten when we left, but I didn't expect to feel the way I do.'

'And how's that?'

Berry shrugged. 'It's hard to put into words. Things feel so familiar. I've been hit with a whole lot of memories that I'd forgotten.'

'Memories?'

'Nothing very earth-shattering or unpleasant, just stuff I'd forgotten,' Berry said. 'You know, like us not being able to swim in the dam unless Mum was there to keep an eye on us. Or just how much I liked playing in the orchard—I used to pretend it was some sort of magical forest.'

'It's good to remember, especially the nice memories. Even though it was cut short, we had a lot of fun when we were kids,' Jodie said with a smile.

'Yeah, we did. So, how's uni going? Your mum said you're doing Teaching?'

'Yeah. It's been a bit full on but I love it. I'm really glad I decided to go after all. I took a few years off after school. The problem was that I just couldn't figure out what I wanted to be. I worked at one of the supermarkets in Castlemaine and then spent half of last year just doing a bit of travel. I spent a month up in the snowy mountains, and then decided it was way too cold and followed the sun up to Byron Bay and finally all the way to Airlie Beach in Queensland.'

'Sounds wonderful,' Berry said with a smile.

'It was. Anyway, I sat on the beach, stared out to sea and tried to work out what the hell I was going to do with my life.'

'Well, I guess it worked.'

Jodie grinned. 'It's the only way to tackle a problem—go to the beach. Maybe that's what you need to do. It's all the sea air and tranquillity, you know. It clears your head.'

'Sounds like more fun than being in the middle of a reno.'

'I rest my case. So, other than fixing up the old place what are you up to?'

Berry dragged in a breath before blowing it out in a sigh. 'I don't know. That's the problem. I think I jumped at doing this because I haven't really got any idea about what I want to do with my life. I thought I had a plan but ever since I found out what actually happened to my parents . . . it's weird, I feel a bit lost or something, I can't really explain it . . .' She finished with a shrug.

Jodie looked at her. 'That doesn't sound weird at all. I didn't realise that you didn't know what happened.'

'My uncle and grandparents apparently thought it was best not to say anything. All I was told was that there had been an accident, a tragedy, and both my parents and my grandparents had died.'

'When did you find out?'

'Not until a couple of years ago. My uncle rarely talks about my mum—he gets too sad—but I was asking a lot of questions and basically badgered him into talking about Mum. It's one of my greatest fears that one day I'll wake up and will have forgotten what she looked like and her smile. I try really hard to hang onto her voice, but I can only recall it now when I'm halfway between dozing off and asleep.'

'I'm so sorry, Berry. That must be hard ... for Jess too,' Jodie said. 'She must remember even less than you.'

Berry nodded. 'There's only so much that we can share, and Tom doesn't remember anything before the move to Melbourne. We've asked our grandparents, as well as our uncle, but they always seem unwilling to talk about Mum or what our life was like in Harlington. It upsets them too much.'

'It must be hard on them too.'

Berry nodded. 'Yeah, I get that, I do. My grand-parents lost their only daughter and my uncle his sister. But we lost our mum, and I hate the way everyone wants to pretend she never existed. Finally, though, my uncle sat all three of us down and told us the truth.'

'Geez.'

'Yeah, I don't know what I thought I'd hear, but it defi-nitely wasn't that Dad was responsible for all of it.'

Jodie reached over and patted Berry's hand. 'The whole town was rocked by the news. No one could believe it. Your dad was a well-liked person, and this landed like a bomb on the community. I can't begin to imagine what it must have felt like for you.'

'Well, it certainly had us reeling. Tom doesn't remember anything, which is probably a blessing. Jess has some memories but she was only eight. Whether you remember or not, though, it's heavy information to carry around with you. Uncle Dave said he didn't want to burden us with the truth, but then he realised we had the right to know. He still grieves for my mum. And he spent so many

141

years being angry at my father for what he'd done, he thought it was best to say nothing or else he'd end up colouring what memories we had of our dad.'

'That's a valid point,' Jodie said. 'I don't know what I would have done in the circumstances. I mean, the father you remember and idolise is suddenly turned into a monster; that's a lot to deal with.'

Berry let out a sigh. 'The problem is, Jodie, I don't think I've still really come to terms with it. I know I should hate my father for what he did, what he took away from us, but something inside me can't. It's stupid, isn't? I mean, he shattered our lives and yet that's not the man I remember.'

Chapter Seventeen

It was a clear morning and the winter sun was doing its best to warm the air. Not that Berry needed any help keeping warm because she was already hot, flustered and about to lose it. For what seemed like the tenth time, she attempted to back the trailer close to the shed.

Andrea had been kind enough to lend her the ute and trailer so she could finish the job of cleaning out the sheds, but so far it had been more or less a disaster. Berry wrinkled her nose and frowned; she should have known this was going to be more problematic than she'd imagined.

Winding down the window, she stuck her head out and glared back at the almost jack-knifed trailer. She let out a loud and exasperated sigh, then drove forwards in an attempt to straighten the trailer. Once in position she inched the ute backwards until she finally got the damn thing where she wanted it, almost—sometimes close enough is good enough.

She got out of the car to survey her handiwork—well, it would have to do. She gave the trailer one last dirty look and suppressed the urge to kick it. She grabbed her phone and pulled up one of her favourite playlists, then popped her earphones in. It was going to take several trips to the local tip to clear everything out, and maybe the music would make it go faster. She hit play, shoved on her work gloves and headed to the first shed, walking in time to the thumping beat.

The morning passed quickly but Berry barely noticed as she was intent on clearing out the shed. As she dumped the last stack of mouldering papers, she turned to the sound of a vehicle, then broke into a grin as she saw her uncle's sleek black car. She ran to meet it, and as she got closer she could make out her sister waving from the passenger seat. Waving back, she picked up her pace.

Her uncle was just getting out of the car when she launched herself into his arms and hugged him tight. For a moment she was overcome and just needed to feel the safety of his embrace.

'Hey kid, are you okay?' he asked before he bent to kiss the top of her head.

Berry nodded but couldn't seem to form any words thanks to the lump in her throat. They stood in silence for a moment as Berry tried to get a hold of herself. As she heard the other car doors open, Berry took a step back and wiped her filling eyes with the back of her hand.

'Sorry, it's just I didn't expect you and ... and I didn't realise how much I missed you all.'

'Geez, Berry, don't cry,' Tom said as he walked over

and gave her a brief, almost awkward hug. 'You're meant to be glad to see us.'

'I am,' she said as she took a step back and studied him for a moment. The family resemblance was strong. She, Jess and Tom shared the same chocolatey brown hair and grey–blue eyes. 'Have you grown?'

Tom rolled his eyes as he stepped out of Jessica's way. 'Don't be ridiculous—you haven't been gone that long,' he quipped.

Before she could reply, Jess barrelled into her arms, causing her to stagger back.

'I've missed you!'

Berry grinned and squeezed her sister tightly. 'I've missed you too.'

'Oh, come on, Jess, let her breathe,' Uncle Dave said with a laugh.

Jess loosened her grip and looked into Berry's eyes. 'Are you sure you're okay?'

'Of course I am,' she nodded with a smile. 'Even better now that you're all here.'

Jess stared at her for another moment until she was convinced she was telling the truth. 'All right then, good.'

Uncle Dave took a look around the place, seeing it for the first time in a very long while. 'So, are you going to show us what you've been up to?' Uncle Dave asked.

'Yeah,' Berry said with a bright smile. 'Although most of the credit has to go to the contractors. Follow me—I'll give you the grand tour.'

Berry linked arms with her sister and they all walked towards the house.

When they reached the front door, Jess paused for a moment. Berry frowned as she turned her head and looked at her sister.

'Are you okay?'

Jess looked at Berry. 'I'm not sure. Stupid, isn't it?'

She shook her head. 'Of course it's not stupid. I had the same reaction when I first came here. Just take your time. And if you don't want to go in . . . don't.'

'No, no, I want to. It's just that it feels weird,' Jess answered. She looked over at her brother and uncle. 'Is it just me?'

'No,' Uncle Dave said. 'It's not just you.'

She glanced back to Berry. 'It feels familiar but at the same time it doesn't—like I recognise it from a dream, or maybe a nightmare.'

'You were only eight the last time you were here. That's a long time ago,' Uncle Dave said gently. 'You don't have to go in.'

'No, I want to,' Jess repeated before taking a deep breath and looking to Berry for reassurance.

Berry took her by the hand and gave it a squeeze. 'You'll be fine.' And with that they both walked through the door.

A small smile flickered across Berry's face as she breathed in the scent of new wood and paint. The house smelled so different from when she had first arrived. It was clean and fresh, the renovation giving the house a new start.

Berry and Jess walked into the lounge room, which was now bright, the old curtains long gone. The windows were opened wide and fresh air filled the room. The heaviness of the past was beginning to lift, at least that's how Berry felt.

'It's funny, you know,' Jessica said as she looked about the room. 'I don't remember this room at all and yet there's something familiar about it.'

Berry wrinkled her nose. 'I know what you mean. It looks very different from when I arrived. Transformed.'

Uncle Dave walked up behind her and laid his hand on her shoulder. 'It looks great, Berry. I hardly recognise the place—and that's a good thing.'

Berry turned her head towards her uncle. 'I know,' she said.

Tom wandered into the room. 'It's bright, and if you look that way, it has a nice view of the paddocks.'

Berry gave her brother a smile. 'It does, doesn't it? Come on, I'll show you the rest.'

* * *

After a tour around the house, Berry led everyone down the steps and into the back yard. There was an awful lot she still didn't remember from when she was a child, but the memory of her riding her brand new bike around the old clothesline had never dimmed. Sometimes when she lay in bed and closed her eyes, desperately trying to recall her mum's voice, that was the image which always surfaced.

This spot was still one of the hardest places to face. But now, looking at her family, she pushed the memory aside.

'So, Uncle Dave, are you staying tonight or going back home?' she asked.

'We're going to stay,' he answered with a nod. 'I rang the lady at the Cumquat B&B and she said she'd be happy to have us.'

'Andrea's the best. I don't know what I would have done without her,' Berry said as she pointed down towards the sheds. 'She even lent me her ute so I could drag all that rubbish to the tip.'

'You know, I don't want to sound whiney,' Tom said as he sidled up next to his sister, 'but is there anywhere we can get something to eat? I'm starving.'

Uncle Dave let out something that sounded like a cross between a chuckle and a snort. 'Tommy, you had break-fast and we stopped for food on the way—how can you possibly be that hungry already?'

'Starving,' Tom said with a grin.

'Well, I'm sure I can find you something,' Berry said. 'Although, it's probably going to have to be a snack—the general store's the only option. The Queen's Arms does counter meals but only at night.'

Tom looked a little disappointed. 'There's really nothing here, is there?'

Jessica gave his shoulder a nudge. 'Yeah, let's condemn the entire place because Tommy can't get a drive thru,' she said and rolled her eyes.

'Geez, Jess, can you get any more salty?' Tom asked as he wrinkled his nose. 'Besides, you've been through the place, there really isn't anything there. We're out in the middle of nowhere with nothing to do.'

Uncle Dave let out a low chuckle. 'Sounds like someone has a touch of culture shock. You'd better give your brother a moment. I guess it's my fault anyway; it's not like we've ventured into the country often.'

'But there really isn't anything here except for one half-empty shop, a handful of houses and a shitload of trees.'

'Hey, watch your language,' Uncle Dave said with a shake of his head. 'You're not with your mates now.'

Berry slung her arm around Tom. 'It's not as convenient as where we live but I'm sure there are pretty much the same things here, you might just have to travel a bit to reach them. Besides, I bet there's a whole lot of stuff you can do here that you can't do in Melbourne.'

'Yeah, like what?'

Berry opened her mouth to answer but got distracted by a ute turning into the drive.

'Who's that?' Jessica asked.

Berry raised her hand and shielded her eyes from the sunlight. 'I do believe it's our neighbour, Nate Tarant.'

The ute swung in and parked next to Uncle Dave's car. As soon as the door opened, Berry saw Nate's sandy blond hair as he stood up.

Jess gave her a gentle nudge in the ribs. 'No wonder you're lingering in Harlington.'

'Oh, shut up,' Berry whispered back. 'I hardly know him.'

'Sure,' Jess said with a smile. 'You just keep telling yourself that.'

Nate walked over, his two sisters following in his wake.

'Hi Berry. I guess we should have given you a ring earlier,' he said.

Berry shook her head. 'It's fine. Uncle Dave, this is Nate Tarant and his sisters Lia and Em. They live up the road from here.'

Uncle Dave shook Nate's outstretched hand. 'Ah, yes, I remember. It's a horse stud, Tarant ... um, Tarantale Downs, is that right?'

'Yes, I'm amazed that you'd remember.'

'I met your dad a few times, back in the day,' Uncle Dave explained.

'Nate, this is my sister, Jess, and my baby brother, Tom,' Berry said as she gestured to her siblings.

'*Berry*,' Tom hissed under his breath before reaching out and shaking Nate's hand, while his gaze was drawn to Lia and Em, who were both staring back at him with interest. 'Hi, I'm Berenice's younger brother.'

'Nice to meet you all,' Nate said. 'Look, Berry, I'm sorry, we didn't mean to interrupt. We'll take off.'

'It's okay, you're not interrupting. My family decided to surprise me but that doesn't mean you have to leave.'

Nate seemed to relax a little. 'Um, well, the girls and I just thought we'd drop by to see if you were up for a picnic? Last time we were here we talked about going over to the island in the dam.'

Berry smiled. 'We did, didn't we?'

'We've packed plenty of food—there's enough for everyone,' Lia chimed in.

'That would be lovely but I have to go to the tip,' Berry said. 'I've borrowed Andrea's ute and I have to get it back to her.'

'I can do that,' Uncle Dave said before adding, 'but you'll have to tell me where to go.'

'Are you sure?' Berry asked.

'Of course. I think I'm capable enough to drag a load of rubbish to the tip,' he said with a shrug. 'Besides, afterwards I'll swing by the Cumquat, return the ute and get everything set for the night.'

'That would be great, if you don't mind.'

'Good, it's settled, then.' He reached into his pocket, grabbed his car keys and handed them to Berry. 'Here, swap keys and I'll see you later.'

'But don't you want to stay and eat with us?' Berry asked.

Uncle Dave gave her a wink. 'Oh, I think you'll have much more fun without me,' he said before he gave a wave and walked towards the old sheds.

Berry turned to Jess. 'What's got into him? I mean, he seems almost relaxed.'

'Weird. Maybe it's the country air.'

Chapter Eighteen

'Look, I'm sorry I didn't organise this with you. I should have thought it through and not put you on the spot,' Nate said as he fell into step next to Berry.

She turned her head and smiled. 'It's all right, really. Besides, you know I always wanted to check out the island.' Berry looked over her shoulder and saw Tom and Lia carrying an inflatable kayak between them. 'Are we going to all fit in that?'

Nate grinned and shook his head. 'Nope, we'll have to take at least a couple of trips but it'll be fine.'

'Well, I guess I'm going to have to trust you on that,' she said.

'You can you know—I'm trustworthy,' he answered with a wink.

Berry kept walking down the narrow track towards the dam and desperately tried to ignore the sudden flash of heat in her cheeks. She took a breath and mentally tried to pull herself together. Out of the corner of her eye she swore that she saw Jess smirking—so much for her sister having her back.

'What did you pack in here?' she asked, holding up the basket she was carrying. 'Everything including the kitchen sink?'

'No, just the stuff we needed for a picnic,' Nate replied. 'I may have gone a little overboard, but I wanted to make sure we had enough to eat.'

'Well, it feels as if we'd have enough to feed half the town.'

'Point taken—next time you can pack the lunch,' Nate said as he reached down and took hold of the basket handle, causing another wave of heat as Berry's fingers tingled at his touch.

Berry shook her head. 'Thanks, but I can manage.'

'Come on, then,' Nate said with a smile.

There was a collective sigh of relief when they finally made it to the old wooden jetty that poked over the deep waters of the dam. They sank down on the rough boards and caught their breath.

'It looks deep,' Tom said.

'I guess,' Berry replied. 'Not that I know anything about dams.'

Nate chuckled. 'I'm not sure about the depth exactly—all I can tell you is that as far as I know it doesn't dry out in summer.'

Jess put her hand up to shield her eyes from the sun as she looked across to the island. 'So, the only way over is by boat?'

'Sure is,' Em answered. 'Who's going first?'

'I'll take Berry, Jess and the food over first and then come back and get you guys,' Nate said.

'That's a lot of rowing,' Berry said as she glanced across the water in an attempt to work out just how far it was.

'Nah, it's fine. Besides, Lia and Em can row us all back later.'

'Way to volunteer us,' Em said. But before she could say anything else Lia piped up, 'That's fine. Tom and I can row back later.'

Tom gave her an apologetic smile. 'Um, I've never done that before.'

'It's okay, it's easy. I'll teach you. I've been mucking about in boats ever since I was little,' Lia reassured him as she ignored her sister's surprised look. 'Really, there's nothing to it.'

'Well, come on, then—this food isn't going to eat itself,' Nate said as he walked over to the discarded dingy.

It didn't take long before Berry found herself skimming over the water towards the island. There was something incredibly pleasant about being in a boat, lulled by the rhythmic sound of the paddles hitting the water. She couldn't help but smile as the crisp breeze tugged at her hair. She tore her gaze from the nearing shore and smiled at Nate. 'It looks smaller than I remember.'

'Time will do that,' he said as he rowed.

'True,' Berry answered as she looked back to the island. It appeared wilder than she remembered too, which was no surprise after so many years of neglect. There were a couple of weeping willows growing close together near the water's edge, their bare branches hanging over the surface. Berry could only imagine what they would look like when their leaves returned. Aside from the willows, there was a gum tree in the centre of the island, then only rocks, reeds and a tangle of undergrowth as far as Berry could see.

'Nate, I was just thinking,' she said, 'no one's been over here in years. There might not be anywhere for us to set up a picnic.'

'Well, we'll soon find out. If it's too overgrown, we'll just eat on the jetty,' he said before adding, 'I probably should have checked that out first.'

'No, it's fine,' Jess said, nudging Berry's leg, which she chose to ignore. 'I'm just enjoying the ride—aren't you, Berry?'

Berry nodded to her sister. 'Yes, I never realised how relaxing this is.'

'Glad you both like it,' Nate answered with a grin.

After a few minutes the boat skimmed into the shallow water at the base of the island. Berry looked over the side of the boat and saw a bed of pebbles beneath the water. There was a small flat area that mainly consisted of rocks and a couple of large boulders. From what she could see there was little vegetation on this part of the island, other than a few straggling weeds growing around the base of the larger rock.

Nate jumped out, turned around and held his hand out towards Berry. As their hands touched, a now-familiar warmth travelled up her arm. With it came a picture of

Nate edging closer and wrapping her in his arms. Berry shook her head as if to dispel her imaginings and the flush of heat that engulfed her body like a tidal wave.

'Thanks,' she said as she quickly stepped from the boat, but when she lost her footing and lunged forwards, Nate reached out and steadied her.

'Are you okay?'

Berry nodded as she righted herself. 'Yeah, I'm fine, thanks,' she mumbled.

'I guess we'd better watch out. It doesn't look like anyone has been here for a long time,' Nate said as he let her go.

'Who would come here? I mean, it's private property,' Jess asked as she got out of the boat by herself.

'That wouldn't stop some people,' Nate replied. 'Besides, it was a well-known fact that your dad stocked this dam with trout. I'm not saying it's right, but I'd bet my last dollar that you've had more than one trespasser over the years.'

Berry glanced around the area to where the island sloped up from where they were standing.

'That's a track, isn't it?' she said as she pointed to it.

Nate looked in that direction. 'Looks like it, though it's pretty overgrown.'

Berry started towards it. 'Come on, let's check it out.'

'When you guys were little, did you ever come over here?' Nate asked as he walked behind Berry.

Berry thought for a moment. 'We did, but not very often. Mum didn't think it was a good idea for the two of us to come here by ourselves.'

Jess let out a laugh. 'You mean you don't remember the trouble we got in when we snuck over here and Mum found out? It's funny, you know—being balled out is one of the strongest memories I have.'

Berry turned and looked at her sister. 'When did that happen?'

'It must have been the last summer we were here, maybe soon after Christmas. We snuck into the shed and borrowed the little wooden canoe and rowed it over here.'

'Actually, now you mention it, I do remember taking the boat.'

'But not the trouble we got into as soon as we got back to shore.' Jess stopped and pointed to Tom and the girls on the jetty. 'Mum was standing over there waiting for us so she could read the riot act.'

Berry shrugged. 'I can't remember her telling us off at all.'

'From what I can remember, she generally didn't. But that day was a whole other thing,' Jess said. 'We must have given her a fright or something because she was so cross. I don't know, I just remember her going off about the leaky boat and being responsible enough to do what we were told.'

'Hang on—were we banned from coming down here?' Berry asked as she wrinkled her nose. 'I think I remember something about that.'

Jess's laugh ended in a sigh. 'Hell yes, we were banned from swimming in the dam all summer and we weren't allowed to go any further than the back yard. You know, there's a lot that I don't remember from when we lived here but that is burned into my memory.'

'It sounds as if she was worried about you, rather than angry,' Nate said. 'Boats can be tricky and if you were only little . . . well . . .'

Jess blew out a breath as she stared back to the shoreline. 'Yeah, I kind of get that as well. All my other memories—and I'm the first to admit I don't have that many—but in the rest, Mum's always kind and quietly spoken. Guess we must have really frightened her.'

'Sounds like it,' Berry said, but at the same time wondered what had really happened; it seemed so out of character from the mother she remembered and kept in her heart. 'Come on,' she said, in an attempt to shift the melancholic mood that had settled over them. 'Let's find somewhere to have this picnic, so Nate can go back and get the others.'

Jess gave her brother a wave. 'Yeah, I'm sure they're anxious to come over.'

'And I have to tell you that my sisters aren't that great when it comes to waiting,' Nate added.

'Right, then, let's see where this track takes us,' Berry said.

Just over the rise there was a clearing that was sheltered by several wattle trees.

'This is it,' Jess said as she pointed to the spot.

'Yep, I reckon that'll work,' Nate replied.

'Perfect,' Berry said. 'It's perfect.'

Chapter Nineteen

Somewhere down Folly's Track, 1906

Neddy had been walking for a while but he wasn't worried. The bunny disappeared every now and again, but he was still able to follow it. The rabbit didn't seem scared at all but rather to be enjoying a slow ramble in the summer sun just as much as Neddy.

They had been following the dusty track down the hill, further away from the cottage as well as from Harlington.

Neddy stopped for a moment and looked behind him. He wasn't that far from home and for an instant he wondered if he should turn around and go back. His father would be coming home soon, as well as his brothers.

But when he thought about it, he grew annoyed all over again. Why his brothers had to be so mean sometimes was beyond him.

'Don't see why I couldn't have gone swimming too,' he said quietly to the rabbit. 'It's not fair.'

The rabbit looked up from the piece of grass it was nibbling, but it didn't look particularly concerned by Neddy's plight.

He briefly debated about turning around and going home. But Mam was busy with the baby and supper would be ages away, so perhaps he still had a bit of time. Neddy took a step towards the bunny. He wished it would stop hopping away; he really wanted to pat the rabbit and keep it as his friend.

As soon as the rabbit sensed his approach it hopped a couple of jumps further away but this time it changed direction. Up until now, it had been leading Neddy down Folly's Track, but not anymore. Instead the rabbit left the edge of the track and veered into the tangle of bush.

'Come back,' Neddy called out but the rabbit ignored him and, as if to prove a point, took another defiant hop into the undergrowth.

Neddy took one last glance up the track towards his home before following the rabbit through the dry grass and beyond the skinny eucalypt saplings. He hurried, not wanting to lose sight of the animal—it wasn't scampering off but had certainly increased its pace. The further Neddy wound his way through the bush, the more the heat of the day was lessened by the shade of the trees. He was so intent on following the rabbit as it zigzagged through the dry scrub, fallen branches and clumps of dead grass, that he didn't take notice which way he was heading.

The rabbit disappeared behind a tumbled log and Neddy stopped to catch his breath. He'd come so far, he didn't want to lose it now. By the time he made it to the old log and peered behind it, he realised that the rabbit had gone. He sat down on the log with a bump and the sense of loss washed over him. Looking about he saw that he was in a small clearing ringed with tall gums whose branches and grey–green leaves seemed to reach up to the sky. It wasn't until that moment Neddy became uneasy. The breeze danced through the trees making the bough creak and the leaves rustle. Apart from an unseen bird singing in the distance, the clearing was quiet.

A shiver skimmed down Neddy's back as he grasped the fact that there was a good possibility he was lost. There was an itch at the back of his throat and hot tears began to well in his eyes. Maybe following the bunny hadn't been such a good idea; all of a sudden he felt very alone.

The first tear trickled down his cheek. He wiped it away with the back of his hand, but another one followed quickly after it. He dashed that one away as well, but his eyes kept filling up. His lips started to tremble when he heard a rustle not far away. Neddy looked up and saw the little brown rabbit sitting at the base of a gum tree as if waiting for him.

Neddy stood up and wiped the remainder of the tears away.

'It's all right, bunny,' he said, 'I'm coming, I'm coming.'

Chapter Twenty

'Berry and Jess are so pretty,' Em said as Nate's car bumped up the dirt road.

Nate kept staring out the windscreen not knowing if he should comment or not.

'I know, right,' Lia said. 'And did you see that jacket Jess was wearing—I want one so bad. Wasn't Lanny Terka wearing the same thing on her Insta last week?'

'I don't know, you follow her, I don't. Besides, as if that jacket is the only thing you want,' her sister laughed. 'I mean we all heard the *Tom and I can row back later* comment.'

Nate shifted positions in his seat and wished he was wearing earphones or had turned on some loud music. The last thing he needed to be privy to was a discussion about hot boys. God, his sisters were silly at times.

'There wasn't anything wrong with that,' Lia snapped.

'Nope, there wasn't. You can have Tom and I'll take Justin,' Em said with a grin.

'As if! I don't know why you always have to—'

'Can we just change the topic,' Nate butted in. 'I gather you both had a good time today?'

The girls nodded in unison. 'Yep, absolutely,' Lia said.

'Did *you*?' Em asked.

Nate nodded with a slight smile. 'Yeah, it was fun.'

The girls grinned at each other, a fact that wasn't lost on Nate.

'Can we do that again, Nate?'

He shrugged. 'I guess that depends on Berry.'

The girls shared looks and Lia mouthed, 'Berry,' silently before the two of them broke into giggles.

Just kill me, Nate thought as he flicked on his indicator and turned into Tarantale Downs. He spotted his father as soon as he drove up to the front of the house. He was standing at the top of the stone steps and was wearing his obligatory frown. Nate blew out a breath; he and his sisters had just had a great afternoon with Berry and now there was a good chance it was about to be ruined. He parked the car and glanced at his sisters. Whatever buoyancy and light-heartedness they shared on the drive back quickly disappeared and was replaced by the tension that appeared whenever Nate and their father were together.

'Where the hell have you been?' Sam Tarant said as Nate stepped out of the ute. 'We've got to ready the stalls for the two new horses arriving tomorrow, and did you forget that Mr Wallace is bringing Silver Moon to get serviced by Sunstorm this week?'

'No, I hadn't forgotten,' Nate said with an air of weariness as he started up the steps. *Here we go again.*

'I should have guessed that you'd be skiving off some-where rather than doing any work,' his father bit back.

Em and Lia gave Nate a sympathetic look before Em squared her shoulders and opened her mouth, but Nate cut her off with a shake of his head before she could say anything. He waved his hand and gestured for them to get out of there before their father turned his attention towards them.

Lia took Em by the hand and tugged her away—both giving Nate one last glance before retreating inside the house.

'I'm well aware of the work that has to be done,' Nate said. 'But it's the weekend and I figured that the girls and I could take a few hours off.'

Sam Tarant shook his head, accompanied with some-thing that sounded like a snort of disgust. 'You'll never be ready to run Tarantale Downs with that sort of attitude. If this place is going to continue to succeed you've got to put your heart, soul and every bloody minute of your life into it.'

'I love this place, Dad, but that's no way to live. I'm willing to put in the hours, but everyone's entitled to some down time, it's the only way to survive,' Nate replied as he faced his father. 'You know that there is actually life outside the boundary fence, don't you?'

'What the hell are you talking about? None of us will have anything if this place crumbles into the dust.'

'Dramatic much?' Nate studied his dad's face to see if the barb hit—it did and that gave him a spark of pleasure. 'I doubt the place will fall just because one of the stalls hasn't been mucked out. I promised the girls I'd take them on a picnic, so I did.'

'*Pfff*, and eating lunch takes you three hours, does it?'

'Apparently so,' Nate said before he turned to walk up the stairs.

'Are you telling me you spent three hours by the dam eating sandwiches?'

'No, I spent three hours at the dam at Stone Gully with Berry McCalister and her brother and sister. And by the way, I'm an adult—I don't question you on your where-abouts, so I figure you owe me the same courtesy,' Nate said as he walked away.

Sam Tarant turned around just in time to see Nate's back. 'Wait, you were with the McCalister kids?'

Nate paused but didn't turn around. 'That's what I said, didn't I?'

'And you were at the dam?'

'Yes . . . so?'

'It seems a strange place for them to go, considering that's where their mother died.'

'It was?'

'Yeah. How could they stand to be there and have a picnic?'

'Wow. That's intense . . . maybe they don't know.'

'Yes, of course, why would they?' His father suddenly changed his tone. 'Why were you with them?'

Nate frowned and glanced behind him. 'Where is it stated that you get right of veto on my plans, or my friends for that matter?'

'Friends—are they really?' his father said quietly.

'What the hell is that meant to mean? Look, as far as I'm concerned Berry McCalister is a friend. I only met the rest of her family today but they all seem great.'

'The rest of her family?'

'Yeah, her brother, sister and her uncle.'

'He's here too?'

Nate turned around and stared at his father. 'He didn't have lunch with us but he's here. They've come up for the weekend to check on the progress of the renovation.'

'Did they say if they're going to sell it?'

Nate shook his head, trying to fathom why he was so interested. 'As far as I know it's undecided. I suppose they'll fix the place up and then see what it's worth. At the moment, I don't think they have a clear idea.'

'I see.'

'I didn't think you'd be interested.'

His father shrugged. 'I'm not. I just hope they work out what they're going to do and move on. Although, I did say I'd buy the place if she needed to sell.'

'You did *what*?' Nate couldn't hide the surprise in his voice.

'You heard me. I just offered, it's not as if we really need more land but I'd rather buy it from the McCalisters than put up with neighbours we don't know.'

'Neighbours? God, Dad, we've never had a problem in the past. It's not as if Tarantale Downs is small, so why would this even be an issue?' Nate asked.

166

'I'm just covering all bases, that's all. Besides, I didn't want Berry to be stuck with a place she doesn't want,' he replied.

'Since when do you care about things like that?'

'That's enough! Remember who you're talking to. We may rub each other up the wrong way from time to time but I'm still your father,' Sam said as he pointed his finger in Nate's direction. 'And if you must know the truth, I said I'd buy the place because her dad was my friend and I didn't want to see her or her family stuck with a place filled with bad memories. And that's the end of it.'

Nate studied his prickly father for a moment. Sam Tarant had acquaintances, but not mates.

'Well, you probably don't have to worry about that,' Nate said eventually. 'From what I've heard, Berry's had plenty of offers for the place. The first couple were pretty insulting but apparently the price is beginning to rise.'

'Where did you hear that?' His father seemed a little taken aback, a little upset.

'Oh, come on, Dad—this is Harlington, gossip spreads like wildfire,' Nate said with a slight smile. 'Everyone knows what everyone else is doing, and if you don't, then you can get a catch up at the pub or the general store.'

'I suppose you're right,' his father said.

Nate sighed and pointed over his shoulder. 'Look, I'll see you later. I'm taking off.'

'Where?'

'Well, apparently I have a stall to muck out,' he said, before turning and heading across the wide verandah to the front door.

* * *

Jess followed Berry up the hall of their childhood home and into the bedroom they once shared. It was an empty shell except for two boxes in the corner. Despite the bareness, lingering memories fought their way to the surface.

'I always thought it was bigger,' Jess said as she looked around the room.

Berry gave her a smile. 'That's because we were little—everything looked bigger.'

Jess nodded but said nothing as she wandered over to the window and stared out.

'Did you enjoy today?' Berry asked.

'Yes, but probably not as much as you did,' Jess said with a grin.

Berry rolled her eyes, crossed her arms and leaned against the doorframe.

'Aw, come on, Ber—I saw the way you kept glancing at Nate.' She held up her hand to stop her sister interrupting. 'And I saw the way he kept looking at you. There's something there and don't you try to convince me otherwise.'

Berry was silent for a moment and then shrugged. 'You're right, I *am* drawn to him, but nothing's happened and it's not going to.'

'Why not?'

'Because what's the point of starting something when there's a damn good chance I'm not staying? It would just make everything awkward and probably even sad if things started to work out.'

'You could just have a bit of fun while you're here,' Jess countered. 'It doesn't have to be forever.'

'I know but I'm not that person. Sometimes I wish I was but I'm not.'

'Well, that's a shame because I thought there was definitely more than a spark there,' Jess said as she moved over to the boxes in the corner. 'Is this some of our stuff?'

Berry shook her head. 'No, it's just some things I found in the shed. I took a box back to the B&B to sort through and just shoved these in here until I could get around to them.'

'Did you find anything interesting?'

'Not much. There was a teacup, a few old magazines and some of Dad's paperwork.'

Jess wrinkled her nose at the mention of their father. 'Why didn't you just chuck it out?'

'I wanted to go through it, just to make sure there wasn't anything important in there,' Berry said.

'And was there?'

'I don't know yet—I haven't sorted through the papers. Did you want to have a look?'

'No, not at all,' Jess said as she glanced at Berry. 'I don't want to be reminded of him.'

'That's fair enough.'

169

'And I don't understand why you'd want to be either. He ruined our lives and stole Mum from us,' she said with a crack in her voice.

Berry walked forwards and pulled Jess into her arms. 'Since I've been here, I've come to realise that I need to understand what pushed him over the edge—it's the only way I can deal with what happened to us. I have to re-concile the man I remember with what he did—or more importantly why he did it. Do you understand?'

Jess sighed. 'I do, but don't ask me to help. I just want him erased from my memory. Forever.'

***

That night the McCalister family sat in The Queen's Arms mulling over the day.

'I never thought I'd say this but I kind of like Harlington,' Uncle Dave said as he reached for his wine. 'It funny, because I do believe I vowed that I'd never come back.'

Berry laughed. 'Well, some vows have to be broken.'

'Have you all thought about what you want to do with the place?' he asked as he looked at his nieces and nephew.

'We haven't really had a chance to talk about it,' Jess answered.

'You know there's no rush,' Uncle Dave replied. 'If you want to sit on it for a while, that's okay.'

Tom fiddled with his salad. 'Look, I don't know how much my opinion counts . . .'

Berry gave him a nudge. 'Don't be an idiot—your opinion counts just as much as ours. Even though you might not remember anything about it, Stone Gully Farm is still yours.'

'In that case, I know I said some harsh things about the town, but hanging around the farm today was good— you know, kind of peaceful,' he said. 'I'm not saying that I want to live here but maybe I don't want to get rid of it either.'

'Okay,' Berry said as she sat back in her chair and glanced at her sister. 'Jess, what do you think?'

Jess took a moment to ponder the question. 'I think I agree with Tom. If we're not in a hurry to sell it, then maybe we should keep it as a holiday place. We can always change our minds and sell it later on. What do you think, Uncle Dave?'

'It was never my decision. Stone Gully Farm belongs to the three of you. If you want to keep it, then that's what we'll do. Berry, how do you feel about that?'

'I think that it feels right to keep it. That's not how I felt when I arrived here, I just wanted to get the place sorted so we could get rid of it. I thought we'd all been through enough and the house would hold too many memories. That it would drag us all back into the past, the one place we've spent years trying to escape. But I think maybe I was wrong,' Berry said. 'There are good memories mixed with the bad, some of which I had forgotten. There's also been a change in the atmosphere at the house. The day I arrived, despite all my bravado to Jess, it was a bit sad and uncomfortable. Nate told me that the kids around here reckoned it was haunted, and I have to admit the first time I walked through the door I got chills.'

Uncle Dave sighed. 'How long before the house will be finished?'

Berry shrugged. 'The bathroom still needs to be done, the kitchen finished off and we've got people coming next week to redo the roof.'

'Well, keep me updated,' Uncle Dave said. 'It was a bit of luck that Andrea had room for us, wasn't it? I'm glad I don't have to drive back tonight.' He looked around at his nieces and nephew. 'Maybe keeping the old farmhouse isn't such a bad idea. It's not that far away from home and could be an ideal bolthole for weekends away.'

Berry smiled. 'Looks like we've got a plan.'

Chapter Twenty-one

A peace had settled over Berry by the time she waved her family off the next afternoon. The decision not to sell Stone Gully Farm felt right. She hadn't wanted to admit it, but the longer she stayed in Harlington the harder it was to face the prospect of selling up. It wasn't so much that Berry saw herself starting a new life here as it could be a backstop—the property would always be there if she needed it. She felt that she'd just found the place again and maybe it meant a little more to her than she ever thought it would.

The visit from her family had energised her, and by the time she arrived at Stone Gully on Monday morning she was itching to get going with the reno. She waved good morning to the contractors as she walked through the house.

'Hey Berry,' Dan the head contractor said. Dan was in his forties with sandy-coloured hair and a beard that matched. 'The marble benchtop's arriving today. So, by this afternoon all the appliances should be in. Jacko has to finish off the splashback, but that should be done by lunchtime.'

'That's fantastic,' Berry replied.

'Once everything's plumbed in and the stove arrives, you should have a working kitchen by probably tomorrow.'

Berry grinned. 'Thanks so much, I can't wait to cook in here.'

Dan looked at her for a moment. 'Look, I hope you don't mind me asking, but are you still going to sell it?'

'No, we've decided to hang onto it.'

'Great! I'm happy to hear that.'

'Why?'

He gave her a smile. 'Oh, I don't know—I guess it would be a bit sad to go to all the trouble of fixing an old place up and then not be able to enjoy it,' he said. 'Besides, it seems like a good opportunity to make some better memories. I reckon the house could do with that.'

Berry nodded. 'I reckon you're right.'

'I see that you got rid of all the junk out the back,' he said, gesturing in the vague direction of the sheds.

'Yeah, we did that on the weekend. Anyway, I'd better crack on—I'm going to paint the bedrooms,' Berry said as she started to edge away. She liked Dan and he was very good at his job, but he was also a bit of a talker. If she stayed there much longer, she was sure he'd start regaling her with stories about his rambunctious kids, and if that happened there was a good chance that most of the morning would slip by.

She managed to excuse herself and headed to her old bedroom, where a large tin of paint, a drop sheet and several rollers and brushes were stacked in a corner waiting for her. Berry prised the can of paint open and stood back to contemplate the colour. She'd chosen white for pretty much the entire house. Perhaps it was a bit boring, but she'd only been thinking about brightening the place up. Now that they were keeping the house, maybe she could afford to be a little more adventurous. Sitting back on her heels for a moment, she toyed with the idea of going and buying some different paint, but the thought was fleeting. She'd already bought this, so she'd better use it—boring or not. Maybe she could shake things up a bit in the lounge room and paint a feature wall?

Decision made, Berry rolled up her sleeves and reached for the nearest paintbrush.

By eleven o'clock, Berry had managed to get the first coat up on one wall and was beginning to cut in around the window. It had been a fairly successful morning and she was pleased with her progress, helped along by the music pumped out by the contractors in the kitchen, the mix of eighties and new music floating into the rest of the house.

Berry dipped the brush into the white paint and started to hum along with the radio when she heard someone clear their voice behind her. Turning around, she saw Nate standing in the doorway. He was wearing a blue plaid shirt with jeans and the type of smile that made her heart skip a beat.

'Hey, what are you doing here?' Berry asked as she put the brush down.

'I had a couple of hours spare and I thought you might need a hand,' Nate answered, his smile broadening.

'I know the contractors are doing the kitchen but I figured you wouldn't have anyone to help you with the painting—at least that's what you said the other day. So, do you want some company?'

As Berry stared at him, a swarm of butterflies took flight in her belly. Trying to pull herself back together, she dropped her gaze and started dipping the brush into the paint. 'Well, that would be great if you can spare the time,' she answered with what she hoped was a nonchalant tone. She glanced back up at him just in time to see the corner of his mouth curve up, and something about it made the room suddenly a little too warm.

'You can start over there, if you want,' Berry said, pointing to the adjoining wall.

Nate looked at the wall and then turned back to her. 'Hmm, how about I start here instead and work my way back to you?'

Damn.

'Sure, if you want,' Berry said as she turned back to the window. The room seemed a little smaller with Nate in it and Berry couldn't work out if that was a good or a bad thing. She tried to ignore his movements but she tracked him with her peripheral vision all the same.

He grabbed a brush and stood next to her and she did her best to concentrate on not dripping paint all over the place. He was too close, or perhaps she was just too aware of him.

'I hear that you've decided to keep the place,' Nate said.

Berry stopped painting and looked at him. 'How did you hear that? I mean, yes—but I haven't told anyone except Andrea.'

'Oh, Andrea doesn't gossip,' Nate assured her.

'Then how did you . . .'

Nate tilted his head towards the door. 'Dan told me when I arrived.'

'Oh.'

'Did you fail to realise that you've hired one of the town's biggest gossips?'

'No. I mean . . . yeah, I guess I did,' Berry said.

'Well, there you go. It'll be all over town by tonight,' Nate said as he glanced at her and grinned.

'Seriously—how is that anyone's business but mine?'

'Oh, it's not malicious. It's just that Dan likes to talk . . . to anyone.' Nate leaned over to dip his brush into the paint tray she was holding. A jolt rippled through her, but as she gave him a fleeting sideways glance she was relieved to see that he didn't seem to notice.

'I'm glad you're keeping it,' Nate said quietly.

Berry stopped painting for a moment. 'So am I.'

'I guess it will give you an excuse to keep coming back to Harlington,' Nate said as he turned and fixed his gaze on her. 'That's good.'

For a second Berry found it hard to pull her eyes away from his. 'Yes, it is.'

* * *

'Miss McCalister, I was hoping to have a word with you.' Laurie Worth was striding towards her.

'Hello, I'm a little pressed for time at the moment. As you can see I've just come home,' Berry said as she tried to sidestep him and keep walking. Unfortunately, she wasn't quick enough and he managed to block her path.

'Really, I only need a moment,' he said quickly. 'I heard that you've decided not to sell—that can't be right, can it?'

'Actually, it isn't really any of your concern,' Berry said. 'But that's correct. My family and I have decided to keep Stone Gully Farm, at least for the time being.'

'But surely that's not what you want. Why would you want to keep a place up here? Harlington is hardly a bustling metropolis.'

Berry took another step to get by him but he mirrored the movement. 'You're right, it's a quiet, sleepy little town, which makes it the perfect spot for a holiday house. I'm sure we could all do with a place where we can recharge our batteries,' Berry said. 'Now if you'll excuse me I have to—'

'I'll be willing to make you an offer—a substantial one,' he countered. 'Why don't we go inside, or better still let's go to my office.'

Berry shook her head. 'No thanks. I appreciate your offer, but as I said, we're not selling. Goodbye Mr Worth.' She moved to the right but as he shadowed her move, she quickly changed direction and slipped past him through the front door and closed it behind her. She stood quietly for a second before Andrea's footsteps distracted her.

'Oh, you're back. I'm so sorry that I couldn't get rid of him,' she said with a smile as Darby trotted next to her.

'There's something about that man I don't like,' Berry said.

Andrea looked a little shocked. 'Who—Mr Chester? I always thought he was nice.'

Berry frowned. 'No, I'm talking about Laurie Worth. He was waiting for me when I arrived.'

'Oh, I agree with you on that,' Andrea said as she peered through the leadlight window. 'I didn't realise he was out there. Maybe I should have set Darby on him.'

Berry grinned and patted Darby on the head. 'Darby's got more taste, don't you, fella. He wouldn't want anything to do with him. So, what about Mr Chester?'

'He's waiting for you in the lounge. I think he wants to make an offer on Stone Gully Farm. I told him that you'd decided not to sell, but he was adamant that he wanted to talk to you,' Andrea explained.

'Damn, all I wanted was a cup of tea and a hot shower,' Berry said as she looked down at her paint-splattered clothes. 'Nate said this would happen.'

'What do you mean?'

'That my contractor would gossip about us not selling,' Berry explained.

'Well, it may have spread quicker because Dan has a big mouth, but it would have circulated sooner or later.'

'Yeah, I know.'

'Listen, you go and talk to Mr Chester and I'll go and put the kettle on.'

Berry nodded. 'Okay, good idea—well, the kettle bit anyway,' she said as she took a step towards the lounge. 'Wish me luck.'

'You'll be fine, just be firm,' Andrea said as she headed towards the kitchen with Darby by her side.

Berry waited for Andrea and Darby to disappear before she fixed a smile onto her face and walked into the lounge.

'Mr Chester, did you want to speak to me?'

A man in his sixties stood up and stretched out his hand. 'Miss McCalister, it's a pleasure to meet you. I hope that Harlington has welcomed you with open arms.'

'Thank you, yes, everyone has been lovely. Now, what can I do for you?'

'Oh, you're direct—I like that. Well, I'm here to make you an offer on Stone Gully,' he said with a bright smile. 'I assumed that you would want to go back to your life and put the past firmly behind you.'

'That's very kind of you, but my family and I have decided that we're going to keep the property. You see, it's our family home and our only link to the past,' Berry said. She saw that he was about to interrupt so she quickly hurried on. 'Even though the place does hold sad memories—there are happy ones as well. We're just not ready to let it go yet.'

He nodded. 'I see. No, I understand completely—I'm sorry if I disturbed you.'

'Not at all, Mr Chester. Thank you for the offer,' Berry said as she shook his hand again and watched him move towards the front door.

He paused as he put his hand on the handle. 'If you ever change your mind and wish to sell, I hope that you will keep me in mind. I promise to make you a decent offer,' he said.

'Of course,' Berry said. 'Goodbye.'

He gave her a nod. 'Miss McCalister,' he said as he opened the door and left.

***

Berry pulled back the curtain as she sat on the window seat. There was a fine rain misting Andrea's cottage garden. It was twilight but still light enough to see the cumquat tree near the lovers' seat. There was a stillness in the garden and the only sound she could hear was the accumulation of raindrops as they dripped onto the flat slate paving stones.

For a moment, Berry's mind wandered to earlier that day. Briefly closing her eyes, she recalled the sensation of Nate's body close to hers.

I guess it will give you an excuse to keep coming back to Harlington. That's good.

His words circulated around her head and wound their way towards her heart. The more she saw Nate, the stronger the enticement became. Perhaps, even if she went back to Melbourne, maybe there was a chance of something.

She shook her head as if to clear it. *Don't be ridiculous,* she scoffed silently. *Long-distance romances are doomed to fail before they even begin.*

Berry turned away from the window and glanced around the room looking for something to take her mind off Nate. In the corner was the box filled with some of the things she'd taken from the shed. Other than one of the magazines, she hadn't looked at it. She wandered over to the box, knelt down and started sorting through it. There was an old battered briefcase filled with a stack of handwritten papers. Berry knew that they were her dad's—she remembered his bold writing style.

As she stared into the case her hand hovered over the papers—partially because she was scared about what she might find. Her mind whirled with crazy ideas, but she slowly worked up the courage to start.

At first she wasn't sure what she was looking at. There were snippets cut from old newspapers, a fragile-looking map of Harlington, her father's handwritten notes and a small paperback about the town's early history and local legends.

Berry frowned. Who knew that a place as small as Harlington would have legends.

She sat down and started sifting through the material to try to work out exactly what her father had been working on, because clearly it had been something. There were some old invoices and a small hand-drawn map of Stone Gully Farm. On closer inspection, Berry saw that it showed a snapshot of what the land had been used for. The house was meticulously drawn and she could easily make out the sheds and the sheep shed in the bottom paddock. The other thing the map showed was the layout of the orchard and all the different varieties of trees that had been planted there.

She flicked through a slim volume of odd stories and possible tall tales from around the area. She skimmed over the first couple of stories, but the title 'Hidden Gold and the Lost Child' caught her attention.

Berry settled on the bed as she started to read the entry.

Back in the summer of 1906 a rumour circulated through the town that Harlington was sitting on hidden treasure. A local boy who wandered away from home was said to have discovered a gold seam in the quartz reef.

Berry looked up from the pages. Something about it sounded familiar. It took her a moment but then an image sparked in her memory of an old man in the pub.

'Young Ned—that's what he was talking about,' Berry said quietly. 'The lost child must have been Young Ned's ancestor.'

Berry searched through the box for an old newspaper clipping she vaguely recalled seeing in her dad's papers. Among the clippings were several accounts of the same story. A few were from 1906 when the child went missing, and others were later. But most surprisingly was an actual newspaper clipping from 1906 confirming that it was indeed Little Neddy Doherty who had been lost.

A smile flickered across Berry's lips. She'd been right about the kid being related to Young Ned. Intrigued, she kept searching through the box and discovered that a lot of the papers centred around this one event. It was interesting to read all the firsthand accounts about the search through the bush, but Berry couldn't understand why this story seemed to resonate with her father. As far as she could make out, her dad had been obsessing about this in the lead-up to his death. Added to the books and papers, she had found her father's notebook, filled with scribbles about the old legends. She could understand being interested in local history, but her dad had collated an entire box of research all on one small incident.

One moment it was a respectable ten o'clock and the next time she bothered to check it was 2.27 a.m. Reluctantly Berry pushed aside the box and crawled into bed, only to have her dreams filled with a gleaming seam of gold and a little boy lost in the bush.

Chapter Twenty-two

Somewhere in the bush, 1906

Neddy was completely turned around. He'd been so intent on following his bunny that he'd forgotten where he was. That was the problem with rabbits, they didn't seem to care where they were heading.

He thought of it as *his* bunny now as they had spent hours in each other's company. He should give it a name, as all pets were supposed to have names. Neddy thought about it for a moment as he leaned against a big gum tree. Maybe he'd call him Peter, just like the one in the story his teacher, Miss Warren, had read to the class.

Neddy tilted his head back and looked up into the spreading branches of the tree. Its grey–green leaves danced in the breeze. He reached out and plucked a leaf and brought it to his lips. Neddy tried to remember how Gabe had told him to hold it so the leaf would make a loud whistle. He blew on it gently but couldn't make a sound; he tried again but got the same result—nothing.

Neddy dropped the leaf and frowned. It wasn't fair that his brothers always seemed to be able to do everything better than he could. Gabe could play tunes on gum leaves—why couldn't he?

He glanced up through the branches and to the sky. It was getting late, and he knew he should think about going back home. The sun wouldn't set for a while, but it must be almost time for supper and he was beginning to feel hungry. The problem was that he wasn't sure which way home was.

He looked over and saw Peter nibbling a bit of grass near a small copse of trees. Maybe there was still enough time to see where Peter wanted to take him, and besides, he wasn't that hungry . . . well, not yet. He was about to walk towards Peter when a faint sound drifted through the bush. Neddy wasn't sure exactly what it was, but it sounded like snatches of a faint faraway voice. Closing his eyes, he tried to concentrate on the sound but it disappeared like a waking dream. He waited another moment or two, then, with a shrug, he started walking towards Peter; as he neared, Neddy saw that the ground fell away into a deep gully.

Just as he reached the trees, the ground seemed to shift. Neddy tried to grab one of the saplings but the earth collapsed beneath his feet and both he and Peter tumbled towards the gully below.

Chapter Twenty-three

Nate walked into the main house and was greeted by the familiar scene of his family's morning routine. As always his mum was flitting around the kitchen getting breakfast ready with one of the twins in her wake.

She smiled as he stepped into the kitchen. 'Morning darling, how are you?'

Nate walked over and gave her a kiss on the cheek. 'Fine, how are you going?'

'Running a little late but other than that I'm okay. Now, would you like some breakfast?'

Nate looked over and saw eggs and bacon and French toast. He'd already had a bowl of cereal but the aroma was just too much to resist.

'I won't say no,' he answered with a smile. 'If there's enough.'

She patted his arm. 'Of course there is. Sit down and I'll grab you some.'

'I can do it,' Nate said as he took a step towards the stove.

'No, no, sit down,' his mother assured him.

His father glanced up from his newspaper as Nate pulled out the nearest chair.

'Where were you yesterday afternoon? Did you forget that the Turners were bringing two horses to be stabled?'

'Of course I didn't forget. I got the two stalls cleaned and ready before I left,' Nate said as he reached for the jug of orange juice in the middle of the table. 'I figured you would have seen that.'

His father studied him for a moment before continuing. 'I did.'

Nate sighed. 'So, what's the problem, then?'

'The problem is that we advertise this place as a family-run establishment. The Turners expected to see you when they dropped the horses off.'

Nate sat back in his chair. 'Yeah, right, do you mean the Turners or their brat of a daughter, Penelope?'

Em giggled from somewhere behind the kitchen bench.

'That's no way to talk about our customers,' his father said firmly.

'Oh, come on, Dad. Mr Turner couldn't give a damn if I was there or not—this is all about Penny,' Nate said with an air of exasperation. 'She's a spoiled brat who has a thing for me. I've never encouraged her.'

'You could do worse,' his father replied. 'The Turners aren't short of a penny and they seem to like you.'

'So, am I meant to marry them or Penny? Seriously, Dad, you sound like someone out of the Dark Ages.'

'Look, all I'm saying—' Sam began but Jackie broke in.

'Sam, Nate's not interested. Penny is a nice girl but she can be difficult at times—you know that,' she said.

'That's an understatement,' Lia mumbled beneath her breath, but it was loud enough for her father to give her a look. 'She's totally up herself and a pain in the arse. Look how she carries on at every horse show—like she's the only one who can ride a horse.'

'Lia!' her mother admonished. 'Is that how we speak about people?'

Lia wrinkled her nose and pursed her lips. 'I'm just being honest, Mum. You might think she's nice but she isn't. Em and I are friends with her little sister, Bethany, and she's just awful to her.'

'It's true, Mum. She is pretty terrible,' Em added. 'And according to Bethany, Penny has wanted Nate for years. She's always talking about him and Bethany reckons she'll do anything to get him.'

'Aw, cut it out, Em—you're making me feel like some sort of hunted animal,' Nate said with a laugh. 'I think I can take care of myself.'

'Yeah, well, don't say I didn't warn you.'

Sam set aside his newspaper. 'You still haven't said where you were?'

Nate took a deep breath. 'I was helping Berry paint.'

'Oh, right,' his father said. 'Because spending time with her is more important than being present in the family business.'

Nate bristled at his father's tone and implication, but before he could respond, his mum chirped in.

189

'I'm so glad they're going to keep the farm.'

Sam stared at his wife. 'What?'

'They're going to keep Stone Gully Farm. I stopped at the servo on the way to pick up the girls from netball—Ken told me,' she explained.

Sam frowned. 'How the hell would Ken know?'

Jackie shrugged. 'I don't know—I guess he heard it from someone.'

'Probably just a baseless rumour,' her husband said as he picked up his coffee cup.

'It's not,' Nate said. 'Berry and her family are keeping the place. They decided the other day.'

'And you're only telling us now?' Sam said.

'She only told me yesterday. I didn't think it was a big deal. I'm happy with the decision—it means that Berry has a reason to keep coming back to Harlington.'

His father studied him for a moment and then slowly nodded. 'Ah, I see. You like this girl, don't you?'

All of a sudden Nate felt the need to inspect his glass of juice more intently and the sound of both his sisters sniggering didn't help.

'I get it now—that's why you're not interested in the Turner girl,' Sam replied as if he'd just uncovered a great mystery. 'Well, you might have said something earlier.'

Nate glanced at his sisters and saw that he'd get no help from them at all. He sighed and put his glass down. He might as well own it.

'Yeah, I do like Berry. Is that a problem?'

'No, it's your life—it's got nothing to do with me,' his father answered.

Nate heard the words but doubted their sincerity. If there was one thing he knew about his father, it was that he needed to control Tarantale Downs and everyone in it. For a second he held his breath and waited for him to say something else; probably about how rich Penny Turner's family was. Or that there wasn't any scandal attached to them, unlike the McCalisters. He waited but the words didn't come, which was even more perplexing.

'So, are you seeing her today?' his mum asked as she handed him a plate full of food.

'Yeah, I'll head over there later,' he said. 'Thanks, Mum.'

She placed her hand on his shoulder. 'I know it sounds like we're prying—we don't mean to, sweetheart. I just want you to be happy,' she said before walking back towards the stove.

He glanced back to his father only to see that he'd picked up the paper again and was immersed in it. With another barely audible sigh, Nate started eating.

***

Berry yawned as she looked over the paddocks. She'd stayed up too late going through her father's paperwork, but as drained as she was she could sense spring in the air.

As she stared across the rolling hills, she could almost see a little boy running through the paddock towards the bush. She smiled—she was being fanciful, but the story she'd read last night kept playing on her mind. It was silly, really, she knew that the little boy had lived through his ordeal and gone on to have a long life—Young Ned was testament to that. But the thought of the little kid being out there in the bush all alone pulled at her heartstrings.

However, the one question she wasn't any closer to answering was why her father was so interested in this story.

The contractors had already been hard at work by the time she arrived. She was off to a late start and there was an entire house to paint, but Berry was finding it difficult to work up the energy just to walk into the house. She looked down at her watch and saw that it was already ten-thirty. Her grandma would say the morning was nearly over, and that's kind of how Berry felt.

She yawned again as she stretched her arms over her head. Staring off across the paddocks or mentally painting the walls wasn't going to get her anywhere. Using up a considerable amount of willpower, Berry headed towards the house and hoped that Nate would turn up and save her.

She wasn't disappointed, because not long after lunch Nate arrived with coffee. For a second Berry wasn't sure if she was more excited to see him or the steaming cup of coffee—nah, it was him.

'Hey, I thought you might need this,' he said as he strolled into the newly painted room.

Berry grinned as she reached out and took the coffee. 'You have no idea.'

'So, it looks as if it's coming together,' Nate said as he surveyed the paint job.

'Yeah, I'm really happy with it, and thanks for helping out yesterday. One room down and only . . . well, the rest of the house to go.'

'Well, I guess I'd better get on with it, then,' Nate said as he walked over and snatched up a brush. 'Where do you want me?'

It was an innocent enough question, but all of a sudden Berry found the room a little warm. 'Um, well, I guess we just have to finish around the door and then move on to the next room.'

'Right, I'm on it,' Nate said.

'Nate, do you know much about that story Young Ned was telling us in the pub? You know, the one about his grandfather?' Berry asked.

Nate laughed. 'That's the only story he tells once he's got a couple of pints in him.'

'Really?'

'Yep, the old guy is fixated on what happened. I get it, but sometimes I think that he tends to live in the past rather than the here and now. Look, I could be wrong but Ned is desperate to convince everyone that the story about the gold is true.'

'And it isn't?'

'I can't say either way. I guess there's a grain of truth in it. I mean, the little kid did go missing, but as to finding Harlington gold, I not so sure about that,' Nate said with a shrug.

'What makes you think he didn't find it?' Berry asked.

'I guess if it were true, someone would have found it by now. Have you read any of the reports about what happened?'

'I have. From what I can gather, the kid wandered off from home and there was a big search party formed to find him—and it took two days before they actually did.'

'Hmm, not quite. According to the accounts I've heard, most of the people in the party were really worried that they hadn't found him by dark. He was only six or something. I guess they were lucky it was summer and the nights were warm, but still you could only imagine all the terrible things that could have happened. You're right about the search party but they never found him,' Nate replied.

'What? I mean, what happened to him?'

'Apparently, Little Neddy managed to get almost home on his own. He ran into the search party not far from his own gate. And that's where the story about the gold first appears and is a bit sketchy.'

Berry put down her paintbrush. 'Why's that?'

'Because the kid told everyone about the gold he'd seen, but couldn't tell anyone where it was. My favourite bit about the whole story is when they asked him how he found the gold, he said that the rabbit showed him,' Nate said with a grin. 'I mean, surely that's enough for most adults to realise that the kid made the story up.'

Berry paused for a moment in thought. For reasons she couldn't explain she felt compelled to defend the boy.

'That's a bit harsh, isn't it? I mean, the poor little thing was lost for two days. I'd find it hard to believe he'd make up a story just to trick people.'

'Okay, you're right,' Nate conceded. 'I don't think he did anything malicious. Maybe he saw something and took it the wrong way, or hell, maybe he dreamed it. Anyway, after the story came out there was a rush to go and find the gold. According to legend—or, more importantly, editorials in the local paper—half the town went gold mad. They scourged the area from the hills behind Sunlight Flat to Patterson's Gorge and everything in between.'

'And no one found anything, right?' Berry asked.

'That's right—not a seam or a nugget or even a damn speck. This entire area was meant to be goldmining country; back in the 1850s, there was a gold rush and towns were founded and then prospered because of it. Castlemaine was one of the epicentres and that's not too far away from us, but Harlington hasn't been blessed with even a pinch of gold dust,' Nate said.

'So, if there *was* gold out there, you'd think someone would have found it by now,' Berry said as she settled down next to the paint tin and reached for her coffee.

'Exactly. People didn't stop looking once the story died down. We've had prospectors here, both local and blow-ins, all searching for Harlington's gold on and off for years. Every now and again if the story is mentioned or gets a bit of exposure, there'll be another wave of gold hunters turn up with their metal detectors.'

'Annoying?' Berry said.

Nate gave a shrug. 'Oh, I don't know. It usually doesn't last long, and they bring business to the town. The Cumquat fills up, so do the couple of spare rooms at the pub, and the servo and shop get an increase in trade—so it's not all bad.'

Berry took another sip of her coffee. 'I suppose we'd better get on with the next room,' she said with a sigh. 'Personally, I'd rather sit here, drink coffee and listen to Harlington gossip, but I suppose that won't get the house painted.'

Nate flashed her a smile. 'You might be right about that.'

Berry stood up and stretched her arms before glancing back at Nate. 'So, I have another question for you,' she said.

'Oh?' His eyes lit up with expectation as he turned his head and focused his gaze on her.

Berry paused and teasingly let the moment linger for a second and then another. 'Do you want to paint the window frame or roll the wall?' she asked with a grin.

Chapter Twenty-four

Stone Gully Farm, 2007

Jordy McCalister had spent the past two weeks scaling every inch of Stone Gully Farm. He left the house every morning just as the sun was coming up and didn't return until it was dark. Cath had noticed, but up until now hadn't said anything.

A smile played across his mouth as he replayed the scene he'd been concocting in his head. How he'd tell her that finally after all these sad years he'd actually come off on top and all their worries would soon be a thing of the past.

Jordy had already planned where he'd take her to tell her the news—the setting was important and he wanted everything to be perfect. Like always, he had a tendency to get a little carried away and this time he was going to try to keep things in check—at least that's what he told himself. The problem was, it was so damn easy to paint a rosy picture, a snapshot of how things should be, of how he wished they were.

But this time it was different. This time he had something concrete to base his hopes on.

For the sixth time Jordy opened up the old map he'd liberated from the local historical society. He continued waging the argument in his mind as he ran his finger over the map and tried to get his bearings. It wasn't as if he'd actually stolen the map, he told himself again, it was more like he had just borrowed it—maybe indefinitely but he had every intention of returning it one day. Albeit anonymously, because the Society President, Mrs Strickland, was utterly terrifying. He wasn't a thief; he needed this particular map because it was from 1899 and had details that didn't appear on the modern editions. Added to that, there were also handwritten annotations and comments included on the back. Whoever he was, the original owner knew the area like the back of his hand.

Jordy studied the map, trying to work out where the hell he was. Around here wasn't like the rest of the farm; this consisted of pebbly dirt, gullies, rocks and struggling saplings. This part of the property was always problematic because it was rugged and rocky and you couldn't plant any crops because of the poor soil and the quartz reef that ran through the area.

He hadn't told anyone that he was chasing a legend. Firstly, because most people would think it was another one of his harebrained ideas, and secondly, he didn't want to see the disappointment in Cath's eyes if it all turned to naught.

Jordy folded up the map and pulled a small journal from his jacket pocket. He opened up the volume to one of the marked pages.

Harlington Gazette, *March 1906*

The boy was interviewed by the authorities but no amount of prodding could unlock the whereabouts from his head. All he could remember were tall gums, a rocky outcrop and a deep gully. Unfortunately, these landmarks could be used to describe most of the countryside around Harlington.

Jordy shut the book and rammed it back into his pocket.

'But it's here,' he whispered to himself. 'It's here—I know it.'

He pushed himself off the rock and was about to go in a northwest direction towards one of the gullies that snaked their way through the property when he thought he heard a low whistle.

Turning around he saw the silhouetted figure of a man walking towards him. He raised one hand to cover his eyes from the sun but still couldn't work out who it was.

'Hey Jordy! Cath said you might be out here—whatcha up to?'

Chapter Twenty-five

The weeks began to fly by for Berry. The contractors finished up and so did the guys who redid the roof. The transformation of the old house was amazing and it was getting harder for Berry to remember what it used to look like—which wasn't a bad thing. The only remnant of the past was the height chart on the wall between the lounge room and the kitchen. She had ummed and ahhed over the decision to keep it, worried that it could bring back memories which needed to be forgotten. But it hadn't and Berry was glad that it was still in place. If she closed her eyes, all she could hear was laughter: hers, Mum's and Jess's as they marked off each other's height. It was good and it made her happy.

One of the biggest changes for Berry was moving out of Cumquat Cottage and back to Stone Gully. She and Andrea had driven up to Bendigo and purchased the bare essentials for the house, including a bed, linen and most importantly a coffee maker. It had been a fun day and watching the deliveries roll up Stone Gully driveway was equally exciting. However, the whole idea of staying in the house by herself did worry her a little—which was ridiculous as she spent most days there on her own. Anyway, it was a small but persistent thought that she couldn't seem to shake.

She had been a bit worried about staying that first night. Berry figured if she could get through that, then everything would be fine. She had, and it was.

As spring arrived, she sensed hopefulness in the air. But maybe this feeling had less to do with her mind or the change of season than it did with Nate Tarant.

Before she even realised it was happening, both she and Nate seemed to fall into a rhythm that gave way to a habit—and she knew just how hard they are to break. Nate would come over most days and help her paint. At first it was only when he could get away from work, but as the days progressed, he carved out a couple of hours around the middle of the day. His presence had become expected and Berry looked forward to each afternoon.

There was a tension between them that was punctuated with a little teasing, but still neither of them had acted upon it—it was as if they were dancing just out of each other's grasp. Berry had been adamant when she arrived in Harlington that she had no intention of starting any sort of relationship, but now things seemed different and every time she looked at Nate she felt an invisible pull towards him. Putting aside her daydreams of what could be, Berry still had to work out what she was doing with her life. It was all very well to take three or so months to do up the house—none of which would have been possible without her uncle's help—but at some stage she had to sit down and work out a path for her future. The question she had to figure out was if Nate was part of that.

***

Berry was standing in the orchard, admiring the budding blossoms on most of her plum trees. Some of the flowers were white while others were a delicate pink. According to the planting map she had found in her father's papers, there appeared to be a variety of different trees, which included Satsuma plums and Golden Gage. Not sure about the difference between them all, Berry figured she'd work it out once they bore fruit.

There was a gentle cool breeze blowing through the orchard, causing the new blossoms to quiver as it passed over them. The sun hung high in the clear sky and Berry could almost catch the hint that spring was beginning to materialise.

'Hey.'

She turned to see Nate striding towards her from up the hill. Damn it, she swore that her heart did a weird little tremble.

'Hey yourself. What brings you here?' she said with a grin.

He smiled in return, one of those ones that can melt a target at twenty paces.

Berry drew in a deep breath.

'Well, I've been busy at the farm for the past few days and I wanted to make sure that you were okay.'

Berry gave a shrug. 'I'm fine. How about you?'

'Not bad,' he said. He glanced around the orchard. 'It's a pretty spot.'

'Yes, yes it is,' Berry replied. 'The orchard was planted about sixteen years ago. I remember as a little kid helping plant one of the trees over there with my mum.' She tilted her chin in the direction of a row of trees to her right.

She prattled on about finding the map of the orchard's layout in the box of her father's papers, all the time trying to ignore the fact that Nate was standing only two steps away from her. His proximity was making it hard for her to concentrate.

'Do you always do that when you're nervous?'

Berry glanced up at him. 'Do what?'

'You talk faster,' he asked.

'No, I don't,' Berry said quickly before adding with laugh. 'Well, maybe I do.'

He looked down at her with a hint of a smile. 'Do I make you nervous?'

'Oh, don't be ridiculous. Listen, I should get back to the house,' Berry said as she went to take a step away.

'Stay . . . please.'

She halted in her tracks and turned to look at him. 'Why?'

'Because there's something between us. I can feel it— can you?' Nate spoke softly with an open, earnest look on his face.

'I don't know what you mean . . . I . . .'

'Yes, you do.'

The heat rose in her cheeks. Half of her wanted to stay and the other half run away as fast as possible.

'I like you, Berry, and I'm fairly sure you feel the same way,' he said.

Berry was trying her best to avoid his gaze, knowing she could almost drown in those eyes. 'Um, maybe we shouldn't complicate things. I mean, I don't even know how long I'll be here,' Berry said with a shrug and a half-apologetic smile. 'It's probably wiser if we leave things as they are.'

Nate smiled gently. 'That aside, you feel the same way I do?'

Berry raised her head and looked back at him. 'Yes . . . but as I said I'd better go back to the house.'

She had walked about three steps past Nate when he reached out and gently grabbed her wrist. The warmth of his fingers seemed to burn into her flesh. One moment melted into another as they stood in the flowering orchard.

'Stay,' he repeated softly. 'Please.'

They were the same words he had said minutes before, but this time they carried a longing she hadn't heard before in his voice. She could have easily pulled her hand away and kept walking but she didn't—she couldn't.

Nate tugged her wrist and she spun around into his waiting arms. He drew her closer and searched her face, giving her one last chance to break away. But in that moment, there was nowhere else Berry wanted to be.

Slowly he inched closer until his lips touched hers.

Their first kiss was slow and hesitant, as if Nate were giving them both a chance to stop. But after so many weeks of tiptoeing around each other, that was the last thing on Berry's mind. Her arms wrapped around his waist and pulled him closer to her, close enough for her to feel the firm planes of his body.

Nate's hand trailed up her back and cradled the nape of her neck as the kiss deepened. Berry was acutely aware of the sensation of being both on the brink of jeopardy and utterly safe as he held her in his arms. The pressure of his lips and the scent of his watery aftershave spun her into a seductive trance that she hoped wouldn't end. She ran her hand up his arm, to his hard bicep and then over his shoulder. As the heat began to unfurl within her, the knowledge that she wanted him, that she needed him, hit her. Perhaps it was the whole delayed pleasure thing but all Berry knew was that she wanted more.

The tip of her tongue ran across Nate's lip and caused something that sounded like a soft growl from the back of his throat. He lifted her up and Berry instinctively wound her legs around him as they continued to kiss. She wasn't sure where he intended to take her but at that moment she didn't give a damn.

They clung together as a breeze danced through the orchard, taking handfuls of blossoms as it went. The petals in the wind may have been a pretty sight, but all Berry was aware of was Nate. It was a perfect moment and one she intended to treasure—but all good things come to an end, especially when you don't want them to. Unfortunately, Berry could vaguely make out a voice in the distance calling her name. At first she did her best to ignore it, but the voice was persistent and appeared to be getting closer.

A sigh escaped her mouth as she and Nate broke apart and he lowered her to the ground. He gave her a wink and they stood side by side as someone entered the orchard.

'Miss McCalister! Oh, there you are. I tried at the house but I thought I'd look around. I didn't want to miss you.'

Berry let out a groan and screwed up her face as she glanced at Nate. 'Well, that's all we need,' she muttered. 'Laurie Worth. Worst timing ever.'

'Yep, I never liked that guy,' Nate whispered back as he reached over and smoothed out a lock of her hair.

It was a small gesture but it made her smile. The feeling was short lived, though, as Laurie Worth hurried up to her.

'Miss McCalister, I really need to have a word with you,' he said as he looked pointedly at Nate. 'In private.'

Berry shook her head. 'No, we're right. What do you want, Mr Worth?'

'Well, I have a business proposition for you. I really think it's best if we talk alone,' he said quickly.

'Like I said, we're right,' Berry answered as she squared her shoulders and stood her ground. 'Whatever you've got to say, you can say it in front of Nate.'

He was silent for a second before giving Nate another look that couldn't be called pleasant on any level. 'Oh, I see how it is.'

'I'm not sure what you're implying, but did you have something to say to me or not?' Berry said.

'I want to renew my offer for Stone Gully Farm. I know that you said you're not selling, but I've generally found that everything has a price—I'm sure this won't be the exception.'

Berry gave Nate a sideways glance before continuing. 'I promise you that we've made our minds up. There's no way we're selling at present. I'm sorry you wasted your time coming all the way out here.'

'I don't think you understand. I'm willing to give you a *substantial* price for the property,' Worth said. 'You won't get a better offer.'

Berry took a deep breath. 'No, I don't think that *you're* listening to *me*. My family and I have decided not to sell, and that's the end of it. You badgering me won't change my answer.'

Worth appeared taken aback for a moment but he recovered quickly. 'Right—I'm stupid, I should have seen this coming. It just goes to prove that sometimes you really should believe the rumours.'

'Mr Worth, I have no idea what you're talking about,' Berry said as she took Nate's hand and started walking away. 'Please excuse us, we have work to do.'

'Just so you know—at least I was up-front about wanting to buy this place and give you a fair price.

Whereas he—' Worth said as he pointed to Nate '—he's just trying to romance the place from under you.'

Berry stared at him coldly. 'I think you'd better leave—we're done here.'

Chapter Twenty-six

In the Gully, 1906

Neddy tumbled down the steep side of the gully, the sharp rocks and brambles scratching and pulling at him as he hurtled past. He rolled and skidded all the way to the bottom and landed with a bump.

For a moment he lay there, staring up at the blue sky— his heart pounded and he wasn't even sure if he could move. The tears welled in his eyes as he tried to sit up; everything seemed to hurt. Looking down he saw that his pant leg was torn and a big red scratch arced up his shin. He hands were filled with dozens of tiny cuts and nicks where he'd tried to grab on to anything as he fell.

Hot tears splashed down his cheeks. He wrapped his hands around his legs, and rested his head on his knees as he cried. Slowly the tears began to subside but the feeling of wanting his mam's arms around him didn't. The warm breeze blew over him, ruffling his hair as it passed.

Neddy looked up and wiped the tears away with the back of his hand. The gully was narrow with tall sides running along its length, the ground was dry and rocky with only a few straggling plants trying to cling to life. A ribbon-thin trickle of water splashed its way through the almost dry creek bed. In winter the creek would have gushed its way through the gully, probably all the way up to where Neddy was sitting, but this was summer and the fact that there was still water was a miracle in itself.

At the end of the gully was a clump of wattle trees, and on the other side of the creek a series of rocks that stood higher than Neddy's father against the far gully wall. Not far from Neddy was a tangled bush of blackberries. Another puff of wind blew against him and he could smell the sweet scent of the sun-ripe fruit.

He glanced at a fragile everlasting daisy, which seemed to be growing against the odds in such a hard place. He reached out and touched its pink petals but left it alone. Normally he would have picked the flower and given it to his mam because she always said that they were her favourite. But this time he left the little daisy; his mam wasn't here but somehow it made him feel that maybe she wasn't that far away.

Neddy slowly stood up. The scratches were still stinging a bit, but other than that he was fairly certain that he was all right. He scanned the gully and wondered just how hard it was going to be to get out of it. As he turned around he spied his friend the rabbit not far away.

'Did you fall down too, Peter?' Neddy asked as he walked towards the rabbit. He expected it to hop away like it had done for most of the afternoon, but this time the animal stayed put. Encouraged, Neddy slowly edged his way closer.

'It's all right, I won't hurt you,' he said quietly. 'I promise.'

The rabbit went to hop but it was clear that one of its legs was hurt and made it impossible for the animal to scurry away.

Neddy scooped the rabbit up in his arms. It struggled for a moment but then settled down.

'I'll look after you. Don't worry, you don't have to be scared,' he cooed as he patted it gently. 'We'll be fine, I promise.' Neddy said the words but maybe they were more for him than the rabbit. The sun was dipping and the shadows were beginning to lengthen. All he wanted was to be home and show Mam his new friend—and hoped that she'd let him keep it. But the night was coming and he wasn't sure which way was home. Staying here by himself was scary but walking around in the bush at night might be even worse.

He patted the rabbit. 'Well, Peter, what should we do?'

Neddy walked over to the trickle of water, there were a few little clumps of long grass. He picked a couple of blades and held them up to the rabbit, which nibbled on the end of one.

Neddy smiled. Even if they stayed here tonight, at least he wasn't alone.

Chapter Twenty-seven

Berry hadn't visited The Queen's Arms in weeks but she felt like a local when she walked in and was greeted by name.

'How's the reno going, Berry?' the owner asked. 'House all sorted yet?'

She gave him a smile. 'Yes, thanks. It's all coming together nicely.'

'That's great. Now, what can I get you?'

'Um, can I just have a lemon squash . . . oh, and a chicken parma?'

'You got it,' he said.

But before he could turn away Berry asked, 'Is Young Ned here tonight?'

'Sure—he's sprawling on his favourite chair. If you want to talk, you probably should do it before he gets through that pint he's cradling.'

'Thanks,' Berry said as she gave him the money. 'I'll just be over there.'

She walked over to the end of the bar and found Young Ned sitting on a stool with his back against the wall.

'Hello, do you remember me? I'm Berry McCalister.'

Young Ned stared at her for a moment but then the recognition sparked in his eyes.

'Of course I do, girly,' he said as he pulled out the vacant bar stool with one hand. 'Sit down. Can I get you a drink?'

'Thanks, but I've already got one coming,' she said as she sat down.

'Good-oh. Now, what can I do for you?' the old man asked.

'Well, actually I was hoping you could tell me the story of your ancestor finding the gold,' Berry said. 'You've told me before but I'd like to hear it again if that's okay?'

Young Ned grinned. 'You got a case of gold fever, do you?'

Berry shook her head. 'No, it's not really that. I found a box of my father's papers. A lot of it was to do with your story.'

He gave her a sympathetic look. 'It was a bad business. I'm sorry that it happened to you. I have to say that your dad was one of the best people I knew. I reckon I could think on what happened for a hundred years and still not be able to work out why Jordy did what he did.' Young Ned took a mouthful of his beer. 'It was right out of character. The man would have done anything for your mum. Never seen a bloke so whipped before.'

Berry took a deep breath. This wasn't what she wanted or needed to hear. Thankfully, the barman arrived with her lemon squash and that stole Young Ned's attention for a second.

He wiggled his half-full glass in front of the barman. 'Can I get another one of these?'

'Only if you promise to eat something. You know what you get like if you drink and don't eat.'

Young Ned gave the barman a scowl before he finally nodded in agreement. 'Oh, all right, might as well if you're going to harp on about it.'

'Nah, I don't harp—I'd just tell your dad next time I see him,' the barman said as he gave Berry a wink.

Berry bit back a smile. The whole thing was ridiculous—the barman was threatening to dob a seventy-odd year old man in to his father.

Young Ned wrinkled his nose. 'Oh, bloody hell—fine, give me a steak sandwich.'

'A good choice,' the barman said with a laugh as he walked away.

'He's always so pushy. I don't know why I bother coming in here every night,' Young Ned said. 'So, you want to know about the gold, do ya?'

Berry smiled. 'Yes, I do.'

Ned looked at her for a second. 'Well, the first thing you'd better know is that most of the people who live here don't believe in it. They think it's just an old story made up by a little kid. Added to that, there's been people snooping around for decades looking for the gold seam but no one has found it yet. And, lastly, you're not the first one from your family to ask me about this stuff.'

Berry's eyes widened. 'What?'

'Your father asked me a whole lot of questions all those years ago. In fact he'd pester me for any little detail that would help him build a better picture. I was never sure what he was doing but after a while I started to think that maybe he was on to something.'

'On to something? You mean like he'd found a clue to where the gold was?' Berry asked excitedly.

'Well, I'm not saying that as a fact—it was just a feeling I got. You see, he already knew the legend, just wanted other details about the family. I told him everything I could, but you have to realise that the story was my great-grandad's to tell, not mine.'

Berry took a sip of her lemon squash as she tried to process the information. 'So, what you're saying is that you're not sure about what happened?'

Ned gave her a smile. 'I know that Little Neddy found the gold, if that's what you're asking. But the story was handed down through the family. Some details were embellished, some were added, and sometimes things are forgotten altogether.'

'Okay, so what makes you think the gold exists?'

Ned held up a finger. 'One, it's the family legend. We know for a fact that Little Ned went missing. It was documented in the local newspapers of the time.'

'Okay, sure, that works,' Berry said.

Ned held out two fingers. 'Two, the family never wavered in their belief in his story. And three,' he said as he held up a third finger, 'there was proof.'

'Proof? Really?' Berry said.

'I say it's proof—others say that it was just a coincidence,' Ned answered. 'Not long after Little Neddy was found, the Doherty farm got a few upgrades.'

'Such as?' Berry asked with a frown.

'Another couple of rooms were added to the house and a big verandah wrapped around the entire thing. My great-great-grandad stopped working as a carpenter and started building up the farm. All of a sudden they purchased another three acres and bought some sheep. But you have to understand just how poor they were before Neddy's disappearance. So my question is, if he didn't bring home some gold, where did the money come from?'

'That's intriguing. Have you looked into where else the money might have originated?'

'I've tried but I couldn't find anything. At first I thought that maybe my great-great-grandad had been working on a big project and got paid in a lump sum, but I haven't found any evidence of that. He had a few jobs around the same time—he fixed a roof, built a new counter for the general store and a cupboard for a local woman—but not enough to buy the extra land,' Ned explained.

'So, you think Little Neddy found some gold and brought it back home with him?' Berry asked.

'Well, I don't see how to explain it otherwise.'

Berry was silent for a moment. 'I think my father might have come to that same conclusion.'

* * *

Berry went over and over what Young Ned had said as she drove back home. She didn't want her imagination to run away with her, but the more she thought about it, the more she began to believe that her father had found a clue about the elusive gold.

It was a dark night with only a sliver of moon hanging in the sky and Berry tried to pay extra attention as she left the bitumen and turned down the dirt road that led home. She was always wary of the kangaroos. Sometimes she'd see them on the side of the road, hopping parallel to the car—the frightening thing was never knowing if they would change direction and jump in front of the car.

Berry slowed a little as she caught sight of a shadowy outline of a roo in the nearby paddock. She kept checking the road ahead and the paddock as she headed towards Stone Gully, when out of nowhere she was blinded by oncoming headlights on high beam. She flicked her own lights on and off high beam to tell the other driver to turn theirs down but they ignored her. She put her foot on the brake and used one hand to try to shield her eyes from the intense white light.

'What the hell,' she said. 'Turn your damn high beam off!'

But the driver didn't, instead they sped up and seemed to head straight for her. Berry tried to pull off the road but the car came at her and purposely swung into her vehicle, causing a sickening thud. Berry's car was cata-pulted off the dirt road and into one of the metal fence posts of the bottom paddock. The impact made her slam her head against the wheel, and it hurt like hell as she tentatively reached up and saw that her fingers were covered in blood. Trying to focus, she looked out the window to see the other car tear off down the road, kicking up a cloud of dust as it went. She screwed her eyes shut for a moment in the hope that it would clear her vision; then, she unbuckled her seatbelt and slowly opened the door. Berry dragged in a couple of quick breaths and brought her eyes back into focus. She reached out a trembling hand to grab her phone.

Berry managed to climb out of the car. She was a little light-headed, but she steadied herself against the open car door and managed to scroll through her phone until she landed on Nate's number. Three rings felt like an eternity.

'Hey, what's up?'

Perhaps it was the relief of hearing his voice, but a lump formed in Berry's throat and she just couldn't seem to get any words out.

'Berry? Honey, is everything all right?' Nate asked quickly.

'I . . . I . . .' Berry stammered.

'Berry? What's happened? You're scaring me.'

'I was run off the road. Can you come?'

'I'm on my way. Where are you?' Nate said. 'Are you hurt?'

'I'm okay, just a bit shaken up. I'm somewhere near the bottom paddock.'

'Okay, hold on—I'll be there in a minute.'

Berry ended the call, stuffed the phone in her pocket and waited. She was sore and shaken but above all having a hard time stopping the tears from flowing. The night was cold, her breath palled in the still air. Maybe it was the shock of the accident but she couldn't stop shivering.

When she saw Nate's headlights in the distance just minutes later, she thought she'd managed to pull herself together, at least a little. He pulled up and clambered out. Before he said a word he took her in his arms and held her tight. It could have been the physical contact or the flash of worry in his eyes, but it was too much for Berry and as soon as she leaned against his chest she started to cry.

He was silent for a minute, just holding her tightly and letting her cry. Then slowly he started rubbing her back. 'Can you tell me what happened? Did you skid on the soft edge of the road?'

Berry shook her head. 'No, there was another car. It ran me off the road.'

He took her by the shoulders and gently eased her away from him, so he could look at her. 'Geez, you're bleeding—you should have said something,' he said.

'It's okay. It hurts but I don't think it's very deep,' Berry assured him as she looked him in the eye. 'But there was another car, it had its lights on high beam and it ran me off the road.'

She hadn't even finished her sentence before Nate took out his phone.

'Who are you calling?' Berry asked.

'The police—you were run off the road and the other car didn't stop.'

When the patrol car arrived twenty minutes later, Berry and Nate were leaning against his ute. Berry had stopped shivering thanks to Nate's presence and the fact that she was wearing his jacket across her shoulders.

Senior Sergeant Rob Mendez walked towards them and raised his hand in greeting. 'Hi Nate, Miss McCalister,' he said.

'Hey Rob,' Nate replied.

'So, are you guys alright? What happened?'

Berry took a breath and nodded. At this point all she wanted to do was go home, have a cup of tea and crawl into bed. 'I was run off the road by another car. They had their headlights on full, they rammed into the side of my car and then took off.'

'I see. And did you manage to recognise the car or anything about it?'

'No, I was blinded by the lights. I flicked my lights on and off a couple of times just in case they had just forgotten to turn them down, but that did nothing.'

'And you'd slowed down?'

'Yes, and I started to pull over to the side of the road. I thought he was just being a jerk who wanted to drive down the middle of the road, but then he hit me and sent me into the fence,' Berry said as she pointed in the general direction of the accident.

The policeman looked towards where Berry pointed and nodded. 'And you're sure that you can't think of anything else about the car?'

Berry closed her eyes for a moment and frowned. Maybe there was something when she saw it drive away. 'I can't be sure but I think it was a dark colour and it wasn't a ute. Sorry I can't be of more help.'

'That's fine, you've had a shake-up. It's always hard to remember details when things like this happen.'

'Listen, Rob, do you mind if I take her home?' Nate asked as he slung his arm around her shoulders. 'I need to check out that cut on her forehead.'

'Sure. Don't worry about the car, I'll get Kev from the garage to come and get it after we've finished collecting evidence. Take care, Miss McCalister and I'll be in touch sometime tomorrow,' he said.

'Thank you,' Berry said with a smile as Nate opened the door of his ute.

Senior Sergeant Rob Mendez handed Nate a business card as Berry climbed in. 'Just in case she remembers something else.'

'Sure thing,' Nate answered as he pocketed the card. 'See ya later.'

Nate got into the ute and flashed a grin at Berry. 'How does a cup of tea sound?'

'Like heaven,' Berry said.

'Good, let's go,' he answered as he turned on the ignition and pulled out onto the dirt track.

They were only a couple of minutes from the house and Berry couldn't wait to get home, but as Nate turned into the driveway she was hit with a sinking feeling. As the ute bumped up towards the house its headlights flickered over the front door.

'What the hell!' Nate cried as he looked at the house.

Berry reached over and grabbed his hand. 'Oh, my God—is that *blood*?' she whispered as her eyes fixed on the large red word scrawled across her newly painted front door.

The word was simple enough but it sent a chill through Berry.

LEAVE.

Chapter Twenty-eight

Senior Sergeant Rob Mendez walked back to where Berry and Nate were standing. 'No, it's paint, not blood, but I get why you thought that when you drove up.'

'Do you think the car that ran me off the road had something to do with this?' Berry asked, thankful that she had Nate's warmth beside her. Things had gone from bad to worse and she was rattled.

'We won't rule anything out. Have you had any altercations with anyone?' Mendez asked.

She shook her head. 'No, everyone has been really welcoming since I arrived in Harlington.'

'Maybe not everyone, honey,' Nate said as he glanced down at her. 'What about what happened yesterday, with Worth?'

'Oh? What happened?' Mendez asked.

'Laurie Worth came around and tried to pressure me into selling Stone Gully Farm to him,' Berry explained. 'I told him the other day that we weren't selling, but clearly he thought he knew better.'

'So, he turned up yesterday to try to convince you?'

'That's right. He got annoyed when I said that it wasn't going to work, and then he implied Nate was trying to "romance" the place out of me.'

The Senior Sergeant looked at Nate. 'I see. I suppose if you bought Stone Gully it would expand Tarantale Downs.'

'What are you getting at?' Nate's eyes narrowed. 'Yeah, it probably would be a bonus if we bought it—only because it would make for a pretty horse trail. It's not like we need more land.' He paused before continuing. 'But for total disclosure I should tell you that Dad said if Berry was stuck, he'd buy the place.'

'I'm just following a line of questioning, that's all. We have to know the details so we can start eliminating some of them,' Mendez said. 'So, why would your dad make Berry an offer if you didn't really need the land?'

'I asked him the same question,' Nate said, relaxing a little and taking Berry's hand in his. 'He said that Jordy McCalister had been his friend and buying Stone Gully Farm seemed a way he could help the family.'

Mendez's eyes widened. 'I hadn't realised they'd been that close. I know he was upset on the night of the . . . well, you know,' he said, looking away from Berry.

'Yeah, I hadn't known that either, but apparently they were friends,' Nate said, turning to Berry. 'Tarantale was going through a bit of a rough time and your dad helped.'

'Really?' Berry said. 'I had no idea.'

'What sort of trouble?' Mendez asked as his dark eyes fixed on Nate.

'Financial, I think, but I'm not a hundred percent sure—I was just a kid. I remember something about an accident and some of the horses got hurt.' Nate rubbed his head as if trying to stir up old memories.

Berry looked at him for a second as a frown flitted across her brow. 'If it was financial trouble, I'm not sure how my father could have helped. From what I can remember, we weren't great in that department.'

'Maybe it was emotional support. My dad is a very private person, but if they were mates maybe he was just able to share his troubles with a friend,' Nate said. 'As it was, my grandmother was able to help us out. She sold up everything and saved Tarantale.'

Berry smiled. 'That's incredible.'

'I know. It was just the type of woman she was. She lived with us for a long time—we only lost her last year. I still miss her,' Nate explained.

'She sounds like she was a wonderful person. But that thing with our fathers, giving each other support is really precious. I don't know why but it kind of makes me happy to think that they were friends,' Berry said before turning to Senior Sergeant Mendez. 'Would it be all right if I go in? I think I need to sit down.'

There was a flash of concern in his eyes. 'I don't think that's a good idea. This is a crime scene, and besides that, I don't think you should be alone tonight.'

'It's all right, Berry can stay with me for a couple of days,' Nate said as he reached down and took her hand.

'Are you sure?' Berry asked. 'I could go to the Cumquat, but it's getting late and I don't want to disturb Andrea.'

'Of course it's okay. Besides, I'll feel better knowing you're safe.'

Berry looked up at him and, despite the shock and drama of the evening, smiled.

* * *

Nate and Berry drove in silence all the way to Tarantale Downs. Nate spent most of that time trying to get his emotions in check. He figured that the last thing Berry needed tonight was him ranting. Instead, he played out a whole lot of scenarios in his head about what he would do to whoever was responsible for this. He was fairly sure that it was that oily Laurie Worth who was behind this, but he wanted to be sure before he slammed the bastard up against a wall. As they turned into the driveway of Tarantale he glanced over at Berry. She was staring out the window as if in a trance—she seemed a million miles away.

'Hey, how are you holding up?' he asked.

She turned to look at him. 'I'm okay, really. Are you sure this is all right—I mean, about staying here?'

'Of course it is—why wouldn't it be? My place isn't as grand as the main house but I like it better,' he said as he pointed to the elegant lines of a two-storey house, which loomed in front of them.

They drove for another minute or two, past new stables and a riding arena. Nate veered the car away from the main drive and turned down a small track. Ahead a large peppercorn tree gently swayed in the night breeze and behind it stood an old brick building. It was two storeys but not particularly big. An outside staircase ran up the side of the building to a glossy black painted door. On the ground floor, two separate horse stalls were still evident.

'It's amazing,' Berry said as she looked up at it.

'Yeah, I love it—it's got so much character,' Nate replied. 'Come on, I'll show you around.'

He led her up the staircase to the small landing at the top, then opened the door and stood aside as Berry walked in.

'Basically, it's a one bedroom, but I pretend it has two because there's a small room over there that I use as an office,' Nate said, pointing to a door off to the right. 'Other than that, there's the bedroom, bathroom, and this is the kitchen/living space.'

'It's gorgeous, I love all the exposed brick walls,' Berry said.

'Take a seat,' he said as he gestured to the dark grey couch. 'I'll make you a drink and then organise where you're sleeping.'

'Please don't go to any trouble. I could just stay here,' she said as she sank into the couch. 'It's really comfortable.'

'No, you take my bed and I'll crash on the couch.' He held up his hand as she opened her mouth in protest.

'I insist. You've had a shock and an awful night—just take the bed.'

She gave him a smile and nodded her head. 'All right. Thank you.'

'Not a problem,' he said as he walked into the small kitchenette to switch on the kettle.

***

Nate left her sipping her tea as he headed into the bedroom and did a quick tidy up and changed the sheets. It didn't take him long, but by the time he got back to the lounge room, Berry had fallen asleep. Nate sighed and took a moment to watch her. Her quiet breathing seemed to accentuate the soft lines of her face, and he felt a warmth inside, and a basic desire to protect her, and hold her close. He closed his eyes for a moment to clear his head before lifting her up and taking her into the bedroom. He placed her on the bed and marvelled at the fact that she didn't even stir.

He removed her shoes and covered her with the thick doona, taking another second to brush a strand of hair from her face before leaving her.

***

Berry woke with a start as the sound of the front door banging open resounded through the entire place. For a moment she was confused, unable to remember where she was. But almost instantly the events of the previous evening flooded back. Sitting up, she looked around the room and realised that she was in Nate's bed—the problem was that she couldn't remember how she got there.

She smiled as she stretched her arms above her head. He had been there for her when she needed him the most and there was something very comforting in that. However, her warm and fuzzy feeling evaporated as she heard angry voices waft into the bedroom.

'Where the hell have you been? We're going to be late if we don't leave in the next twenty minutes.'

'Dad, can you keep it down! I messaged you and told you I'd be a bit late. Not that it should matter— everything's ready for when Constantine arrives.' Nate's voice was lower than she had heard it, as if he were trying to placate his father.

Berry threw off the covers and sat on the edge of the bed in confusion.

'I know the stable's ready for him—I double-checked it last night,' his father snapped. 'We're meant to be on the road already if we're going to get to Heritage Stud by midday and pick him up.'

'Look, can you take Justin or one of the other stable hands with you instead? There was a bit of trouble last night and I think I should stay here,' Nate said.

'What sort of trouble?'

'I did send you a message explaining everything, but I guess you didn't read it,' Nate said, and Berry could hear the thinly veiled frustration in his voice.

'No, I didn't.'

'Berry was run off the road last night,' Nate said.

'What?' his father snapped. 'Why am I only hearing about this now?'

'Well, if you'd read your messages . . .' Nate started and then stopped. 'She was run off the road and called me to come and get her. It wasn't an accident.'

'Are you serious?'

'Unfortunately, yes, I am,' Nate answered. 'Some jerk purposely ran into her car. Thankfully, except for a cut on her forehead, she's okay. I thought that was enough, but when I drove her back to Stone Gully, someone had painted a warning over her front door in red paint.'

'A warning?'

'They wrote *Leave*. It looked like blood.'

Berry listened—though she didn't really have a choice as both Nate and his father's voices carried.

'God, who would do such a thing?'

'I don't know for sure, but probably someone who wants her to sell up and leave Harlington,' Nate said.

'You've got someone in mind?'

'The police will have to look into it but, yeah, I have my suspicions.'

'Like who?'

'Anyone who offered to buy the place and was annoyed when she turned them down—the top of the list has to be Laurie Worth.'

'Why him?'

'Because I was with Berry the other day when he turned up at Stone Gully. Let's just say he was doing his best to talk her into reconsidering his offer and then got shitty about me being there. So much so that he even accused me of trying to get the place myself,' Nate said.

'That guy has always been an arsehole.'

'That's what I thought,' Nate agreed.

Berry opened the door and walked out of Nate's bedroom just in time to catch Sam Tarant glare at his son.

'Chill, Dad—I took the couch,' Nate said quietly.

'Good morning, Mr Tarant,' Berry said with a smile. 'I'm really grateful that Nate let me crash here last night. As you can imagine I was a bit rattled.'

Sam gave her a smile. 'Of course. I'm so sorry about what happened. You must have been scared.'

'I was when the car ran me off the road, and the graffiti was, let's just say, unnerving.'

'And do you think you know who did it?' Sam asked.

'No, I don't. A lot of people offered to buy Stone Gully. Which means there are a lot of people annoyed that we're not going to sell it. Mr Worth was the most vocal about it, but that doesn't necessary mean he did it,' Berry said.

'We told the police about him,' Nate said as he glanced at Berry and managed a smile. 'They'll be in touch when they know more.'

'Well, I guess it will be a while until you can go home,' Sam Tarant said. 'Feel free to stay here as long as you want. In fact, it's probably a better idea that you do—at least that way we know you'll be safe.'

'Oh, Mr Tarant, I couldn't.'

'Of course you could. Stay, at least until the police catch the culprit.'

'Thanks, Dad,' Nate said. 'I think that's a wise idea.'

Sam nodded. 'You don't want to take any risks. I'm sure that everything will be wrapped up pretty quick—it's not as if Harlington's the crime capital of Victoria. You can stay here if you want, or if you'd rather, there's plenty of room in the house.'

'Thank you, Mr Tarant, I really appreciate it,' Berry said.

'It's fine,' he answered, waving his hand as if to brush off her thanks. 'Now, I've got to get going—I've got a horse to pick up. You stay here, Nate. Berry might need you. I'll take Justin with me or go by myself.'

Nate looked at his father for a moment. 'Are you sure?'

'Of course,' Sam said as he started to turn away. 'I'll see you both when I get back.'

'Bye Dad,' Nate said but his father was already walking out the front door. He sighed and then turned back to Berry. 'Well, it looks as if that's all sorted. Are you okay here or would you prefer to go into the house?'

Berry gave him a smile. 'I think I like it here—if that's okay with you?'

He took her by the hand and looked into her eyes. 'More than okay.'

Chapter Twenty-nine

Berry and Nate were sitting together having a coffee when Senior Sergeant Mendez knocked at the front door.

'Oh, hey,' Nate said as he took a step back and swung the door wide open. 'I didn't expect to see you so soon.'

The sergeant nodded as he walked in. 'I was going to come earlier but things got a little crazy. How are you, Miss McCalister?'

Berry smiled as she looked up from the couch. 'I'm fine, thanks. And please call me Berry.'

'Right, Berry it is,' he said. 'I just thought I'd let you know that we've been looking into the events of last night.'

'And?' Nate asked.

'And . . . there have been a few developments. The main one being that Laurie Worth has taken off. According to his girlfriend, he packed a bag in the wee hours and told her he had an emergency meeting.'

'He has a girlfriend?' Nate said probably a little louder than he intended.

'Apparently so,' Mendez said with a smirk. 'Anyway, of course nothing has been proved yet, but it's interesting that he's done a runner. I just wanted to suggest that maybe it would be better if Berry wasn't alone at Stone Gully.'

'You don't think he'd try something else, do you?' Nate said with a frown.

Rob shrugged. 'I don't know. But the thing is, Worth has a reputation around here, and we can think of any number of reasons he'd fly the coop, so to speak. I just think that it would be unwise to presume that everything's okay now that he's gone. He's not the only bad element around.'

'What do you mean, Rob?' said Nate. 'This is Harlington. We don't have that kind of problem here.'

'Really?' the policeman answered. 'I think that Berry might disagree with you. Now—'

'Look,' Berry interrupted, 'I'm freaked out enough about this. Let's not start talking about multiple suspects, okay? I'm fine, and I'll just stay here with Nate for a while till things are sorted out.'

'Of course', said Mendez, 'I didn't mean to alarm you. It probably is that Worth character. But I would feel better if you had people around you, okay?'

'Yeah, so would I,' Nate said.

* * *

After Senior Sergeant Mendez left, Nate took Berry's hand in his and gave it a squeeze.

'Are you okay?'

She nodded. 'Yeah, I'm fine. I have to admit, instead of being frightened, the more I think about it, the angrier I get.'

His fingers laced between hers. 'Anger's good—it's better than fear.'

'You know, Nate, we've assumed all this has to do with Laurie Worth. And, yes, it doesn't look good that he's run off somewhere, but it might not be him.'

Nate thought about this for a second. 'You're right. But he does fit the bill. Besides, who runs away in the middle of the night? And what's all that business about having an emergency meeting? The guy does real estate in a small country town—just how many midnight emergency meetings can there be?'

'Yeah, it does sound dodgy,' Berry agreed. 'But even more surprising is the fact that he has a girlfriend. The guy makes my skin crawl. He's phoney and I wouldn't trust him if he was the last man in town. But we may have to acknowledge the possibility that he had nothing to do with it.'

Nate rolled his wide shoulders. 'I guess that could be true—though unlikely.'

'We're just assuming that it has to do with Stone Gully Farm,' Berry argued. 'But what if it wasn't about selling the house? It could be about some other random thing that's not related to it at all. I'm not saying that's the reason—all I'm saying is that it's possible.'

'In other words, we need to stop jumping to conclusions,' Nate said.

'Exactly. I'm sure we'll find who is responsible.'

'Well, it can't come soon enough.'

* * *

The last thing Berry wanted to do was alarm her family, but she figured they had a right to know what was going on. As Nate rustled up something to eat, Berry slipped outside and rang them. The conversation with her uncle didn't go very well, and the one with her sister even worse. As far as both of them were concerned she should hightail herself back to the city straightaway. She did point out that her car was banged up and then wished she hadn't mentioned it as Jess and Uncle Dave both vowed to jump in the nearest vehicle and come to get her. Eventually, with a whole lot of reassurance and fast talking, she managed to get them to dial it down.

'Are you sure you don't want me to come up and get you?' Uncle Dave asked for what seemed like the hundredth time.

'No, I'm fine. The police have got everything under control and I'm happy to stay here with Nate. So, please don't worry,' Berry said.

'Hmm, well, I'm not happy about this. I want you to promise to call me if anything happens—even if it seems small or silly,' Uncle Dave said.

'Okay, I will. You don't have to worry—I can take care of myself. Besides, I've got Nate and Andrea keeping an eye on me.'

'I still didn't hear a promise,' Uncle Dave said.

Berry laughed. 'All right, all right—I promise. There, are you satisfied now?'

'No, but I guess it will have to do. Keep me updated and, no, I don't care if you call me at three a.m. Just be careful.'

'I will. I'll talk to you soon,' Berry said.

'You'd better,' Uncle Dave warned before he added, 'I love you.'

'Love you too.'

Just as she was popping her phone back into her jeans pocket she saw Nate's sisters hurrying towards her. Both were carrying bags and had grins on their faces.

'Hey Berry!' they called out in unison.

Berry held up her hand, waved and waited for them.

'Dad said that you were staying here,' Em said. 'So Mum sent over some things.'

'Yeah,' Lia chimed in. 'She says about the only thing Nate has in the house is usually cereal or cold pizza.'

'Is that right?' Berry laughed.

'Yep. Anyway, Mum raided the fridge and pantry, so, here you go.'

'Oh, that was really kind of her,' Berry replied.

'She also said, if there's anything else you need just come on over,' Em added as climbed the stairs with the bag of food. Lia and Berry followed but as they almost reached the small landing the front door opened.

'Are my two pesky sisters annoying you?' Nate said with a smile as he stood by the door.

'Aw, shut up, Nate,' Em said as she passed him.

'No, not at all,' Berry assured him.

Nate glanced at his watch. 'Why aren't the two of you in school?'

'Curriculum day,' the girls said once again in unison.

'Dad said before he left that some idiot ran you off the road. You must have been really scared,' Lia said as she glanced over at Berry.

'Um, I guess I was but to be honest it happened so quickly. I think it didn't really sink in until afterwards and I was waiting for Nate to come and rescue me.'

Em gave Nate a nudge. 'Rescued, huh?'

He curled his lip and scowled but only got a grin back in reply. Berry thought it was kind of sweet that they had a teasing bond between them. From what she'd seen, Nate might call his sisters silly or annoying, but it was obvious that he doted on them.

'So, are you going to be staying here from now on?' Lia asked.

'Maybe just for another night. It depends when I can get back into the house,' Berry said.

'Did something happen to it?' Em asked.

Before she could answer Nate stepped in. 'Some idiot scrawled graffiti over Berry's front door—you know the one we just painted.'

'Really? I wonder who would do that,' Em said with surprise. 'You don't suppose it was just some sort of prank, do you?'

Berry shrugged. 'It could be. The police are looking into it, so we'll find out soon enough.'

'That's awful. You've worked really hard to get the house all fixed up,' Lia added.

'Yeah, I have to admit I'm quite cross about it,' Berry said with half a smile. 'Maybe when they catch the person I'll be allowed to paint him.'

Both Lia and Em giggled.

'I'd like to see that,' Nate said.

'So, what are you doing for the rest of the day?' Em asked as she started unpacking the bag, taking out numerous plastic containers and stacking them in neat piles on the bench.

'I don't know, other than I promised to drop in at Andrea's later this afternoon,' Berry answered.

'I'll drive you over there, if you like. Oh, and we have to check in with the garage about your car,' Nate said.

'Thanks,' Berry answered as their eyes met and lingered for a moment too long. This wasn't lost on the girls, who both giggled.

Nate rolled his eyes and said, 'So, have you met my silly sisters?'

Lia chose to ignore him. 'I was just asking because maybe we could go for a ride?'

Nate glanced at Berry. 'I don't know. You did agree to me giving you riding lessons, and today is as good as any other to start. Would you like to?'

Berry looked at Lia and Em, who were staring at her with expectation in their eyes. It was too hard to say no.

'You know what? You're right . . . today is a perfect day to start, although I hope you have a really gentle horse for me.'

The girls looked at looked at each other. 'Maggie! You can ride Maggie,' they chimed.

'Yeah, she's a good choice,' Nate said before turning and giving her a wink. 'Don't worry, she's really sweet and I promise I won't leave your side, okay?'

Although maybe not quite convinced, Berry nodded. 'Okay.'

* * *

Later Lia led Berry by the hand to the riding yard where Nate was bringing out a dappled grey mare.

'Maggie is Mum's horse. She rescued her when she was a couple of years old. They're devoted to each other and she's the sweetest horse,' Lia said.

'And your mum doesn't mind me borrowing her?'

Lia shook her head. 'Not at all,' she said as she opened the gate and walked into the training area. 'Come on, it'll be fun.'

Berry felt a little apprehensive but she took a deep breath and followed Lia over to Nate.

'Hey,' Nate said quietly as he glanced her way. 'This is Maggie, give her a pat.'

'She's beautiful,' Berry said as she slowly reached out her hand and stroked the side of Maggie's neck.

'She is,' Nate answered, staring at Berry for a little too long. 'We'll get you up and I'll take you around the arena

240

a couple of times. Then, and only if you're comfortable, we'll go for a short ride up the track by the far paddock. Are you ready?'

'I think so,' Berry replied.

'Good, let's give it a go, then,' Nate said as he handed her a riding helmet. 'Here, you'd better put this on—you know, better safe than dead.'

Berry took the helmet and put it on, fastening the strap beneath her chin. 'That's not exactly comforting, you know.'

Nate chuckled. 'You'll be right. Maggie is the gentlest mare we have. Come over here to the left side and step up on the mounting block. Okay, good. Now hold onto the pommel of the saddle with your left hand along with the reins and place your left foot into the stirrup. Don't worry, I've got Maggie and she's not going anywhere. Right, now swing your right leg over the saddle and sit down.'

Berry followed his instructions and swung into the saddle. She gave him a smile, pleased that she hadn't managed to fall off.

'Excellent. Okay now we're just going to go forwards,' Nate said as he walked beside Maggie holding onto her bridle. 'You're good?'

'Yep,' Berry said.

They did a circuit of the arena, and just as they were beginning another, the girls led their horses down from the stable.

'How's it going?' Lia called out as Nate and Berry neared.

Berry gave her a thumbs up. 'Good.'

'Nate, we're going up the track and taking the trail past the dam. You don't mind, do you?'

Nate brought Maggie to a halt. 'Why would I mind?'

'It's just that we said we should all go together but . . .' Em let her sentence trail off.

'You shouldn't worry about me. I don't think I'm up to going for a long ride,' Berry confessed. 'What are your horses' names? They're very beautiful.'

The girls beamed.

'This is Jinx,' Lia said as she glanced at her brindle-marked chestnut mare. 'She's my best friend—other than Em, that is.'

'And this is Stormy,' Em added as she gestured to her dark grey mare. 'She can be a bit of a handful but she's lovely.'

'Well, they're both gorgeous,' Berry said.

'Go on, off you go and have a good time,' Nate said and then added, 'And don't get into trouble.'

'Geez, what sort of trouble can we get in going for a ride at home?' Lia said with a good pinch of salt.

He shrugged. 'I don't know but the two of you always seem to find trouble, or it finds you—wouldn't you say, Justin?' he called out as Justin wandered out of the main stable.

Em whirled around. 'Nate, shut up,' she said in a harsh whisper, but Nate just grinned.

'I thought you might have gone with Dad to pick up the horse?'

'I offered but he said he'd be okay,' Justin replied. 'He said he was in a hurry.'

'Hmm, I guess he just decided to go by himself,' Nate said. It didn't really surprise him, his dad tended to prefer his own company. 'He'd probably be on his way back by now.'

'Anyway, we're taking off,' Lia said. 'We'll see you later.'

Berry gave the girls a quick wave before they walked their horses away from the fence and towards a mounting box that stood by the hitching rail nearby.

Justin watched them go before turning back to Nate. 'Did you want me to saddle Ronin for you?' he asked.

'Do you want to go for a longer ride?' Nate asked as he looked up at Berry. 'Or are you happy just staying here?'

'Actually, I think I'd rather stay here. Maybe another day?' Berry said.

'Sure, whatever you want,' Nate replied before he turned back to Justin. 'Thanks, but I'll take Ronin for a run in the morning.'

'No worries,' Justin said with a smile. 'I'll leave you to it then.'

'He seems nice,' Berry said as they watched him walk away.

'Well, my sisters certainly think so,' Nate said as he glanced up at Berry. 'No, he's good. I just think the girls have a thing for him.'

'Is that such a bad thing? Most girls have crushes—I know I did.'

Nate had started walking Maggie again but her comment made him pause. 'Oh, really? On who?'

'That's a secret,' Berry said with a broadening smile. 'And don't look at me that way, because I'm not going to tell you.'

Nate was silent for a moment. 'Well, what did you think of me back then?'

'You? I . . . I was just a kid, and you would never have even looked at me.'

'So . . . was I your crush?'

Berry turned red and looked away. 'Nate, I said I wasn't going to tell you.'

Nate grinned. 'So I was!'

She looked at him with her eyebrows raised. 'Are you gloating?'

'Absolutely!' Nate started walking the horse again. After a short silence he said 'So, are you willing to give this a go on your own?'

'Yes, yes I think I am,' Berry said as Nate let go of Maggie's bridle and Berry took control of the reins.

Chapter Thirty

It was mid afternoon when Berry saw a large car pulling a horse float drive slowly towards the stables.

'Looks like Dad's back with Constantine,' Nate said.

'Constantine?'

'Yep. He's a roan stallion with great bloodlines and the latest addition to our stud stable.'

His father slowed down to a stop alongside Nate and Berry.

'Hey Dad, how'd it go?'

'Good,' Sam replied, his arm resting on the open window. 'I was surprised the traffic around the city was pretty light—well, light for Melbourne. Anyway, it was a good run and I was down the peninsula before I knew it. Everything all right here?'

'Yeah. I'm about to take Berry to see Andrea,' Nate said.

Sam glanced at Berry. 'Any word from the police?'

Berry shook her head. 'Not really but the garage has been in touch and my car will be ready in a couple of days, so I guess that's good news.'

'Well, that's something. I thought it could have been out of action longer,' he said with a smile before turning his attention back to Nate. 'Are the girls around?'

'They went for a ride around the trail. I don't reckon they'll be back for at least another hour. Did you need a hand settling Constantine in?'

'No, I'll be right. If I need help I'll get Justin. You should take Berry to Andrea's,' Sam said as he glanced over towards the stables and saw Justin. 'I'll see you later.'

'Come on,' Nate said as Sam drove off. 'I'll take you to Andrea's.'

***

'Oh, my gosh, Berry, you should have called me,' Andrea said as she gave her a tight hug. 'I can't believe this happened.'

'It's okay—it was late and I didn't want to disturb you,' she answered, finding it a little difficult to breathe.

'Silly girl, you can ring me whenever, especially when it's an emergency,' Andrea said as she finally relinquished her death hold. 'Come on in and I'll put the kettle on.'

Berry smiled as she and Nate followed Andrea down the hall and settled onto a couple of the high stools at the kitchen bench as Andrea bustled around the kitchen.

'So, they don't know who was responsible?' she asked as she filled the kettle.

'Not yet,' Berry replied.

Andrea stilled for a moment before turning around. 'Wait. The person that ran you off the road—are they responsible for the vandalism as well?'

Berry glanced at Nate. 'We're not sure but it kind of feels that way.'

She sighed. 'I can't believe that something like this could happen in Harlington. It's always so peaceful and everyone gets on fine.'

Nate leaned his elbows on the bench. 'I guess mostly that's true, but do we really know our neighbours?'

Andrea grabbed three mugs and set about making coffee. 'You're right, of course. I suppose that after living in the city for most of my life, I tend to think that Harlington is idyllic. Well, I've always been a bit prone to looking at life through rose-tinted glasses,' she said with a smile.

'That's not a bad thing,' he reassured her. 'Besides, Harlington is a great place to live. But every place has its secrets. I mean—' Nate's phone rang and he didn't get to finish his sentence.

Berry saw a frown form on his brow.

'Sorry, I have to take this,' he said as he stood up and walked away. 'Lia . . . slow down. What! Where the hell are you?'

Berry swivelled around on the stool and stared at Nate, her eyes rounding in surprise.

'Is Em still with you? Okay, okay, calm down and get the hell out of there. No, I'll call them now, don't hang around. No, Lia, listen to me—just go!'

The hairs on Berry's arm began to quiver.

'What's happened?' she asked as she stood up and faced him.

'There's a fire. Just hang on, I'm calling emergency,' Nate said as he punched in 000 and headed back into the hallway.

Berry's eyes widened as she heard him tell the operator Stone Gully. She glanced at Andrea and saw a shocked look on her face.

'Oh my God, the girls were riding.'

'What?' Andrea asked. 'I don't understand.'

'The trail the girls were on bumps up against the Stone Gully fenceline. They must be close to my place—which means they're close to the fire,' Berry said as she started after Nate.

'Berry, be careful.'

'I will. I'll call you as soon as I find out what's going on,' she called back over her shoulder.

She almost bumped into Nate as he was shoving his phone in his pocket.

'Are the girls okay?' she asked as she caught hold of his arm.

'Yes, I told them to ride back home as fast as they could. We'd better get going. The fire brigade will be coming as soon as possible, but maybe we can do something in the meantime. If it's too dangerous we'll go back to my place and take it from there,' Nate said as they started walking towards the door.

'Nate, is it the house?'

He looked down at her. 'Oh, sorry, I should have said.

No, it's not. The fire's in the top paddock. From what Lia said it sounds like it's near where we fixed the fence.'

Relief overtook her at the knowledge that the house—her house—was still standing.

***

We're lucky.

At least that's what Berry thought as she and Nate watched the firies put out the blaze. All the way to Stone Gully, Berry couldn't help but let her mind jump to the worst-case scenario—total destruction. But that hadn't been the case at all.

Lia had rung Nate as soon as she and Em had made it home. According to her, they had been riding the horse trail and noticed the smoke in the air, which they presumed was just someone burning off until they reached the boundary fence and heard the crackle of fire as it began to eat up the eucalypts in the bush on the other side of the fence. The air was full of acrid smoke but the fire was obviously burning further into the block. After Nate called emergency services, it wasn't long before the first fire engine turned up, followed closely by a second.

Berry watched and could only marvel at the firefighters' dedication and professionalism. The afternoon waned and soon the light began to fade as the smoke rose high in the sky and obscured it.

The atmosphere changed as twilight approached. Before, Berry had been aware of the feeling of urgency as firefighters fought the flames and tried to contain the blaze, but now there was calm. Nate was standing by one of the fire engines and chatting to a couple of the firefighters. After a while, he shook each of their hands before turning away and striding over to Berry.

'Any news?' she asked as he approached.

'Yeah, some. The fire's almost out—they're just wetting down the area and stomping out any spot fires. But they reckon it's done and dusted.'

'Well, that's a relief,' Berry said. 'Anything else?'

'Hmm, there is,' he said as he put his arm around her. 'The fire took out a couple of acres and the old sheep pen. Thank God it's barely spring. We're lucky, because there was more than a decent amount of rain last winter and things haven't warmed up yet.'

'We just have to be thankful that it wasn't too bad. No one was hurt, and I figure if there were any animals about there's a chance that they got away. And as for the sheep shed, it was dilapidated anyway,' Berry said as she leaned her head against his shoulder.

'That's true, but you should know—' he hesitated '—they think it was deliberately lit.'

'What! You're joking!'

He shook his head. 'I wish I was.'

'So, was it connected with what happened yesterday or just some idiot firebug? Either way you look at it, it's bad,' Berry said.

'I swear, people who light fires on purpose need to be chucked in jail and the bloody key thrown away,' Nate said.

A chill slid down Berry's spine. Did someone want her out of Harlington that badly? And if they did—why? Why would Stone Gully Farm be so important to someone that they'd be willing to do anything to get it? This was the question that kept spinning in her head all the way back to Nate's place. There had to be a reason and she was determined to find out.

Nate parked outside his place, got out and walked around to the passenger's side. He held out his hand as Berry stepped out.

'It's been a hellish couple of days,' he said as his fingers interlaced with hers. 'How are you holding up?'

Berry tried to smile as they walked side by side towards the steps. 'To be honest, I'm a bit shaken up. I still can't work out why this is happening,' she said. 'It all seems so . . . oh, I don't know, over the top. These events have to be connected but it still doesn't make any sense.'

'Yeah, I know. Why would someone go to all this trouble to run you off?'

'Stone Gully must be important, but why?' Berry said as she waited for Nate to unlock the door.

'Okay, let's try and think about this logically—why would it be important?' Nate answered as he led her inside. 'Is it worth a lot of money?'

'Doubtful. I love it, but let's be real, it's a farmlet in a tiny town—hardly prime real estate,' Berry answered. 'Unless Harlington is about to be the next big thing for tree changers and there're plans to enlarge the whole place with new supermarkets, housing and schools, I can't see the attraction.'

Nate smiled. 'I doubt it. Secrets around here have a way of getting out, although I have to admit having a supermarket would be nice. There could be some local planning shenanigans, but Stone Gully Farm is located out of town, so I can't see how that would even work.'

'Hmm, I know, right? It's not as if we're a sprawling metropolis. So, what's another reason?'

They stared at each other as they tried to come up with an answer.

'Enlarging your property,' Nate said with a shrug. 'However, that would point the finger at me as Tarantale is your only neighbour.'

Berry tilted her head to one side, put her hands on her hips and asked with a grin. 'Nate, did you burn down my sheep shed?'

He chuckled as he pulled her into a hug. 'No, I didn't.'

Berry placed her head against his chest and let out a sigh. His navy jumper was soft and she could detect the faint smell of smoke mixed with his familiar aftershave. She was content in his arms and she closed her eyes for an instant. As she did pictures of her father's research tumbled through her mind and she opened her eyes wide.

'Then the only other explanation is that someone is hunting Harlington's gold and they think it's at my place.'

Nate let go of her and took a step back so he could see her face. 'What? That's just a stupid old legend. That's crazy—there's no such thing as lost gold.'

She looked at him for a moment before she spoke. 'Isn't there?'

Chapter Thirty-one

In the Gully, 1906

It was getting dark and Neddy was scared. The only thing that gave him comfort and stopped him from crying was the rabbit curled up asleep under his shirt. It was soft and warm and made Neddy think that maybe everything was going to be all right.

The wind had picked up and began whistling through the gully. He wanted his mam but she didn't know where he was—and neither did he. A single tear worked its way from his eye and down his cheek until Neddy swiped it away with the back of his hand. Crying wouldn't help, he needed to think and work out how he and Peter were going to find their way home.

He wasn't hungry because he'd stripped several handfuls of fat blackberries off the tangle of bushes on the other side of the gully by the clump of gum trees. And even though he was worried that the rabbit had hurt his leg, Peter seemed to be fine as he happily accepted the blades of grass that Neddy had collected for him.

Trying to get back home now would be a mistake because he wouldn't be able to see where he was going and would probably end up even more lost. No, he was going to wait until the sun came up. Neddy looked around the gully in the hope of finding somewhere to rest. He didn't want to be out in the open—at least he'd feel safer if there was somewhere he could hide until morning.

Neddy wrapped his arms around the sleeping bunny as he stood up and walked across the trickling creek to the big rocks that jutted out from the gully wall. They were tall, grey and filled with crevices. At first he thought they were attached to the wall, but as he walked around the circumference of the nearest boulder he realised that there was a gap between it and the wall—a gap big enough for Neddy to squeeze through. Behind the rock was a narrow opening in the gully wall and Neddy wondered if it led to a hidden cave. He wanted to go in and explore, but it was almost dark and it looked a bit scary. So, he settled down with his back against the boulder and tried to sleep.

At first the sounds of the bush kept him awake, with wind rustling the leaves and bushes as it passed. In the distance an owl hooted, and somewhere nearby Neddy could hear the strange guttural argument between two territorial possums. It should have frightened him but he knew the sound that possums make because one lived in the peppercorn tree by the sleep-out he shared with his brothers. It often bumped across the corrugated tin roof making a terrible racket and producing the strangest grunting, hissing sounds.

The night air was cool, but Neddy was warm with the rabbit cuddled against him, and slowly his eyes began to droop and he fell asleep.

He woke with a start and for a few moments lay in confusion as he tried to remember how he'd managed to get here. His next thought was for Peter, who was no longer curled up next to him.

Neddy scanned the area, afraid that the rabbit might have run off, but he found him nearby munching on the leftover pile of grass from last night. Behind him, the large rock was still in shadows except for one shaft of morning sun that shone through the gap between it and the gully wall. The light beam ran across the rocky ground and permeated the darkness of what Neddy thought was a cave. As he looked at the ground scattered with white quartz pebbles that glowed in the sunlight, a glint caught in his peripheral vision. Neddy turned his head and saw a golden gleam coming from one of the quartz pebbles.

Standing up slowly, so as not to startle Peter, he went and picked up the rock to get a better look. The stone was about the size of his palm and there were little bumps, veins and speckles of gold throughout it.

'Look, Peter, at this pretty rock,' he said as he held it in the shaft of light. But the rabbit appeared more interested in finishing off the grass.

Neddy put the stone in his pocket and looked at the ground to see if there were any more. To his delight he found a small stone with the same golden inclusion, and then another. He added them to his pocket and smiled.

He was sure his mam would think them just as nice as he did.

The light shaft shone into the entrance of the cave. It illuminated just a fragment of the bottom of the wall. Neddy peered inside, still unsure—there could be anything in there, from a dingo to a dragon or maybe even a monster. But, even so, curiosity won out and he took a few tentative steps into the shadows. His eyes widened in surprise as he saw that the light beam had landed on a thick seam of gold trapped within the rockface.

Chapter Thirty-two

'What makes you even say a thing like that?' Nate asked as he stared down at her. 'That's a big assumption to make and it's coming out of left field.'

Berry shook her head. 'No, I don't think it is. When I cleaned out the sheds, I found a whole lot of my father's papers. He had stacks of notes and research all about Harlington's gold and the story about Little Neddy Doherty finding it.'

'Like I've told you before—it's just a stupid old legend. Sure, we get a handful of crazies every year who hear about it and come to dig around. But they're not going to find anything, because it doesn't exist.'

'Young Ned believes it does,' Berry countered.

'He's an old man who wants nothing more than to prove the story is true.'

'And why is that?'

'Because it legitimises his family. The Dohertys have always been at the centre of this tale. He just wants to prove that his family was right and telling the truth all this time. I get it, because he and the story are generally regarded as a bit of a joke. They both bring a bit of character to the town.'

'I don't believe Young Ned is a joke,' Berry said quickly. 'I believe him.'

He placed his hands on her shoulders. 'I don't mean I don't like him, I do. It's just we've all grown up with the tale and heard it so many times. Ned recounts it to anyone who'll listen.'

'That may be, but it doesn't mean it's not real. I believe that most stories and legends have a tiny grain of truth in them,' Berry said. 'Besides, I think he has some proof.'

Nate raised his eyebrows in surprise. 'Proof? What do you mean?'

'Well, I've been over my father's research and apparently the Dohertys were pretty poor around the time the little boy went missing. Even though they had a small holding outside of town, their father worked as a carpenter rather than running their own farm,' Berry explained.

'Okay, but I don't see—'

Berry cut him off. 'But after Little Ned was found, things changed and the family's fortune was turned around. I'm not saying that they were uber rich, but something happened because they bought extra land and Mr Doherty started working it.'

'That's not proof they found gold,' Nate responded.

'I know but it's definitely something to think about. I talked to Young Ned the other night, and he said that my father had spoken to him numerous times about the legend and the Dohertys in general. He was keen to find out anything he could.'

'So, what are you saying exactly?'

'What if Dad had worked out the mystery—what if he knew where the gold was?'

Nate took a deep breath and then slowly blew it out. 'That's kind of a long shot, don't you think? Besides, if he'd found the gold—and let's just say that it was even on Stone Gully—why would he have done what he did? If a man hits that kind of jackpot, what reason would he have to go crazy?'

Berry stared at him for a moment. 'I don't know, but I'm going to find out.'

***

Nate finished his coffee with a satisfied sigh. 'That was great.'

'Yep!' answered Berry enthusiastically. 'I've gotta say, I'm enjoying the meals here. You may never get rid of me!'

'Okay with me,' he replied with a smile.

Berry was just about to expand on that thought when her phone rang.

'Hi Berry, it's Senior Sergeant Rob Mendez here. I just wanted to let you know that we've found Laurie Worth.'

'Oh, that's great. Did he say why he left town in such a hurry?'

'Yes, but let's just say the details keep changing. It's not looking good,' Mendez replied.

'So, you think it was him?'

'Well, it's looking likely, although he denies everything.'

'How did you find him?' Berry asked.

'He got spooked when he saw a patrol car. He ran a red light on the other side of Bendigo,' he explained with a slight laugh. 'Anyway, I just thought you'd like to know.'

Nate looked at her from across the table as she ended the call. 'And?'

'They've found Worth. Apparently he ran a red light in Bendigo,' Berry answered.

'Well, that's a relief,' Nate said. 'I know it hasn't been proven it was him, but everything is kind of pointing that way.'

'I'm just thankful he was caught before he could do any more damage. And I do really want to know why he did it in the first place.'

'Are you still running with your gold theory?' Nate asked.

She nodded. 'I'm not saying that my father definitely figured out where the gold was, but maybe Worth thought he did.'

'But why now?'

'I don't know, but something must have triggered him. Maybe he stumbled across some new information, or Young Ned told him about my dad going to see him?'

'It could just be that he had a dodgy plan to build something on Stone Gully,' Nate offered.

'Maybe, but either way I'm heading back home in the morning to start going over Dad's papers again. I just wish you'd at least think it's a possibility.'

'I do, sort of. I believe that your dad was fixated on the legend and collated a ton of research on it. But I still think the gold is fictional. But, in saying that, if Worth thought there was a chance that it was real, then that would explain him trying to buy your place.'

Berry glanced at him. 'Okay, I'll take it,' she said with a grin.

Nate returned her smile as he stood up from the table. Berry watched him as he walked up to her and held out his hand. Without any hesitation she took it and rose to her feet. His gaze locked on her and for a second she found it hard to breathe. A little while ago they were talking about theories and missing gold, but now the atmosphere in the room shifted.

His arm went around her waist and he pulled her closer to him, his eyes never breaking contact.

Nate's face lit up with a warm smile. 'I want you,' he whispered as he rested his head against hers.

Berry let the warmth of his body encompass her. Standing there, with her arms wrapped around him felt right. She wasn't sure when or even how it happened, but the last thing she wanted tonight was to be alone. 'I want you too.'

'Good answer,' he said before he lowered his head and kissed her. His mouth was soft and warm and it sent tingles through her entire body.

The kiss started soft and gentle but developed quickly, and the first sparks of passion began to ignite. Still kissing her, Nate lifted her up—again Berry held onto his shoulders and folded her legs around his hips. His strong arms held her tightly as he carried her into the bedroom. He kissed her once and then again before he laid her on the bed.

She scooted over to give him room enough to join her. He turned to reach for her but she was already there. She cupped the side of his face for a moment before leaning in and touching his mouth with her own.

They stayed like that as if they were suspended in time, the only movement was the steady deepening of their kiss. There was a thrill in his touch as his hands began the slow and tantalising discovery of her body.

Berry's senses were heightened as Nate's tongue followed that path blazed by his hands. It was too much and not enough at the same time. Berry bit her lip as his mouth began its agonisingly slow descent down the column of her neck. She pulled and tugged at his clothes as she was ensnared by the overwhelming need to press her skin against his.

'Berry,' he whispered against her throat, 'you want this, don't you? 'Cause if you want me to back off, then tell me now.'

Berry looked at him and smiled. 'Yes, I want this.'

His hot breath blew across her sensitive skin, setting off a tiny maelstrom of tingles that seemed to spread and trigger over her body.

His hand found hers and he interlaced their fingers. He looked down at her. 'I want you so bad, Berry. I've never felt this way before.'

Berry gazed into his eyes. 'Then what are you waiting for?'

Chapter Thirty-three

Finding a way home, 1906

Neddy looked around and around as he walked through the bush, still not convinced that he was going in the right direction. Sometimes he'd pass a tree or a clump of bushes that seemed familiar, but he couldn't be sure.

It had taken him a couple of tries to get out of the gully as the shale and dirt was summer dry and it moved under his feet. What also made it difficult was that he was carrying Peter under his shirt. The third time had been the charm as he managed to hang onto one of the saplings and pull himself out.

Neddy looked up in the sky, the sun shining brightly down on him. He'd been walking for a long time now and the sun was directly overhead. His stomach rumbled and the walking made him thirsty. He stopped by a nearby gum and stood in its shade.

'It will be all right, Peter—I promise. I think we're going the right way and soon we'll be home,' he said to the rabbit. He didn't expect Peter to answer; it was just that the talking helped—at least he didn't feel altogether alone.

He'd eaten some berries and drunk a couple of hand-fuls of water from the creek before he started off but that was ages ago. He swallowed but it didn't help, his throat was still dry.

'When we get home, I'm going to ask Mam for some of her lemonade. It's got lemons and sugar in it,' he explained to Peter. 'Mam doesn't make it often but maybe she will if I ask.'

Neddy pushed himself away from the tree and started walking hopefully towards home, the thought of the lemonade spurring him on. The scents of the sun-warmed ground, eucalypts and dust were carried on the little breeze that blew past Neddy and ruffled his hair as it went.

One ghost gum looked like the next and then the next one after that, but Neddy persevered and kept going. Another hour passed and his legs were sore and worn out. Those pesky hot tears started to prick at his eyes and he had to stop to wipe them.

As he sniffed, he caught sight of something through the straight trunks of the gums and their grey–green leaves.

'Peter, that's a track!' Neddy said as he hurried towards it. Relief washed over him as he stood in the middle of it and looked across the countryside. Beside him was a fenced paddock that looked vaguely familiar. In one direction the track sloped downwards and followed the pad-dock's boundary fence. Neddy looked over his shoulder: the other way veered off and climbed uphill.

'I think I know where we are,' Neddy said to Peter as he turned around and started walking up the hill. Once he made it to the top he stopped to get his bearings. 'Yes, I know this place. If we keep walking over the next hill we'll be home.'

He picked up speed with every step. The wind carried the sound of voices, but he wasn't sure where they were or how far away. As he reached the dip in the track, a shout sounded.

'Neddy! Neddy Doherty!' came the cry.

Neddy looked around and for a moment all he could see was the bush on one side of the track and the dried-up paddock on the other. But as he looked back to the bush he saw several figures emerge from the trees. Someone was blowing a whistle and people were calling his name.

Mr O'Hare from the general store and stock feed hurried towards him with a grin on his face.

'Jesus, Mary and Joseph—I've found you, boyo. You're safe and sound now,' he said with a laugh as he scooped up Neddy. 'You've led us all for a merry dance, I'll say.'

'You've been looking for me?'

'We have, nearly everyone in town,' Mr O'Hare said with a smile as he sat Neddy on his shoulders.

'Did you hear that, Peter—everyone has been looking for us?'

'And who are you talking to?' Mr O'Hare asked as they were joined by several other men who clapped him on the back for finding Neddy.

'My rabbit, Peter—he's why I left. He wanted me to follow him, you see,' Neddy explained.

'And why would he want you to do that?' he asked with a chuckle as they all walked along together.

'To show me the pretty pebbles,' Neddy explained.

Chapter Thirty-four

Berry opened her eyes as a shaft of sunlight shone in the darkened room. It took her a moment to remember where she was, but as the events of last night came flooding back she couldn't help but smile. Last night had been the start of something, she felt it in her bones. She didn't want to jinx whatever it was between her and Nate by trying to define and give it a label, but she sensed that it had been the first building blocks in a natural progression. One she hoped would continue well past the foreseeable future. She turned over to see that the other side of the bed was empty and frowned as a wave of disappointment washed over her.

'Morning,' Nate said. He banged open the bedroom door as he tried to manoeuvre through it while carrying a tray.

Berry sat up in bed and arranged the covers around her. 'What's this?' she asked with a smile.

'I thought you'd like breakfast in bed,' he said as he triumphantly put the tray down in front of her and revealed a mug of coffee and some toast with jam. 'I never said I was a chef,' he added with a wink.

'It looks fantastic,' she said. Glancing up at him she saw that his hair was damp and he was wearing jeans and an unbuttoned blue plaid shirt. Berry tried to focus on the toast. 'So, you're up early or did I just sleep in?'

Nate sat next to her and gave her a quick kiss. 'A little bit of both. Dad called me earlier, he needs a hand with one of the stallions. So, even though I'd much rather stay here with you, I'd better do the right thing.'

'You should,' Berry said. 'Besides, I was going back home today to finish going through Dad's papers, remember?'

'I do. Are you sure you're okay to go back by yourself? I can get Mum to drive you there and go in with you, if you like,' Nate asked.

Berry shook her head. 'Nah, I'll be fine. Besides, I think I could do with a walk. And as for being by myself— well, I'm not worried. They caught Laurie Worth, so I haven't got anything to be concerned about.'

Nate smiled down at her. 'I suppose so,' he said before he kissed her again, this time lingering.

After a moment or two Berry pulled away. 'You'd better get going,' she said with a laugh. 'You don't want to keep your father waiting.'

'We could make him wait just a little bit,' he said with a glint in his eyes.

'But that's the problem, isn't it?'

Nate frowned. 'What do you mean?'

'That it wouldn't just be for a little bit. If you carry on what you're doing, we could be here for the rest of the morning,' she said with a meaningful look.

'Ah, I suppose you're right but you make it hard for me to leave,' he admitted as he rested his head against hers. 'Can't I stay?'

Berry laughed and gave him a gentle nudge. 'No, you can't. Go and meet your dad and we can catch up later.'

'That's a given,' he said as he reluctantly got up off the bed. 'All right, you win.'

She gave him another smile. 'It doesn't feel like a win,' she said. 'But I'll see you later, okay?'

'Hmm, okay,' he answered as he bent down and dropped a kiss on her head before straightening up and heading to the door. 'Stay out of trouble.'

'I'll try, but I'm not promising anything,' she called after him.

* * *

Berry took her time walking back home, enjoying the peacefulness of the morning. Apart from the singing of several birds in a nearby bush, there was a stillness in the crisp air. It would probably take a good fifteen minutes to walk back to Stone Gully, longer if she kept on with this meandering pace. She paused every now and again to take in the beauty of the landscape. One side of Lyrebird Road was covered in dense bush and a vast stretch of gum trees, and on the other side were the cleared pastures of Tarantale Downs, punctuated by small pockets of bush and the occasional dam. It must have looked like the other side of the road at one time, Berry reflected, but it had been cleared in the past decades and now only a handful of ancient trees still stood their ground.

She paused for a moment where a gnarled plum tree's blossoms cascaded over the boundary fence. She reached up and touched one of the fragile pale pink blooms and was instantly transported back to the moment Nate kissed her for the first time. Berry smiled as she dropped her hand and continued on her way.

As she walked up the drive of Stone Gully the bright red *LEAVE* was still scrawled across the front door. She briefly wondered how hard bright red paint was to paint over and considered changing the colour of the front door, but then she dismissed the thought and let herself back into the house.

She caught herself smiling. *It's good to be home.*

Berry pulled back the drapes in the lounge room, then hurried to her bedroom and carried the box of her father's papers back to the lounge and dumped them on the large coffee table. She looked at the stack of books, maps and notes, some of which she'd already read. With a sigh, she sat down and reached for her dad's notebook— one way or another she was going to work this out.

* * *

Nate leaned on the wooden railing as he watched Justin lead Constantine into the training arena. Constantine had a glossy black coat, stood about sixteen hands and was

271

just as majestic as his bloodlines. He had proved himself in the dressage ring and was considered an up-and-coming champion.

Nate dragged his gaze away from the horse and glanced at his father who was standing next to him.

'He's magnificent,' Nate said.

His father nodded. 'I know—breathtaking. Best stallion we've had since Lightning Bolt. They'll be lining up to get their foals sired by this one.'

Nate looked back at Constantine. 'I don't doubt it. He's beautiful, but pricey.'

'It's true, we've got a lot riding on this one. It took us a long time to recover from the accident. We've been holding our own over the past few years, but that horse,' he said as he gestured to Constantine, 'he could cement our ranking as one of the best studs in the district.'

'I don't remember much about the accident, I guess I was fairly young. We lost our best horses, didn't we?'

Sam Tarant dragged in a deep breath. 'Yeah, we did: Lightning Bolt and Longren. A van veered into our lane, hit the car in front of us and took us out as well.'

'I remember we lost the horses and there was some sort of car accident but I didn't realise to what extent.'

'Yeah, it was bad. I was lucky, I managed to walk away with a dislocated shoulder, a few decent cuts and concussion. John, the stable hand who was with me, ended up with a broken leg but—' Sam stopped himself, then continued with a shake of his head '—no one else made it. Not the people or the horses.'

'It was that bad?'

'It stuffed everything up. The business, our standing and reputation, and even the family. In some ways we never really recovered.'

'But . . . but how come you've never talked about this to me? Why didn't you tell me?'

'Because that's what parents do. It was my job to protect you, and to give you opportunities and a better life than I had. You're my son, and you were just a boy. Why would I burden you with that?'

'Sorry, Dad.'

Sam glanced over at Nate. 'What the hell are you sorry for? It was bad, it happened, but now it's just water under the bridge.'

'Yeah, but it must have made it hard for the business. I remember crying my eyes out over losing Longren, he was my favourite horse, but I never considered what the ramifications were for the business.'

'It was touch and go. They were our best horses. Sure we eventually got a payout, but that was a long time coming and things were pretty grim for a while. I was sure we were going to lose the place,' his father said. 'For a while I was convinced I was the failure who was going to lose the family legacy—it messed with my head. I was difficult and I know I gave your mum a hard time—it was like I was a whole different man; I barely recognised myself. It seemed to me that no matter what I did, I couldn't work out how to save us. The bank was baying for my blood . . . but we pulled through, thanks to your grandmother.'

Nate gave his father a small smile. 'I miss her.'

'Me too,' he replied before inhaling a deep breath and straightening up. 'Anyway, enough of that. I don't like thinking about it. Are you seeing Berry later?'

Nate's smile widened. 'Yeah, she's gone back home for a bit but I'll swing by after we're done here.'

His father nodded as he turned back and looked at Constantine prancing in the arena. 'He's looking good, don't you think, Justin?'

'He sure is, Mr Tarant,' Justin called back with a grin.

'So, what's Berry up to? She won't be nervous to be by herself?'

'I don't think so, not now at least,' Nate answered. 'I mean, since they caught Laurie Worth, what's to be scared of?'

'Oh, they caught him, did they? Good,' Sam said. 'How?'

'He ran a red light in Bendigo.'

Sam's scoffed. 'He always was an idiot.'

Nate chuckled. 'Yeah, I can't disagree with that. Anyway, Berry's going through some old papers to try to work out why Worth was so bent on buying Stone Gully.'

His dad turned back and stared at him for a second. 'What, I don't understand. What papers?'

Nate shrugged. 'Her father's notes. Apparently, he was obsessed with that old Harlington gold story and has a box full of notes and research on it. I don't believe it, but Berry does; thinks that maybe there could be a clue in why Worth wanted the place so bad.'

'Right. You know it's all utter nonsense.'

'Of course,' Nate replied.

'So, where were these papers?'

'I don't know for sure, she stumbled across them when she was cleaning up the place—so probably in one of the sheds.'

'Have you seen them?'

'Yeah, there's a pile of them—books, maps, notes and handwritten scribbles. Her father really went all out, even pestered Young Ned about it. Why are you so interested, anyway? I didn't think it would be your sort of thing.'

Sam shrugged. 'Just curious. I think it's kind of sad that Jordy would have wasted his time on such rubbish.'

'I'd be interested if it were my land. Still, I guess you'd know since he was a friend of yours.'

'He was . . . he was,' Sam said quietly before clamping his hand on Nate's shoulder for a second. 'Why don't we go back to the house and grab some lunch?'

Nate looked down at his father's hand. Signs of affection weren't his thing. 'Um, okay.'

Chapter Thirty-five

Stone Gully Farm, 2007

'What exactly are you telling me?' Cath McCalister asked her husband as she got up from the floor where she'd been playing with little Tommy. Both the girls were at school and this was her special time with the baby. He was a solid little guy who was sitting up and sucking on a teething ring. He was becoming a champion crawler, so she daren't take her attention off him for too long. The shafts of sun streamed into the lounge room through the windows and filled it with light. Tommy was fascinated with the moving shadow on the floor from the rose bush swaying gently in the breeze outside.

Jordy took Cath by the hand and pulled her to her feet before he whirled her around once, and then once more for good measure. 'I'm saying that everything is going to be all right.'

Cath gave him a dubious look and waited for him to launch into another one of his schemes. She was used to it; he was always getting fired up about the next thing that was going to make then miraculously rich. Jordy had a special way at looking at life. It had been this quality that had drawn her to him in the first place—she loved his enthusiasm. But as each grand idea turned sour it was a little hard to stay totally on board. She loved him, there was no denying that, but sometimes Jordy forgot to live in the here and now. He forgot about the bills that had to be paid and that the children really did need to eat. She loved him—but sometimes it felt as if she were bringing up four children instead of three.

'What exactly is going to be all right? Jordy, if this is about the llamas—it's not going to happen, I mean it.'

He grinned at her and pulled her into a hug. 'It's not—and it was alpacas, not llamas. And I still think an alpaca farm would be great—just imagine how much the kids would love them,' he answered.

Cath drew out of his embrace. 'No. No alpacas.'

'Okay,' he answered with a smile as he leaned in and dropped a quick kiss on her lips. 'No alpacas. But this isn't about that. This is something bigger, so much bigger.'

'Please don't say emus.'

Jordy let out a laugh. 'No, nothing like that. I think I've found it, Cath. I think I've found the gold.'

Cath sighed. She should have seen this one coming. He'd been talking about it for the past few months.

'You mean the gold that the little kid found a hundred years ago?'

Jordy nodded. 'That's it,' he said excitedly.

'Sweetheart,' Cath said as she took his hand in hers, 'it's just a legend, there never was any gold. It's just a story.

The only reason we still talk about it is to get the odd tourist or prospector into Harlington.'

'Yeah, but you're wrong, Cath. Little Neddy found the gold, of that I'm certain. I've got proof, I really have.'

'Proof? Okay, tell me,' she said as if she were placating a child.

His story of the change in the Dohertys' circumstances was interesting, but as far as Cath could see it certainly wasn't proof. 'It doesn't exactly prove it, does it?'

Jordy's shoulders slumped a little as if she'd taken the wind out of his sails. 'No, I guess it doesn't. But I've been studying all the different facets of this story and I truly believe that's what happened.'

Cath forced a smile. She felt bad for always bringing Jordy back to earth with a crash. 'Okay, let's say it does. How does that change our lives?'

He looked up at and she could see the light had returned to his eyes. 'Because I reckon I know where the gold is.'

'Jordy, people have been searching for that for years and no one has ever found it.'

He smiled. 'That's because they weren't looking in the right place,' he said as he walked over to the table and shuffled through a stack of paper. He found what he was looking for and brought it back to his wife. He flourished an old map in front of her.

'Wait, where did you get this from?'

He grimaced for a second. 'The local historical society. I'm just borrowing it.'

Cath pinned him with her eyes. 'Do they know?'

Choosing to ignore her question, Jordy pointed to the map. 'It's here, Cath. I reckon it's here . . . on our land. We're going out later to see if we can find it.'

'We?'

'Yeah, Sam said he'd come with me.'

'Oh, Jordy, why would you bother him with this? You know he's been going through a rough time. You know, Jackie was over here the other morning for coffee. She's a mess, she told me that Sam's been acting weird, almost violent,' Cath said.

'Violent? Sam? That's not like him—he's always so level-headed, sometimes even a bit distant,' Jordy said with a frown.

'I know. But Jackie reckons it's the stress of the accident. She told me there's a good chance they'll lose the place. And it's not like he's hurting anyone, it's just all of a sudden he'll snap and slam things on tables.'

'Well, maybe he just needs a bit of time to get his head together. Maybe going on a treasure hunt is just what he needs,' Jordy said with a reassuring smile. 'Don't worry, I'll look after him. Everything's going to be fine.'

Chapter Thirty-six

Berry picked up her father's notebook. She'd read it from cover to cover but still wasn't any closer to an answer. She ran her hand over the black leather it was bound with.

Come on, Dad—what are you trying to tell me?

With a sigh, she opened the book again and flicked through the pages. There were scrawled notes about the gold, stories about Little Neddy and a dozen interviews with some of the older residents of Harlington. Berry had read over them a couple of times, and as far as she could see, there wasn't any definitive proof that the gold ever existed. Perhaps this was just another one of her father's wild ideas that never came to anything. Maybe the realisation that he'd spent months chasing ghosts helped push him over the edge that day—but she would never know.

It didn't matter how much she wished it otherwise, maybe she needed to just come to terms with what her father had done. Logic demanded that no matter how she remembered him, he was still the same man who killed her mother and grandparents. There could be no absolution, the fact was that her loving father turned into a monster that day.

She turned to the back of the journal, where a couple of loose scraps of paper dislodged. She glanced at them, and though neither seemed to be particularly important, Berry noticed a small slit in the heavy cream endpaper. At first she thought it was a tear, but it appeared to be too precise. She ran her finger over it and thought she detected a thin lump, like something was hiding in it.

Berry hurried to the kitchen and placed the book on the bench. With the carving knife she carefully probed the paper slit.

It's probably just a dead bug, she told herself but that didn't stop the tendril of excitement growing within her.

She made the hole a little bigger and saw a corner of a folded piece of paper, which she carefully removed and unfolded. Berry's eyes grew wide as she realised what she was looking at: a hand-drawn map of Stone Gully Farm. Past the paddocks and the dams, up to where that hard quartz reef ran through the property, her father had drawn a narrow gully. There was no X marks the spot but instead the word: *Possibility*.

Berry stared at it for another few seconds as she tried to take it all in. That's all she needed: a possibility.

* * *

Nate was sitting at the kitchen table across from his dad. The house was quiet, with the girls at school and his mum off at lunch with friends. Nate always felt a slight awkwardness with his father, and usually his mum or sisters were there to buffer between them. However, today seemed different and Nate couldn't put his finger on why.

They were eating roast beef and salad sandwiches, using up the leftovers from last night's dinner. Nate had just taken another bite when his phone rang. He quickly tried to swallow as he got up from the table.

'Senior Sergeant, how are you?'

'Good, thanks. Listen, I just thought I'd give you a heads up. Worth has confessed to running Berry off the road and the graffiti. According to him, he panicked when he saw Berry driving back that night—he figured it was her because as he got closer he recognised her red car. He said that he didn't want to hurt her, just wanted to scare her away without her realising it was him.'

'So, running her off the road was the answer? Geez, you wouldn't like to let me alone with him for a few minutes, would you?' Nate asked.

'Hmm, maybe that's not such a great idea. Anyway, when I asked him why he wanted Stone Gully, he said that he'd made a deal with someone, and it was worth a lot to him.'

'A deal—what deal?' Nate asked.

'Well, apparently he had a guaranteed buyer for Stone Gully, who was willing to pay premium price for it. His idea was that he could buy it for a low value, then on-sell it to his buyer. It would have made him a quick hundred grand.'

'Really? Why would this buyer make a deal like that? Wouldn't it have been easier to do it himself and not involve Laurie?' Nate said.

'Yeah, I know, it's a bit strange. I guess this buyer, whoever it is, doesn't want to be known,' Rob Mendez explained.

'Really? That's crazy! Why would anyone go to such lengths to buy the place? There's plenty of other real estate around!'

'Yeah, it's all a bit mysterious. So far, Worth hasn't said who this buyer is, but I reckon I can get it out of him. Anyway, I just thought I'd let you and Berry know,' Mendez said.

'Yeah, thanks. I'll tell her.'

'Okay, great. I'll talk to you later.'

'Oh, just one thing—what did he say about the fire?' Nate asked.

'He says he had nothing to do with that, but I'll get to the bottom of it.'

'So, what was that about?' Sam Tarant asked as Nate sat down again.

'Oh, Laurie Worth has confessed to writing paint all over Berry's door and driving at her.'

'Why?'

'Because apparently he was working on a deal with some mysterious buyer that would make him a shitload of money,' Nate explained.

'Really? Did he say who?' Sam responded.

'Well, if he had, it wouldn't be a mysterious buyer, would it?' Nate said.

'Yeah, right.' Sam said and then asked, 'Hey, but what about the fire, did he own up to that?'

Nate frowned. 'Police reckon it wasn't him.'

'Do you believe that?'

'Not really.'

Sam nodded. 'Me neither. It could have just been some stupid kids, but it was more than a campfire gone wrong, wasn't it?'

'Rob Mendez believes that it was intentional,' Nate said.

'Then I wonder who would do such a thing. Unless Laurie just doesn't want to own up to it because he thinks he's in enough trouble.'

Nate was about to answer when his phone rang again. He gave his dad an apologetic smile before silently mouthing *Berry*. Sam waved his hand as if to tell him to go ahead and Nate disappeared through the kitchen door, but he wasn't gone long.

'That was Berry, she wants me to go over once I'm finished here,' Nate said as he slid back into his chair and put his phone on the table.

'Anything important? Nothing else has happened, has it?' Sam asked quickly.

Nate shook his head. 'No, she just thinks she might be onto something,' he explained. 'She going out to check it out—told me to give her a ring when I come over so she can tell me where to find her.'

'That sounds intriguing,' Sam said as he glanced at Nate and gave him a slight smile.

'Nah, probably not. I keep saying that the whole gold thing is just a fairytale. But at least it will give me some more time with Berry,' he said.

Sam stared at his son for a moment too long. Long enough to make Nate a little uncomfortable, as if he were being studied like a bug under a microscope.

'You really like her, don't you?' Sam said quietly.

'I do,' Nate replied. 'Is that a problem?'

'No, it's not,' Sam said before changing the subject. 'Listen, I know that you want to get over to Berry's but could you do me a favour first? Could take a run up to Bendigo for me? There're a couple of outdoor lights that have blown and we need new ones.'

'Which lights?'

'The motion-detector ones. There's one that isn't working outside the stable and another near the back of the house. Now, I think Laurie Worth is responsible for the fire, but if we're wrong, then I don't want anyone messing around our horses, especially Constantine. You know, sometimes it's good to play it safe.'

'No, you're right. If I leave now, I'd probably be back by three,' Nate said.

'Sorry to do this to you,' his father added. 'I just think it'll be one thing that we don't have to worry about.'

Nate got up from the table and carried his plate over to the sink. He turned around and said, 'I'll take off now. How do I know which ones to get?'

'I put one of the empty boxes on the shelf by the back door so I wouldn't forget,' Sam said.

'Great, I'll get going then,' Nate said as he gave his dad a wave and headed towards the back door.

Sam sat there for a moment and looked down to where his son had been sitting. Nate's phone was still on the table. He heard the back door close and after another minute or two Nate's ute firing up. There was still time to tell him that he forgot his phone but instead Sam sat there, finished his coffee and said nothing.

* * *

Berry took a few minutes to throw some items into her backpack. She packed a foldable spade she'd found in the shed, a torch, a mini first-aid kit, a sandwich, banana and a bottle of water. She didn't know how long she'd be gone but she wanted to have some sort of a plan. Grabbing the map, her phone and her sunglasses, she turned and walked out the back door.

The gully that her father had drawn on the map was right up past the far paddock. It was going to take her quite a while to walk there.

Chapter Thirty-seven

In the Gully, 2007

Jordy had been out searching nearly every day for the past two weeks. He had even managed to drag poor old Sam out for one of the expeditions. None had been successful but that hadn't dampened Jordy's enthusiasm. He knew the gold was out here, he could almost feel it.

As Jordy half-slid down the bank of the gully wall he stopped his fall by managing to hang onto a ghost gum. The ground tended to give way, leaving the tiny pebbles and rocks to slide down the hill. A smile tugged at his mouth as he launched himself towards the next tree; it was the only way to get to the bottom in one piece.

Once he reached solid ground he wandered over to the shallow creek that meandered along the gully floor. He stood there for a moment and watched the water splash and bubble on its way past. It was summer but the little creek still managed to run. It was peaceful; Jordy could very well stay for the rest of the morning, but he knew that if he did that, there would be hell to pay.

It was Berry's birthday and she was having a big party later that afternoon. Cath would expect him to be on deck and help out—which he'd be happy to do; it wasn't every day your daughter turned ten. But this morning something had called to him, just as he opened his eyes before the sun had even risen. He couldn't explain why, but he had an overpowering urge to come and poke around the gully. He tried to ignore it because he didn't want to upset Cath, but he couldn't. So, he snuck out of the house just as the sun was beginning to peep over the distant hill.

Jordy picked his way over the creek without getting even a splash. He wanted to check out the great big rock, which he figured made up part of the gully wall. It was tall, imposing and it intrigued the hell out of him.

As he headed towards it, his mind went back to Sam Tarant. It was true what Cath had said about him being stressed ever since that terrible car accident. Sam was his friend, although many people couldn't fathom how or why. In the eyes of the town, if Jordy was a fool and a dreamer, then Sam would be the complete opposite. He was cool, detached and always level-headed—at least he had been, now maybe not so much. Lately, whenever Jordy met him, he wasn't sure which version he'd get—the original quiet and sensible one or the latest model prone to fly into a rage. Getting angry was one thing and Jordy could understand just how much pressure his friend was under. But the thing that was unnerving was that every now and again he could see a cold light in his friend's eyes and it worried him.

'I'll find the gold and then we'll all be happy,' he murmured.

He walked around the rock, fully expecting it to be part of the wall, but he was wrong. There was a gap, it was narrow but it was a gap nonetheless. Excitement began to bubble inside of him as he dropped his bag and rummaged around until he found his torch. Without a moment's hesitation Jordy squeezed through the space and into the deep shadow of the crevice.

Chapter Thirty-eight

Berry stood on the edge of the gully and looked down. The sides were steep and stony. From here it all looked quite unstable, and she figured if she wasn't careful she would slip and tumble all the way down to the gully floor. Several gums were growing up the slope—maybe that would be her way down. Near the base of the last gum tree was a tangle of blackberry bushes. She only hoped that she wouldn't be propelled down the slope and end up falling head-first into it.

Berry took the first tentative steps off the edge. A cascade of small rocks tumbled down the hill as Berry took another step. She waited for a second in the hope that everything would settle down, then she walked on. The ground seemed to shear away from the gully wall, and for a moment it was as if she were skimming over water or snow, but just as she was beginning to topple and lose her balance entirely she managed to half-grab, half-fall into the trunk of the first tree.

She looked back up to the edge of the gully and frowned. Maybe Berry hadn't thought this one through—if it was this hard to get down to the gully floor, how the hell was she going to get up? But there was no going back now. She'd come this far, so she might as well keep going. Besides, she had her phone and Nate knew what she was doing—somehow or other she would make it out.

Berry turned her attention to the next tree, which was only half a dozen steps away. She lined herself up, aimed for the tree and made a run at it. Once again the ground moved and slipped under her feet, but her trajectory was true and she bumped into the smooth trunk of a ghost gum and hung on for dear life. She repeated the process again and was beginning to congratulate herself on a job well done when she missed the last tree and tumbled down the final part of the slope, landing on her backside with a bang.

She sat for a second trying to ignore the scratches on her hand, the gravel-rashed knee and the fact that her butt hurt. Slowly she got to her feet and looked around. At least she hadn't landed in the blackberry bushes—so, she should be thankful for small mercies.

Berry walked a little slower than normal towards the small creek that was splashing through the gully. The winter rains had made sure that it was flowing but it still wasn't particularly wide. There was a large flat stone sticking out of the water and Berry `wondered whether, if she managed to get to that, she might be able to jump the rest of the way without getting too wet.

But before that, she needed to check her bearings. She took off her backpack, dropped it on the ground by her feet and sat on a nearby rock. Pulling out her father's map, she paused for a moment while she studied it.

'Okay, Dad, I'm here—where do I go next?'

***

'Oh, bloody hell,' Nate said as he went to reach for his phone and realised it wasn't in his pocket. While still keeping his eyes on the road, he moved his hand and checked his shirt pocket just in case—nope, not there either.

Nate flicked on his indicator and pulled off the road. He checked his jacket pocket and between the seats. He already had the sinking feeling that it wouldn't be there, but he looked just the same.

'Damn it!'

Nate was already on the far side of Harlington and on his way to Bendigo. In fact, he was almost at the turnoff for the Calder Highway. He could just keep going, the task of buying the light shouldn't take that long, but then what if Berry or his sisters had to get in touch?

Nate waited for the oncoming car to pass before he pulled back onto the road, did a U-turn and headed back home.

***

The map was no help whatsoever. Berry stared at it again trying to spot any markings or hints as to where the gold might be, but there was nothing. She could see the gully walls drawn in and the path of the creek and even the gums that grew up the slope. Yet there wasn't a hint about where to go now.

Berry wrinkled her nose and thought about it for a second. The writing on the map was where her father had written *Possibility*. She glanced up and saw the big rocks across the creek. With nothing else to go on, she stuffed the map away, picked up her backpack and tried to make it over the creek without getting too wet. Once she got to the rocks, she started to make her way along the gully wall when she spied a narrow opening.

'Well, hello, what have we got here?'

She grabbed the torch from the backpack and was about to go in when she thought better of it. Taking out her phone, she rang Nate—no answer. She rang the number again but he still didn't pick up, so she typed a message.

I'm in the gully in the top paddock. Found a crevice in the rockface. I'm going to have a look. Come find me and bring a rope! B x

Satisfied that at least someone knew where she was, Berry placed the phone in her anorak pocket, switched on the torch and squeezed through the narrow gap.

Once inside Berry could see there was a bit of space—probably enough for her to sit down, maybe even stretch out. But the surprising thing she discovered was a crevice in the actual wall of the gully. There was no way of telling whether it was just a small indent in the rock or a full-on cave.

Crouching down, she shone her light into the darkness and saw that there was definitely an expanse. The light beam was fairly narrow, but as she swept the shaft across the cave's floor she thought she caught a glint. Berry backtracked with the light until it settled on a small white stone with a splash of gold.

'No way,' she breathed.

As excitement outweighed cautiousness, Berry crawled into the cave and picked up the stone. She sat down and studied it in the torchlight. It was the loveliest thing she'd ever seen, not because of what it was but rather what it meant. She shone the light on the ground near her and saw a handful of pebbles glinting back at her.

You were right, Dad. You found it! Gold really does exist in Harlington. Just wait until I tell Young Ned.

She dashed away a tear. She didn't know why she was getting emotional. Maybe it was the knowledge that after all her father's ideas, schemes and plans one actually had substance. Or perhaps it was that Young Ned was finally vindicated.

She pushed the pebble into her pocket and moved to gather up the next one. Her torch arced up over the wall of the cave, and Berry had to blink a couple of times as she tried to comprehend what she was looking at. The more she shone the light on the wall, the more she couldn't believe what she was seeing. On the other side of the cave, a soft glow emanated from a gold vein that ran across the entire wall.

* * *

Nate strode into the kitchen and almost bumped into his mum.

'Hey, what's your hurry?' Jackie said with a smile. 'Everything okay?'

'Sorry,' Nate said. 'I thought you were out with your friends.'

'I was. We'd planned a long lunch followed by a shopping expedition, but unfortunately Kaye was called away,' Jackie explained. 'Anyway, our catch-up day has been postponed until next week. What's happening here?'

'I was meant to pick something up for Dad in Bendigo but I think I left my phone here, so I came back,' Nate said as he walked over to the table and saw his phone taunting him from where he left it. He sighed, picked it up and checked for any messages. 'Where's Dad?'

Jackie shrugged. 'I don't know. He wasn't here when I got back.'

Nate frowned when he found Berry's text. 'Geez, she shouldn't be doing that by herself,' he muttered.

'What's the matter, darling?' Jackie asked.

Nate looked at his mum. 'Berry's gone off exploring. She's asked me to come and to bring a rope—I can only imagine the trouble she's in. I don't know why she didn't wait. I would have gone with her.'

Jackie bit back a smile. 'Oh, I don't know. Berry's a grown woman, I suspect that she can take care of herself.'

Nate gave her a look, slightly annoyed that his mother looked amused. 'Well, she's in the gully and needs a rope, so I'm not sure what exactly is going on. If you see Dad could you tell him that I'll go to Bendigo after I make sure Berry's okay?' Nate asked.

'Of course,' Jackie said with a smile.

'Thanks, Mum.'

Nate pocketed his phone, kissed his mum's cheek and went to find a rope. As he walked towards the garage his phone rang.

'Hello Nate,' Senior Sergeant Rob Mendez said. 'Listen I've just discovered some very interesting information. I think you need to hear this.'

***

Berry carefully made her way from out of the gap between the rocks; it was tight, but she managed. She looked down and saw that her jeans were smeared with damp soil from when she'd been crawling around the cave. She bent down and started brushing the dirt off them, not that it made it much better. Giving up, she went to retrieve her backpack from where she'd left it by the rockface.

'So, you found it, then.'

Berry jumped with fright and whirled around to see Sam Tarant standing not far away. 'I can't believe I never looked here. That opening is so bloody narrow, I didn't think a grown person could get through it.'

'Mr Tarant, you startled me,' Berry said as she picked up her bag and slung it over her shoulder before turning back to him. 'What are you doing here? Has something happened to Nate?'

He stared at her and something in his eyes made the hairs on the back of her neck quiver, but she didn't understand why.

'You really like him, don't you?' Sam asked quietly.

She gave him a small smile. 'Yes, I do. Is that a problem, do you object?'

He let out a long sigh. 'No, I don't. It's just unfortunate, that's all.'

Berry frowned. He was always reserved but he'd never made her feel uncomfortable, until now. There was something wrong, something off and all she wanted was to get away from Sam Tarant.

'I'm sorry but I don't understand,' Berry said as she took a few steps to the side, increasing the distance between them. 'Now, if you'll excuse me. I texted Nate a while ago—I'll go and wait for him.'

Sam turned and stared at her. 'You needn't bother, he's not coming. I've sent him on an errand to Bendigo and he'll be ages yet.'

'What do you want, Mr Tarant? Why are you here?' Berry asked as she backed up.

'What do I want?' he echoed as he took a step closer. 'Come on, Berry, don't pretend. We both know you're not stupid.'

Berry's eyes widened as she realised what he was saying. 'The gold?'

'Yes, the gold!' he snapped. 'I knew that your father had found it. Oh, he denied it, of course—called himself my friend, but pretended that he didn't know where the gold was so that he wouldn't have to help me out.'

'You're not making any sense,' Berry answered. 'I don't understand what you're trying to tell me.'

'I was losing everything!' he shouted. His mouth was flecked with spittle as he spat out the words, and his eyes blazed with an anger that she had never known he was capable of. 'Everything!' He pointed at her. 'And your father was keeping the gold from me. I would've helped him if I could . . . he had a head full of dreams that never got him anywhere, but I would've helped if he needed it. Everyone said he was a good man and I didn't deserve a friend like him . . .' Sam stopped to take a breath, his hands quivering with an almost palpable rage. 'Well, what did he do when I needed him, hey?'

Berry tried to steady her racing heart and keep her voice even. 'Mr Tarant, please . . .'

'He did nothing!' Sam said. 'He hid the gold from me so that he wouldn't have to share it—that's what he did.'

'I don't think he—'

'You don't know anything. You were a child. But I knew.'

'Knew what?'

'That he'd found the gold. And I was going to find out, oh yes. It was only a matter of time before I found out. But then . . .'

'Then what?' said Berry, as she continued backing away.

'He wasn't supposed to die! He cheated me completely. He took his secret to the grave and left me with nothing.

Why didn't he just tell me? Well, I won't be cheated again, you hear me?'

'Okay, well, I'm going to leave now,' Berry said as she jumped over the creek and landed on the flat rock in the middle of the flowing water.

'Why didn't he just tell me? Everything would have been fine—we would have all been happy.' Sam looked over at Berry. 'You should have sold the place when you had the chance.'

Berry looked behind her. 'What?'

'You heard me. I think I've waited long enough, don't you?'

'What the hell does that mean?'

'I've been waiting all these years to buy Stone Gully. If only you'd just sold it to me, all this unpleasantness need not have happened,' Sam said as he started clambering over the rocky ground towards her.

Berry jumped off the rock and landed on the other side of the creek. 'As I said, I'm leaving. And I want you to get off my property.'

'He'd found the gold—I knew it. But every time I asked he said he hadn't. He even dragged me around pretending to look for it, making a fool of me. I was the owner of Tarantale Downs, my family had been on that land for generations. By what right did the likes of Jordy McCalister have to look down on me? I needed the money and he was meant to be my friend but he wouldn't help.'

Berry turned around angrily and faced him. 'This is not your property, and we will never sell it to you.'

Sam paused, and a nasty smile spread over his face. 'No, I don't suppose you will. However, if you were to have an unfortunate accident as you were exploring this gully all by yourself, then I think your brother and sister could be convinced that this place is, well, cursed. I doubt they would refuse an offer, particularly when they were consumed with the tragic loss of their big sister at the same place they lost their parents and their grandparents.' Sam jumped off the rock and landed on the same side of the creek as Berry, then started making his way towards her. Berry backed up, one thought racing through her mind: could she make it back to the gum trees and climb out of here before he could catch her?

'You won't make it,' Sam said as he watched her look frantically towards the trees. 'I'm much more familiar with this territory, and you can see that I'm gaining on you.'

'Go away!' she shouted at him.

'And I haven't even raised a sweat yet.'

'Just leave me alone.'

'Leave you alone? With the gold? I don't think so. No, it's gone too far now, don't you see? I can't possibly let you go now, can I?'

'Please, Mr Tarant . . .'

'I'm catching up, Berry. Just make it easier on both of us, hey? You're not going to get away—you know that.' Berry looked back and saw that he was indeed gaining.

She whimpered quietly to herself as she realised that he was right.

Chapter Thirty-nine

'Back off, Dad. Don't even think about touching her.'

Berry whipped around and saw Nate standing at the edge of the gully.

'Nate,' she breathed as a wave of relief washed over her. Without giving Sam another thought, she raced as fast as she could towards the ghost gums.

'Nate, you shouldn't be here,' Sam said with a frown.

'But I am. Dad, what have you done?' His voice was thick and sounded on the edge of cracking. Berry watched as Nate turned and made his way to the edge just above the trees.

'I'm protecting us. No one has to know—it can be our secret.'

'Really? I think Berry might have something to say about that.'

Berry started to scramble up the slope towards Nate, but the pebbled ground kept sliding beneath her feet. After three attempts, she finally made it to the first tree. She glanced back over her shoulder and saw that Sam was striding towards her. Looking up, she saw Nate appear above her. He gestured to her with his hand.

'Come on, baby, move it,' he said as he glanced down towards his father. Then, more urgently, 'Berry, he's coming.'

Berry pushed off the tree trunk and tried to make it to the next gum, but it was harder going up than coming down.

'Nate, are you really going to side with her? I'm your father, and everything I've done was to protect you and Tarantale,' he said in a soft voice. 'You don't want to do this. What would your mother and sisters say if they find out that you betrayed me?'

'You've already betrayed us—you did that when you killed Berry's family,' Nate said quietly.

Berry froze as the impact of Nate's words hit her. Confusion and nausea swirled in her and she stumbled back onto the tree, unable to grasp the enormity of what she had heard. 'W-what?' she stuttered. 'He killed my family?'

Sam and Nate stared at each other, neither moving, the tension building between them. Suddenly Sam scrunched up his eyes and ran his hand though his hair before flinging his hand back down by his side, a sharp movement filled with such intensity it made Nate flinch. His father stood for a moment and stared at the ground with a frown, and to Nate it almost looked as if the man was grappling with his thoughts. After another second or two he finally looked back up at Nate and sighed. 'So, now the truth is out,' he said. Then he continued, defiance lighting in his eyes. 'Jordy wouldn't tell me where it was, and he knew how desperate I was back then. I was out of my mind with worry and I snapped. I didn't mean to do what I did—it just happened.'

'My father didn't murder my mother,' Berry stated simply, as if by saying it out loud her mind might comprehend the fact.

Sam shook his head. 'Your dad loved her beyond reason—he would never have harmed her. I doubt he'd could have hurt anyone.'

'You killed them all . . . My grandparents.'

'Yes, well, I had to, didn't I? I didn't *want* to, but they saw what happened. They would have sent me to jail, and I couldn't let that happen.'

Berry started to tremble violently as realisation hit home and anger welled up inside her like a volcano. 'All these years . . .'

His eyes pinned her. 'I've wronged you and I'm sorry for it. In hindsight I would have acted differently, but you can't erase the past.'

'You bastard,' she hissed. 'You murdered my family, and you made me believe it was Dad. Everyone despises him and tries to forget him, when he was the most loving and caring man. *You* did this!'

'Berry,' Nate said, 'don't talk to him. Just come up here now—you're not safe.'

'He destroyed my family! He butchered my mother and my grandparents, and set up my father to take the blame.'

'Look,' said Sam, 'I never planned for it to happen.'

'Don't you *dare* speak to me!' she spat at him. 'What sort of a person are you? You've come into my home and talked to me like a friend when all along you had the blood of my family on your hands. You're scum, Sam Tarant. *Scum!*'

Sam glanced up at Nate with a look that resembled sadness and regret, but it was laced with something harder, darker. 'Ah, Nate, this wasn't the way it was supposed to be. How did you work it out?'

Nate looked at his father. 'Well, for a start, your sleazy friend Laurie gave the game away. Oh, he tried to hold out and not say anything, but when the police hinted about how much jail time was up for grabs, he confessed everything.

'He told Rob Mendez that you're the guaranteed buyer and you're the one behind all his actions. That made me wonder why you would go to such great lengths to scare Berry and buy Stone Gully. And then I remembered you told me where Berry's mother was killed. I asked Rob about it and he confirmed she had been found near the dam, but he also said that no one knew about that. But you knew about that, didn't you? The only way you could have known about that is if you had been there when it happened. What was it Dad . . . the gold?'

'Nate—'

'And the fire—that was you, wasn't it?'

'Yes, but listen, son—'

'No!' Nate exclaimed. 'I won't listen to you. Never again. You're a low-life murderer. You destroyed Berry's family and disgraced ours.' Nate straightened and stared down his father. 'When you're locked away for the rest of your miserable life, I'll know that I no longer have a father.'

'It doesn't have to be that way, Nate.'

'Actually, it does. There's no avoiding it now. You have to pay for what you've done,' Nate said as he quickly tied one end of the rope he was carrying around a sapling at the top of the gully.

Berry had just made it to the second tree when she looked behind her and saw Sam had made it to the first.

'Berry, here!' Nate tossed the rope down to her. 'Hold on and I'll pull you up.'

She grabbed the rope with both hands and started walking up the slope. The ground was still moving with each step, but she hung onto the rope and managed to move towards Nate.

'Think about this, son,' his father called out. 'I can make this right. All you have to do is walk away. I can take care of everything.'

'Just shut up!' Nate called out. 'That's never going to happen.'

Nate made eye contact with Berry. 'Just keep moving. You're almost to the top. Don't listen to him, he's talking bullshit—I won't let anything happen to you, I promise,' he said as he pulled on the rope.

Berry grimaced as she pushed herself to keep going. She could hear Sam behind her, but with a final yank of the rope she was almost there. She reached out her hand and Nate took it.

'I've got you,' he said as he grabbed her under the arms and drew her towards him.

But before he could pull her all the way to safety, Sam's hand wrapped around her ankle and clung on with an iron grip.

Berry's eyes widened with fear as she felt herself slip back down.

'Nate!' she called out.

Nate held onto her but his father was almost to the top and he still clutched her leg.

'Just let her go,' his father said as he looked up and managed to grab the edge of the gully. 'Just let her go and everything will be back to how it was. We can put this all behind us and no one needs to know. Come on, son—she's nothing to us.'

'That's not true. She's everything to me—I love her,' Nate said as in one final effort he shoved his boot onto Sam's shoulder and gave him a shove in an attempt to free Berry.

For a second, there was a look of confusion in Sam's eyes as Berry was wrenched from his grasp and he began to fall back down into the rocky gully. The momentum of pulling Berry free sent her and Nate flying backwards until they both hit the ground. They lay there for a moment stunned and wrapped in each other's arms, and the only thought that went through Berry's mind was that he hadn't let her go.

Nate sat up and looked at her. He ran his hand down the side of her face. 'Are you hurt?'

She shook her head. 'No, I don't think so,' she whispered.

'Good,' he said as he got to his feet and pulled her up into a tight hug. 'You're safe now, it's over and nobody's going to hurt you.'

Berry held onto Nate. Her body trembled as she tried to process everything that had happened, but she couldn't. All she could do in that moment was to hang on to Nate and let the warmth and strength of his body enfold her.

Finally Nate let her go. He looked down at her, his hands resting on her shoulders. 'You stay here. I'll be back in a second. Okay?'

'Where are you going?'

Nate glanced over to the gully. 'I have to look.'

'Then I'll come with you,' Berry replied.

'You don't have to.'

'I think I do,' Berry said quietly.

Hand in hand they walked back to the edge and looked down. For a second Berry couldn't see Sam but then she found him, lying at the bottom of the gully near the blackberry bushes. He was alive but Berry saw that his left leg was at a strange angle.

A low-pitched wail echoed through the gully as Sam tried to move. He looked around until he stared up to where they were standing.

'Nate! Nate, help me!' Sam Tarant called out. 'Nate!'

For a moment Berry looked dispassionately down at him before turning and taking a few steps away from the edge.

Berry glanced at Nate as he pulled out his phone and scrolled through and found the number he was looking for. It rang a couple of times before it was answered.

Nate took a deep breath before he spoke. 'Hi Rob, it's Nate Tarant. Could you come to Stone Gully Farm—we've got a situation down here. Berry and I need your help.'

Chapter Forty

Stone Gully Farm, 2007

Sam Tarant was hunched over as he walked through the paddocks towards Stone Gully. He didn't know what he was going to do but somehow Jordy had to help him. Fifteen minutes ago he'd just got off the phone from the bank—they were threatening to take Tarantale Downs unless he came up with money for the arrears. What could he do? You can't get blood out of a damn stone. He tried to tell them that there was a payout coming but it was still going through the insurance companies and the court. But nothing he said would placate them. Jordy was his last chance.

He stopped for a moment and looked up at the sky. *What the hell am I doing?* Jordy wasn't even sure where the gold seam was—oh, he kept boasting that he knew where it was but he hadn't shared that information with Sam.

His hand closed around the object in his pocket. Maybe he'd just make Jordy tell him—that's right, that's what he'd do. He dragged in a breath and started walking again, this time increasing his pace. How could Jordy not share where the gold was? He was meant to be his friend, wasn't he? Why would he keep that sort of secret when it could change both their lives?

The sun was descending towards the far-off hills but the heat of the day still lingered. Sweat trickled down Sam's back but he felt chilled to the bone. Once again he stopped, this time looking back over his shoulder. He should go home and forget that he was going to confront Jordy. This was a mistake, a monumental mistake.

Slowly he turned his head back and looked ahead. But was it? Maybe Jordy was pretending about the gold. Maybe because it was on his land he was going to keep it all for himself. Sam stood as still as a statue as the warm summer breeze blew over him.

But Jordy wasn't like that—if he had the money he would help. It wasn't as if Sam was asking for charity. It would be a loan, just until he got back on his feet. He couldn't lose Tarantale Downs, it was in his blood, his bones, it was what defined him. What would he be without it? Nothing.

And if Jordy McCalister was really his friend, he'd help him.

Another gust blew over him, bringing the scent of dust and dry grass. His heart told him to turn around and go back. Instead he took a step forwards, his boot crushing a small plant struggling to survive in the dried-off paddock. Sam didn't notice, he just straightened his shoulders and kept going.

Chapter Forty-one

It was a rough day, the second worst one of her life. And yet with all the revelations and secrets from the past finally being freed, there was something cathartic about it as well. The past was finally purged clean, and even though the events of her tenth birthday could never be changed, at least the truth had finally surfaced.

The shadow that had hung over Jordy McCalister disappeared. He was no longer the monster; he became again nothing more than what he'd always been—her dad. The injustice still bit at Berry, nonetheless. Sam Tarant had ruined her family, killed his friend and then had the audacity to frame him for it. They say forgiveness is the key to living a peaceful and happy life, but she couldn't do it—at least not today.

Berry rang Uncle Dave and told him what had happened. She assured him that she was okay but didn't try to stop him when he announced that he was going to get her brother and sister and drive up straightaway.

The worst part was having to tell Nate's mum and sisters. Nate asked Berry if she'd go with him. She almost said no because she was still reeling from what had happened but changed her mind. She would go to support Nate, and maybe even more importantly to show his mum that she didn't hold her in any way responsible. She also realised that now it was Nate who had a murderer for a father, and she understood how difficult that was to come to terms with. She more than many others knew what it was like to feel the burden of family shame as well as the loss of a father.

'What?' Jackie asked as she stared round-eyed at Nate. 'What did you say?' She stumbled for a second as she sat down at the kitchen table.

Nate went over, sat next to her and took her hand. 'I'm sorry, Mum, but it's true. Dad killed the McCalisters, and he would have tried to do the same thing to Berry this afternoon if I hadn't turned up.'

Jackie slowly shook her head in denial. 'No,' she whispered, 'he wouldn't do something like that—he couldn't.'

'But he did,' Nate said softly. 'He did. He told me.'

Jackie's face was pale and tears welled then fell down her cheeks. She looked over to Berry, who was standing by the door.

'Oh, I'm so sorry, Berry. I'm so sorry. I never knew, never thought that he could . . .' Her voice cracked and she buried her head in her hands. 'Oh, how can you ever forgive me?'

Berry walked over and kneeled before her. 'It's not your fault. You didn't know and no one is blaming you,' she said as she reached over and hugged her.

* * *

The late afternoon breeze rustled through the pasture carrying the sounds of the stable hands grooming and feeding the horses, and the smell of the evening meal being cooked in the house. Nate was gazing across the fields in deep thought, while occasionally waving away the persistent mosquitoes that came out with the onset of evening shadows. Berry stood beside him, her own thoughts whirling as she came to terms with her new reality. Everything had changed and she was feeling unbalanced and slightly overwhelmed.

Nate broke the silence that had settled over them. 'Where do we go from here, Berry?'

'What do you mean?' she answered.

'My father murdered your family and then put the blame on your dad. Your dad was a good man, a man who loved his wife and his kids, and because of what my father did, he's been despised for so many years. My dad ruined your life, Berry. It's hard to get past that.'

'Nate—'

'No,' he interrupted her, and went on in a rush as if he needed to say his piece now or he wouldn't be able to. 'Listen, I'm the son of a despicable person who destroyed your family and your childhood, and caused so much pain and damage. How can you stand to be with me?'

Berry looked at Nate, and smiled, the first real smile in what felt like forever. 'You're not your father, Nate. He's in prison now and will most likely spend the rest of his life there. You're just as much a victim as I am. You've lost your dad as well.'

'It's not the same.'

'Isn't it? You think I don't know what you're going through at the moment? I know what it's like to have people in town look at you, and to know what they're thinking. When you walk into a room, and everyone goes quiet. When people are overly nice and trying to be supportive, when you know that they're pitying you and, yes, judging you as well. That's what being a victim is. It's not something that happens and then goes away. It carries on for years and years.'

'So, what am I supposed to do?' he asked her, desperation creeping into his voice.

'Hold on to the things that matter. The people that matter.'

'But I'll always be a living reminder of what happened. How can you bear that?'

'No. You're a living reminder of how much I love you. Don't you get it? The sins of the father be damned. We both have a chance for a new start, to leave all of this behind and make something good out of this.'

Nate focused his misty eyes on her face. 'Do you mean that?'

'Yes, I mean that,' Berry stepped into his arms. 'Now, stop talking and kiss me.'

Chapter Forty-two

Berry was leaning against the wooden fence of the training arena when Nate sauntered up and stood by her. They both watched as Justin led around the newest addition to Tarantale Downs. A lot had happened in the past nine months, the biggest thing being that Berry didn't ever go back to Melbourne. Nate had taken over the running of Tarantale; he was still finding his footing but the business was beginning to thrive. All those years of working under his father had paid off, but now he was able to implement his own ideas and the whole place had a different atmosphere. But what made it all the better was that Berry was by his side. She shared his life, his home and his business.

'He's pretty,' Berry said as she watched the silver–grey stallion trot past.

'Sir Tristram or Justin?' Nate said as he turned his head and looked at her.

She gave him an innocent smile. 'Ah, both.'

He cleared his throat. 'Um, are you trying to make me jealous?' he asked as he slung his arm around her shoulders.

'No need to be,' Berry said as she stared up into his eyes. 'I guess you're stuck with me now.'

'How's it looking, boss?' Justin called out as the stallion passed by again.

Nate didn't change his gaze, instead he was focused on Berry. 'It's good—very good,' he said before he bent over and kissed her.

Justin rolled his eyes and decided to lead the horse back into the stable.

By the time Berry and Nate pulled apart, the training arena was empty.

'Well, I guess we found a way to clear a room—or in this case a training arena,' Berry said with a smirk.

'That's not a bad thing,' Nate answered before changing the subject. 'So, is everything set for tonight?'

Berry reached over, took Nate's hand and looked at his watch. 'Yeah, Uncle Dave, Jess and Tommy should be arriving in the next hour or so. And I told Andrea and Jodie to come over at six o'clock. And so is Young Ned. How about your sisters and your mum?'

'Pestering me about what the party is for. I've also invited Justin,' he said.

'Well, that will make the girls happy,' Berry said with a laugh. 'So, no one has worked out why they're coming?'

Nate shook his head. 'Nope, I just kept it vague, told them it was time we all got together and also we could do with a celebration.' He looked down at Berry's hand and the ring of diamonds that encased her finger. The stones danced and glittered in the afternoon sun. 'They've got no idea we're throwing an engagement party. Thank you for saying yes—I love you, Berry.'

She wrapped her arms around his waist. 'I love you, too,' she said as she laid her head against his chest.

'I can't take away the past but I promise that I'll do my best to make you happy,' he said as he held her close.

She couldn't stop her smile. 'I believe you.'

Chapter Forty-three

Dohertys' Farm, 1906

Neddy stood by his mam's side as the whole family waved goodbye to last members of the search party. She was holding his hand in a tight grip as if afraid he might disappear again.

He thought she'd be angry with him, but it seemed that she had been too busy crying ever since he'd arrived home to be cross. When the last of the town folk disappeared down the track, Mam kneeled in front of him.

'You're never to run off like that again, do you understand? You had us all worried sick and most of the town came out to search for you.'

She sounded terse to begin with but that didn't last long. She pulled him into her arms and gave him a hug. When she pulled back there was a look of confusion on her face.

Neddy nodded. 'Yes, Mam. I promise.'

'Neddy, what's under your shirt?'

'It's Peter—he's my friend. He helped me find the way home.' Neddy pulled down the top of his shirt so she could see. On cue the rabbit moved and peeked out. 'Please let me keep him. He's hurt his leg and I have to look after him.'

Mam glanced at his father, who in turn gave a shrug and a nod. He reached over and ruffled Neddy's hair. 'Well, I guess it won't eat that much. Ah, come on, Maggie, it should be all right.'

His brother Gabe piped in, 'But where *were* you?'

'I followed Peter, he took me to see the yellow pebbles,' Neddy explained.

'What yellow pebbles?' asked his father.

Neddy stuck his hand in his pocket and pulled out the stones. 'These!' he said with a grin as he held out his hand and the stones glistened in the afternoon sun.

OUT IN MARCH 2022

Summer at Kangaroo Ridge

NICOLE HURLEY-MOORE

The Carrington family own the only pub in the small town of Kangaroo Ridge in rural Victoria. It's been many years since the five Carrington siblings became orphans but, with the help of their aunt Maddie, twins Sebastian and Tamara stepped up and looked after their younger brothers and sister.

Seb and Tam gave up their own teenage years to make sure the family stayed together, and because of their experiences they have turned into very different people. Now, seven years after the accident, Seb is silent and stoic. Tam, on the other hand, wants to kick over the traces and catch up on the life she missed out on.

To complicate matters, Tam is having a secret relationship which she's sure Seb will question. But can Tam ever give herself a happy future while she still, deep down, blames herself for the accident that killed her parents?

ISBN 978 1 76087 555 8

One

Christmas was a big deal for the Carringtons and the one thing they never took for granted. The entire family always made a point of being together on this precious day.

Tamara looked fondly at the people gathered around the long wooden table. The old kitchen was filled with delicious scents—like cloves, ginger and cinnamon—that she always associated with Christmas. It was noisy as her family chatted, laughed and, in the case of her two younger brothers, squabbled with each other. The Carringtons all shared similar physical characteristics, from their dark hair, oval faces and light coloured eyes, which ranged from a bluey grey to Felix's almost green.

It had taken a lot for her family to get to this point and Tam had had her doubts that they would ever be happy again. Her fingers fiddled with the small gold compass that hung around her neck.

'You all right?' Seb asked as he gave her a gentle nudge with his shoulder. 'You're a bit quiet.'

Tam smiled at her twin as she pushed a lock of her dark brown hair behind her ear.

'I'm just enjoying the scene.'

Seb glanced around the table. 'Yeah. It's good, isn't it?'

Tamara nodded but before she could answer one of her other brothers interrupted.

'Tam, can you pass up the potato salad?' Lix called out from the opposite end of the table.

'Felix, you don't have to shout.' Aunt Maddie gave him a mock frown, picked up the salad and handed it to her little daughter, Rori, to pass up.

'Sorry,' Lix replied sheepishly as he waited for the salad to reach him. 'Thanks.'

Seb turned to Tam with a grin. 'Some things never change. So, after the Christmas Day cricket match, it's time to find out which film is next in our top five Chrissy movies, right?'

Tam gave him a shrug. 'I don't think I can hang around that long tonight. I've got somewhere to be.'

Seb studied her. 'Really?' He gave her a penetrating look from his pale blue eyes. He was tall with a well-built physique and a sharply defined jawline. When he smiled, small dimples appeared in his cheeks; which was known to have a devastating effect on a portion of Kangaroo Ridge's female inhabitants. But he wasn't smiling now. The Christmas movie tradition had started years ago. Each year they would have a heated discussion on which movies should be included. Then for five days they would watch one each night, finishing the marathon on Boxing Day.

'This is a special family thing. We always watch the movies together,' Seb said.

'You can't guilt me into staying,' Tam answered.

'But don't you think—'

She didn't let him finish. 'Just because I have to leave doesn't mean that I don't love you all. I need a bit of time alone this year—I deserve that, don't you think?'

Seb was silent for a moment. 'I thought that we said we'd do everything we could.'

Annoyance sparked in her blue eyes. 'I did—I do.'

Aunt Maddie reached over and laid her hand over Tam's. 'Is everything all right, sweetheart?'

Tam nodded. 'Yes, nothing to worry about.'

Seb looked at his aunt. 'She says that she has to go out later. Won't be here for the movie.'

'There's plenty of us here, Seb,' Maddie said evenly. 'One person missing isn't going to ruin the evening.'

'I guess.' He moved back in his chair.

Tam loved him, she did. But sometimes he drove her insane. She picked up her glass and had a sip of the crisp white wine. Christmas fare for the Carringtons was a cold offering of meats, salmon, salads, cheeses, vegetables and dips. It had taken her, Aunt Maddie and Lix nearly all morning to put the food together and decorate the table but it was worth it. She sat back now and admired all their hard work. The most important thing was the chocolate cake surrounded by miniature gingerbread houses, which her younger siblings Gray and Lucy had made yesterday. It had become a tradition that those two would make the cake and Tam had to admit they were getting better at it with every passing year—this one was fantastic. Seb had been in charge of the bakery, snack and drink run, he got the easy job because he was still working at the pub until late last night.

'I took a call from a frantic bride yesterday.' Tam glanced at her aunt. 'She wants to know if there's any chance we could schedule a tiny wedding next month.'

Maddie blew out a breath. 'Geez, I don't know. We're booked right up until April, aren't we?'

Almost six years ago, Maddie and Tam had come up with the idea to turn the old farm into a wedding venue. Maddie had been desperate to find something that could sustain the family and keep it together. The farm was on one hundred and fifty acres, with a weed-filled garden, one barn, some broken-down sheds, a few grapevines and a dam as big as a lake. Tam had been only nineteen at the time but she had thrown herself into the project without hesitation. All the years of hard work had paid off and now Carrington Farm was a much sought-after venue and they were generally booked out months in advance.

'I feel really sorry for this girl though,' Tam continued. 'She had her dream wedding planned but right before the big day the venue she'd booked went under and she lost her deposit. Then the next venue she booked cancelled and now everywhere else is booked up.'

Maddie nodded sympathetically. 'Let me think about it,' she said. 'How tiny is tiny?'

'They've cut it down to their immediate family—her mum, her best friend and the groom's brother. She said that it didn't need to be big or special, they just want to get married.'

'Well, every wedding is special, no matter the size. Let's have a look at the bookings after lunch and see what we can do.'

'Okay.' Tam nudged her brother in the shoulder. 'Don't worry, it'll be done before the cricket starts.'

'I'll hold you to that,' Seb said with a nod.

* * *

After lunch Tam and Maddie headed to the office to look at the bookings while the rest of the family cleared away the remnants of lunch. Then they all assembled on the flat green lawn at the front of the house for the Christmas cricket match.

The day was warm and Tam sat with Rori in her lap under the dappled shade of the large peppercorn. Gray bowled and

Seb swung his bat, missing the ball entirely as it sailed past and slammed into the wickets.

Seb sank to his knees dramatically and shouted, '*Noooooooooooo*.' Rori laughed while Gray and Lix whooped in victory. Tam smiled—Seb was good at nearly everything . . . except cricket.

The day and the match wore on with laughter and lemonade. After dinner, Tam picked up her keys from the bowl on the kitchen bench. Her sister Lucy peered up from the fridge.

'Not staying for the movie?'

Tam shook her head. 'Nah, I wanted to catch up with some friends.'

'Your loss, you'll be missing the most quintessential Christmas movie,' Lucy said as she grabbed the orange juice.

'Okay, which one?'

'Your favourite—*Die Hard*.'

'Damn.'

'Told ya.' Lucy laughed. 'See you later, then.'

'Don't overdo the popcorn. Remember what happened last time,' Tam called as she shrugged into her leather jacket and headed to the back door. Her red motorbike, an original 1969 Triumph Bonneville, was parked in the backyard underneath a shady willow.

Tam settled on the seat, turned the key and slowly rode out the driveway. The sun had set behind the hills but the sky was still filled with the afterglow of orange, yellow and pink. Tam turned left at the gate and headed further out of town; the gums that lined the uneven bitumen road were bathed in a rosy light.

Not far from Turpin Hill, she turned down a dirt track and kept going, passing the No Through Road sign. Tam rode past an open rusty metal gate and followed the dirt driveway that snaked through the clumps of eucalypts until the small cottage came into view.

She parked in the front garden and walked to the blue front door. It opened before she had a chance to knock.

'I was beginning to think that you weren't going to make it,' a deep voice said from the shadowed doorway.

Tam smiled. 'I said that I was coming,' she said and she stepped into his waiting arms and kissed him.